Joseph Geraci has for many years been a rare book dealer, and is the current Director of the Paidika Foundation in Amsterdam. His previous publications include the novel *Loving Sander* and the nonfiction anthology *Dares to Speak*, both published by Gay Men's Press.

MARRYING TOM

Joseph Geraci

GAY MEN'S PRESS

First published 2001 by Millivres Ltd,
part of the Millivres Prowler Group,
Worldwide House, 116-134 Bayham St, London NW1 0BA

World Copyright © 2001 Joseph Geraci

Joseph Geraci has asserted his right to be identified as the author of this work in
accordance with the Copyright, Designs and Patents Act 1988

A CIP catalogue record for this book is available
from the British Library

ISBN 1 902852 25 7

Distributed in Europe by Central Books,
99 Wallis Rd, London E9 5LN

Distributed in North America by Consortium,
1045 Westgate Drive, St.Paul, MN 55114-1065

Distributed in Australia by Bulldog Books,
P O Box 300, Beaconsfield, NSW 2014

Printed and bound in the EU by WS Bookwell, Juva, Finland

Stalked But Not Courted 7

Courted But Not Seduced 69

Seduced But Not Married 109

Marrying 169

PART ONE: STALKED BUT NOT COURTED

1. TOM ARRIVES IN MADALIN

Tom's house was a few doors down from ours, but as he was Protestant, lived alone with his divorced mother, associated with an older, wilder crowd, and went to the public high school, our lives seemed too much at odds for us to become friends. It was not until many weeks after he had moved into our village that we did.

My desk was perpendicular to my bedroom window, and overlooked the woods out behind our house. Peering out cautiously from the side of the shade, I could catch glimpses of him mowing his lawn, cutting the overgrown weeds, or shooting at squirrels and bottles with equal dispassion. One early autumn evening he and his buddies turned over a garbage can on Dr. Mason's porch because the old man had shouted at them to stay off his lawn; another night they blocked the street with a huge pile of burning leaves. The great plume of acrid, charcoal gray smoke hovered over the village like some trickster genie, warning us of their dark, savage powers. From various upstairs windows, unseen, I had grandstand views. I watched horrified, amused, and excited. I imagined myself the settler boy in the cabin spying on the redskins who, though never quite attacking, lurked threateningly at the edge of his vulnerable world.

Madalin was a tiny mid-Hudson Valley village of seven hundred; it was nigh on impossible to keep anything there secret. No sooner had we heard that the old Dornbush house had been sold and a boy about my age was moving in (something I had dreamed about happening every time a house changed hands), I felt I knew as much about him as he knew himself. His mother was a registered nurse and had secured a position at the county hospital; they had been living on Long Island, out in the Hamptons, which people supposed meant they had money; his father was a career Navy man, his parents had divorced when he was three and he had been raised fatherless, which, according to local lore, was to say wild and unruly. He had been in some sort of mysterious trouble at his junior high school. I heard several versions of this: that he had robbed a store, that he was caught dealing drugs, that he had broken into a house, stolen a car, and even made a sixteen-year-old girl pregnant. For a model Catholic boy like myself – growing up in a small village under hundreds of watchful eyes, who everyone took for granted would become a priest, or carry on for the village doctor – before I even caught a glimpse of him, the rumors would have suggested more than enough Dionysian anarchy to have excited my curiosity, and caution.

I was out in our backyard one warm, early July morning just after the 4th, down by the fringe of trees that separated our property from the woods beyond. It was not eight o'clock yet, but I was diligently doing dry-land, warm-up exercises, even though the school vacation had hardly begun and swimming team practise did not officially start until the 1st of September. Coach had told us that working out in the fresh air would increase our lung capacity. On clear days I dragged a mat outside, bent on being in shape for the new season. Birds flashed red and yellow streaks from tree to tree; chipmunks chattered at me; the wind rustled the upper reaches of the old oak. I liked these mornings, out alone at the bottom of the yard working up a sweat, everything, including me, informed with energy and busy purpose.

I could hear, but not see a large truck out on North Road. We had all been expecting it for the last couple of weeks or so, ever since 'SOLD' had been pasted over the 'For Sale' sign planted in the middle of the Dornbush front lawn. I had no doubt what it was, or where it was headed. I ventured through the underbrush a few hundred feet, close enough to read the black and red lettering on the side of the cream-colored moving van as it crawled slowly along the road looking for the right house. I cut through a grove of sumac and stepped out onto the shoulder to get a better view, and caught my first glimpse of Tom. He was standing at the end of his driveway waving at the truck to turn in. For a moment we stood facing each other many yards apart. I pulled up the bottom of my sweatshirt and wiped my forehead. He was barefoot, and wore only a pair of bright new, beltless blue jeans a size too large and sagging below his navel. His long, straight, blond hair was pulled back tightly from his face and held by an elastic band. He was older than me, I thought, with some disappointment. Sixteen to my thirteen? I was standing south of him. He lifted his hand to shade his eyes from the still low sun. The truck veered in towards him and he jumped nimbly out of the way. I knew that he had also been staring at me. An old, blue Volvo was parked just beyond his driveway and a heavy-set woman wearing khaki-colored work pants was bent half inside, retrieving boxes from the back seat. Like some shy fawn I turned and retreated soundlessly into the cover of the trees.

Some friendships begin on first sight; others grow slowly; a few are precipitated by a seemingly unexpected event. In those first weeks, the long vacation days of summer, I did not see that much of him. No doubt he was still settling in. Every sunny day I was off somewhere with Richie and Jacqueline, and sometimes a group of our friends. Usually we would pack a lunch and make a bike trip to the lake a couple of miles away, encamping on a small patch of dirty sand.

One of those muggy middle or late July days I remember Tom turning up. He stood apart, straddling the bar of his bicycle, looking in our direction, but making no attempt to join us; not dressed for swimming.

The lake was no more than a pond, the beach no more than a few hundred square feet of litter and trucked-in sand. On any one of those hot, sticky afternoons that afflicted the Valley it was as crowded as a Reginald Marsh painting.

I was lying on a wet towel, propped up on my elbows. "There's Corrigan," I said to Richie, motioning towards Tom with my chin.

He lazily raised his head from his arm, and held his glasses to his eyes without putting them on. "Checking us out. Hope he gets an eye-full."

"Looks like a new bike. English racer. They're pretty expensive."

"So big deal. I'm underwhelmed. Christ, look at that fag shirt. And I mean *beads* no less. I suppose he's proving something."

Tom was wearing a black and mustard-yellow dashiki open at the neck, and a strand of African pottery beads.

I said, still staring at him, "Look, he's barefoot . . . I mean, riding a bike barefoot?"

"Weird." Richie tucked his glasses back into his shoe, and his head sank down onto his arm again.

Jacqueline leaned over to see past us. "What are you two talking about?"

"That," Richie said disdainfully, without looking up again.

She looked over our bodies. "Oh, maybe he'll come over. Why don't you call him Richie, you're closest?"

"Call him. What, are you crazy?"

"Well, why not? How would you feel if you were brand new in the village. Look . . . he's staring back at us. Go on wave to him, or I will. I think he's cute."

"Cute! Like a speckled band." Richie was into Conan Doyle these days.

"You're just *jealous* Richie . . . "

"Give me a break. The guy's a loser."

"You're always so negative about everyone. Every time anyone new moves in the village the two of you go around automatically criticizing."

"Not true."

"Leave me out of this," I exclaimed.

"It *is* true. Remember when Donny moved in? Both of you were going around saying what a little pest he was and you would never let him in your club."

"Well he was a pest . . . Still is, as a matter of fact."

"So, you let him into your stupid club didn't you? Three days after he moved in? And even made him president?"

"Not president. Communications Officer. And anyway, Donny's different. Not a criminal type like this Corrigan."

She said disapprovingly, "Always ready to judge. You don't know *anything* about him. Not for sure."

Richie said sarcastically, "I know a bad egg when I smell one."

"You should at least give him a chance."

The banter was making me uncomfortable. "Jeez, it's hot today." I stood up abruptly. "I'm going in again. You guys coming or what?" I looked at my wrist-watch. "Christ! I have to be home in less than an hour."

Jacqueline sprang nimbly to her feet. Sand covered the front of her two-piece bathing suit. She shook it from her halter with her fingertips. Some of it sprayed onto Richie.

She said, "You're awful Richie. You always think people have to prove themselves to you. Well they don't."

He stood up; brushed himself off. "Watch it, will you. You're wrong about me . . . as usual. I don't think Corrigan has to prove anything to me or anyone. Fact is, trouble-maker's a trouble-maker. We all know one when we see one."

I hitched up my cut-off jeans, hand-me-downs from my brother, and glanced one last time at Tom. He was still staring in our direction.

"Come on, I'll race you both."

I sprinted down the narrow stretch of sand, perhaps as much anxious to escape Tom's gaze as I was eager to end the bickering or beat my friends into the silty, warm water of the lake.

If Tom had to prove himself, either to Richie, or to anyone else including me, he did not seem aware of it. He strutted around the village, into and out of the post office or general store, with too much of a cocky, chip-on-the-shoulder air, as if defying us to make him conform. He either pretended not to care, did not care, or simply did not understand that we might be a closed rank against him. As the days passed we continued to eye each other at a distance, from the edges of our yards or across a safe expanse of field, like two young animals, intrigued but wary. Because of something Richie said to me, our lives even suffered the illusion of drawing further apart.

One gloomy, rainy afternoon a few days later Richie and I were in his bedroom making a model airplane together. The rain pelted his window and swept in noisy waves over the roof. We were working by the light of a bare suspended bulb at a pine table set in the middle of the floor. I was gluing a strut to the bottom wing of a Fokker biplane; Richie was about to fit a British bull's-eye decal to the side of the fuselage. He was habitually pushing back the bridge of his horn-rimmed glasses with his index finger. His room was not just his bedroom, workshop, observatory replete with high-powered telescope; it was our clubhouse, briefing room, war/crisis/news center. If Richie were to have been magically transposed into a tribal boy-circle he would have made some anthropologist's perfect informant. Nothing seemed to go on in Madalin, at least in our boy-circle, without him either finding out or being able to find out. I once said with some exasperation, taken as a compliment, "A seed can't fall from a tree around here without you knowing it."

He had heard from Donny the evening before the latest rumors about Tom. Expelling a pent-up breath as the decal slid into place, he rubbed the wrinkle out of it with a clean white handkerchief, then leaned back from the table to inspect his work. Once finished, the biplane would join the six or seven other models already suspended by threads from the ceiling, swaying and turning in the draft from the stairwell opposite his open door.

Boys being as much gossips as girls, or more, we were gossiping about Eleanor. She lived across the street from Richie; her mother owned the general store. She was seventeen: quiet; naive; unsure of herself. She read a lot of romantic fiction. I liked her because she would unexpectedly surprise me with a genuine insight into someone in the village. She also gave me free egg creams and told Jacqueline that I had a beautiful aura.

The rumor was that she was pregnant. The father was supposedly the senior swimming-team jock Matt Palermo. I did not think that Matt could be the father because I would have heard something about it through the team grapevine. He liked to go around bragging about his conquests. I would also have seen them driving by my house at least one night, heading down to the river to park, like all the other village teen couples.

I said sceptically, "Sure she dated him once or twice but she told me Matt wasn't her type."

"He wouldn't care." He leaned back from the table and put his hands behind his head. "I think we got a major mystery here. If Palermo's not the father who is? She even going steady with anyone?"

"Not that she said or I heard."

"My brother Ralph dated her a few times. But he can't even put his pants on straight." He stood up and stretched. "Maybe it is Palermo. She wouldn't necessarily say so if it was. You know, protecting him or something. My mother says if she goes around blabbing to everyone that he's the father it sort of blackmails him into marrying her and then he never would."

"I still think Matt would have shot his mouth off to someone about laying her. You know how he is." I eased the strut into place.

"Maybe . . . maybe not. They might have made a pact or something." Walking over to a wall mirror, he whipped a comb out of his back pocket and ran it through his thick black hair. "Donny's got a better explanation. Says he knows for sure."

Donny was a few months younger and three or four inches shorter than I: thin, wiry, hyperactive, compulsive, and manipulative; not someone I trusted anymore, not after catching him stealing my expensive Swiss army knife from my desk drawer.

Richie had let his remark linger in the air, forcing me to ask, "So, what's Donny's latest cockamamey theory?"

"He says for absolutely fucking sure Corrigan's the father."

"What? Baloney! Donny always wants everyone to think he knows everything. I mean, Tom's only been here a few weeks and he hardly even knows Eleanor. Donny just made that one up."

"I'm not so sure. A couple of nights ago? He's over at Lansing's and Tom shows up acting real smartass. And when they started in joking around about Eleanor getting knocked up Lansing starts needling Tom about how it's funny no sooner does he move in the village than all these chicks start getting pregnant and like . . . maybe the coincidence isn't a coincidence? And Tom didn't actually go out of his way to deny it. In fact he said, 'Just sharing it around.' His exact words."

"Come on, that doesn't prove anything."

Eleanor was working at the soda fountain in the general store for the summer and Tom was hanging out there quite a bit, but so was every other kid in the village.

Richie opened a dresser drawer and pulled out a cotton sweater. The rain had made the room damp, if not exactly chilly. "All I know is, if the baby has platinum blond hair then we'll know for sure . . . "

Matt and Eleanor both had dark brown hair.

I interjected, "Christ, you know how Donny is, you can't listen to anything he says. The next thing we know he's going to try to tell us that Tom crawled in Eleanor's window some night when she was asleep and even she doesn't know Tom's the father."

"Well?"

"Yeah, sure. Maybe it's even a virgin birth."

"That would be cool. Madalin with its own miracle. Anyway, that's not what I was going to tell you."

I groaned with mock detachment. "There's more? Donny's mouth must have been going a mile a minute." I knew that even if I had said I did not want to hear more he would have told me anyway.

"Lansing was bragging about all the stuff he'd done. You know, all those robberies and shit and Tom says 'No big deal' because he was arrested for breaking and entering . . . get this! . . . when he was *ten*! Can you believe it?" As if it were not a rhetorical question, he answered it himself. "Better believe it."

"You mean he went to jail or juvenile? A jail-bird on top of everything else!"

"Donny said Tom told them the judge let him off because his father's like some Navy hero or something and said he'd personally keep Tom in line and off the streets."

I said sceptically, "I heard his father was in Japan, or Vietnam."

Richie went back to the mirror again. Leaning close to the

glass he stretched out the corner of his mouth with his tongue in order to examine a raw red spot. He frowned, opened a tube of cream and daubed the pimple.

He said dismissively, "This is now. That was then. He was probably on leave or something and anyway that ain't the big news . . . ", adding "for *you*." He threw the tube of cream back on the dresser and walking back over to the table, poked me in the shoulder. "The big news is . . . get this . . . Donny says Tom showed up with this huge bag of weed and sort of like goes strutting around the room offering reefers to everyone like big man on the block, real cool. Handing it out. Just like that. For free! It was like the best shit you could get this side of Mexico Donny says . . . Acapulco Gold . . . or better! Zillions of dollars of the shit. So Donny says, sure, why not, and takes one, maybe two hits and gets so totally bombed he can hardly see to walk home it was that good."

"So? Big deal. That supposed to impress me?"

"Hold your horses. He says Tom's talking tough all the time. Real mean. So, here's where you come in. He and Lansing are thick as thieves right now and Donny says Lansing and Tom were cooking up some shit against you. Donny says you better watch out."

"What kind of shit?"

"Like grabbing you alone some day and beating the crap out of you."

"I hardly ever even said hello to Corrigan!"

"Don't matter, does it, not if Lansing is behind it."

Of course, he was right. Lansing seemed to have a grudge against me just for living. Tom conspiring with Lansing was indeed bad news for me, and probably even for Madalin. I said, "He didn't waste no time making friends, with Lansing no less. Donny say when and where they were going to get me?"

"He didn't say. He did say though that Lansing said you thought you were the village smartass and Tom was like nodding and agreeing all the time and saying like you thought you owned the village and the woods and had to be taught a lesson and be brought down a peg or two."

I expelled a loud breath, and exclaimed, "Man! Lansing

and Tom."

"Birds of a feather."

Lansing had a single-minded hatred of me, which stemmed from my publicly embarrassing him when I was in the first grade. I was six and he was about thirteen at the time. The Bishop was paying one of his biannual diocesan visits to our little village school and the nuns had staged a spelling bee in the school auditorium. When Lansing left the 'h' out of 'catechism' I was asked to spell it and did so correctly. The kids laughed at him because a first-grader had shown him up, which, of course, the nuns knew I would do. Not known for their sensitivity they wanted to show off their bright student; feelings be damned. Later on that day or week, Lansing caught me alone in the schoolyard and, grabbing me by the shirt collar and practically choking me to death on the spot, said that if I ever crossed him again like that he would finish me off. He had pushed me backwards and I had fallen on the gravel tearing my trousers, but I had never told a soul who had done it.

His words still rang in my ears. "I'm warning you Wyant, you even look at me the wrong way you're dead meat!"

I was sure he meant it. He did not have the opportunity to make good his threat because a few months later he was arrested for robbing a gas station and sent to a juvenile detention home. When he was released a couple of years later, supposing that the threat was still valid, I went out of my way to avoid him.

In spite of my doubts about Donny as a trustworthy source of information it made sense to me, from all I had heard, that Tom would have gravitated towards Lansing's gang.

The boys in the village fell roughly into two opposing camps, one centered around Lansing and the other around Richie and his brothers. Of course, I belonged to the latter. Between the two a hostile truce existed, a state of war in suspended animation.

Lansing's clique was several years older. The protocols of age demanded that they treat us with disdain. We went out of our way to avoid them. Brief skirmishes would flare up now

16

and then, as when Lansing bought an air rifle and started shooting at us from his car on our way to school, but for the most part, open war never broke out, though a truce was never declared. One or two of us, like Donny Kitzel, motivated by the occasional joint or two, the sex talk, or just plain boredom, floated the news back and forth between bases; exposed double agents. Everyone knew that at the first opportunity they would blab everything they had learned to the other camp. If it was Donny's way of gaining attention and acceptance – arriving at Richie's or Lansing's door brimming with the latest 'secrets' – it proved convenient and added interest. Everyone was always planting rumors by telling them to him. Sorting out the facts from the lies was half the game.

Lansing might have gathered that Tom was a source of good grass. A stranger to village ways, he could also be someone Lansing could manipulate. They were both outsiders; their houses were also only a stone's throw apart. He had to go by Tom's every day. He might have taken it for granted that Tom's reputation spelled a comrade in crime.

Lansing's house was just a few symbolic feet over the village line, a fact I heard referred to many times as if Madalin did not want them to belong. His father was an alcoholic and a petty fence; his mother was also an alcoholic. The house was the county eye-sore: plastic where there should have been panes of glass; rusting metal patches where there should have been neat shingles; nothing painted, nothing clean. Hardly a blade of grass could crop through their front yard, a conglomeration of car parts, old sofas, broken crates, brass lamps, stacks of old rubber tires; an unlicensed junk shop. They centripetally gathered everyone's detritus, displayed to general horror.

Such flaunting of chaos must have appealed to Tom. Over the summer he was seen everywhere with Lansing. It did not sit well with the villagers. After all, the Dornbush house was not only within the village line, but was also rather historic, having belonged to the first village mayor before the Dornbush family had bought it. People began to talk against him. Father, for example – soon after Tom moved in – said sometime about catching him down by the river breaking bottles with some kid he had never seen before, "sort of dark and Indian-looking?" I did not know whom he meant, although I took it for granted he must be part of Lansing's gang. "I rolled down my window to tell them to stop and they gave me the finger!" My brother Charlie remarked that his friends were saying that Tom "was a real asshole." They had been over at the Mall and had seen Tom getting into a bad fist fight. "The other kid was pretty damaged. Blood everywhere. Not a scratch on Tom though. The perfect friend for you, Butthead."

Summer waned; September began. In the first week of school I had an encounter with him that did not bode well. It was about three thirty in the afternoon and I was walking home alone down the main road towards the river. Our house was at the top of the big hill, before the main road descended to the railroad tracks and river front.

I was almost to the corner of North Road, Tom's turn. Our house was just beyond; our acre of property extended to the corner, though more as uncultivated field than yard. I heard the whirr of bicycle wheels and turned, thinking it was Richie. But it was Tom. He skidded around 180 degrees on the gravel to stop in front of me. He had on a blue and black check flannel shirt, Levi's and old, torn sneakers. He must have been biking hard to catch up with me; his forehead and upper lip were beaded with sweat. He rested his forearms on the handle bars of the forest green, three-speed Raleigh, a rather elegant bike for Madalin, and one which I would have envied; I had been handed down my brother's scratched and battered, ten-year-old red Schwinn.

He looked younger close up. I decided he was hardly fifteen. His eyes were long, almond shaped, dark blue almost black; a dusting of freckles at the top of his high oriental cheeks; wisps of white gold hair by his ears, parted in the middle, tightly pulled back, accenting the sharpness of his chin, the height of his forehead. His mouth was thick and full. He licked his lips, wetting them, making them redder. His shirt was open a couple of buttons and as he leaned forward a leather cord with a single African bead fell out. He stared at me without saying anything. He looked intelligent, not at all stupid and thick like Lansing. He kept squeezing and releasing his hand-brake; it made me feel threatened. His fingers and hands were long and esthetically thin, even delicate.

"Hey, Danny . . . That where you live?" he asked, jerking his head towards my house, the first words we had ever spoken. I nodded. "Thought so. I seen you a couple of times out back in the woods." I shrugged, but said nothing. He was confusing me. "You've got some kind of fort or something."

I shrugged again. "So?"

He turned his head to the side and spat. "So, I suppose if that's your house then that was you I seen spying on me from behind the curtains."

He was more agitated than threatening.

"So? It's my house. Besides I wasn't spying. I was just seeing who was making all that stupid infantile racket out back."

"Wow! In-fan-tile. Three-syllable word no less. That what you call guns and shooting at things?"

He rocked the bike back and forth nervously. He cleared his throat.

I nodded. "Sure, that's what I call it. What else?"

"I heard about you. Like you think you're some kind of big-shot boy wonder around here."

"Thanks for the compliment. That what Lansing said?"

"Him and a few others. I heard all about you, Junior Diving Champion of the Universe, like an altar boy since you were six, teacher's pet, flag raiser, best grades. All that shit. Like you just stepped off a holy card. Unreal."

He spat a second time, the ritual gesture, the sign of male dominance, the signal not to resist aggression.

"What's it to you? I hear things about you too you know."

"You and that Richie. Real close buddies I hear. *Real* close." Quite unconsciously I think, he suddenly hitched up his crotch.

"So, what are you trying to say?"

"What I'm trying to say is, just stay out of my way."

"Suits me," I said.

He put his foot on the pedal. "And stay out of our part of the woods."

No one in all my thirteen years and eight months of life in Madalin had ever warned me not to go into the woods. My mother's Italian blood boiled in my veins. I had as much right to those woods as anyone. More maybe. I was almost born in them.

I said, "Free universe."

"Yeah, well, someone and something new has arrived in town. Just stay out of my way."

He stepped down hard on the pedal, did a wheelie, and sped off.

That conversation with Tom must have taken place in the first week of school, and I can most probably date the following conversation to the middle or end of the following week.

I was lingering after classes. It had been an unusually warm day. The boys had been allowed to remove their suit jackets and ties. My shirt was wet and clung uncomfortably to my sides and back. I was eager to get home to change and was hastily stuffing books and papers into my book bag when Sister Francesca asked me to stay a moment. I glanced wistfully at the backs of my friends as they disappeared through the door.

"Daniel? Can you please come up here a moment?"

This would have seemed perfectly normal to me. With their usual efficiency the nuns doled out assignments and privileges in the first week of school, even typing them out on a sheet of paper and posting them on the bulletin board. I had been made a patrol boy and given one of those official, white canvas belts that empowered me to stop cars and direct the other children safely across the street. This was an especially choice task coveted by all the boys each year as it allowed you to come ten or fifteen minutes late to catechism class, so long as your grades did not suffer. I was also an altar boy and served the evening Benediction. No doubt, I thought, Sister wanted to discuss one or other of my duties.

I turned and walked back up the row between the low, wooden, ink-stained desks to the front of the room. Sister was stooped over gathering up her papers, her face hidden beneath the stiff, black head-dress her order still insisted its nuns wear despite Vatican II. Several years later they finally made the change to simple street wear, the original historical intention of the habit.

I was hoping against hope that she was not going to ask me to have a talk with the Pastor, Father Simone, about becoming a missionary. I had no inclination for doing that, and I did not yet know how to say no to such pressures.

She smiled and asked me to take a seat at one of the front desks. She was large, Swedish-born, big-boned, with rough, masculine mannerisms and hands. She came around her desk and sat on the edge nearest me, swinging her ugly black shoe back and forth, playing with the large black wooden rosary attached to her black cincture. I wondered how she was not suffocating in the heat. She put her hand to her mouth and cleared her throat. I had seen her once squatting down on the ground playing marbles with some first-graders. One of the boys, I suppose. I had heard from others who had previously been in her class that she bragged about being the youngest child in a family with eight boys, which seemed hardly worth bragging about. Apparently everything she wanted to imitate when young was male. She identified with athletic prowess. In June, at the close of the last school year, she had approached me to tell me that she was very pleased she would be teaching me the following year and that with God's grace and hard work she was sure I would become the regional junior diving champion, something even my father was not pressuring me about. Perhaps, because I had been motherless since the age of three, or because I was bright and responsible, the nuns had expectations for me; and made demands.

"I saw you on the road yesterday talking to that new boy. I hear he's a neighbor of yours?"

"He lives on North Road, just past the church."

She nodded, obviously knowing very well where he lived. "The Dornbush house. He's your age, I think."

"A couple of years older."

"Have you been talking to him much?"

I felt relieved. She was going to pump me for information, which the nuns frequently did with the village children, not badger me about my vocation. I was quite willing to share whatever I knew about Tom, which was probably less than she knew already.

"I only said hello a couple of times."

"I've heard that he's been up to no good. You know they had to leave where they were living."

I smiled and nodded. We had no doubt all heard the same things. She continued, "Not at all a good influence. Not the kind of person that would make a good friend, don't you agree?"

I shrugged. "I suppose so." I was not intending on having Tom as a friend.

"Yours is such an impressionable age, and that boy's a wild one. He's already been in enough trouble for four boys and two lifetimes." She laughed a little, and I think she meant this as a joke. I did not see the humor but I smiled politely. "That poor mother of his must nearly have died with worry ten times over. And the poor thing is divorced and has to work so hard. I heard his father's in the military somewhere?"

Now here was a chance for me to add something that I had heard which she had not. "He's in the Navy, a doctor on a destroyer or carrier or something. He's in Japan. Or Vietnam."

She shook her head, "Fatherless. Protestant too."

I was beginning to warm up to the subject, "I saw his mother go into Trinity last Sunday . . . but not him though."

She shook her head again, disapprovingly. "No doubt a boy like that doesn't believe in anything . . . He'd be too filled with himself."

She adjusted the wide, half moon shaped, starched white bib by sliding it back and forth until it was centered again, and continued, "You can tell from his appearance just what sort he chooses to be."

I imagined she meant his tie-dyed shirts, beads, and two-foot long ponytail. She reached under her bib into a breast pocket and pulled out a tiny silver watch on a thin metal chain, then slid it back in again. She swung her raised foot down onto the floor and gripped the desk with both hands. She said she happened to know for a fact that he had been in with a bad crowd and had broken into a house.

"He has a record, you know."

I said I did. The Sisters of St. Joseph had a convent in the

Hamptons so it would have been easy for her to find out about him, simply by phoning one of the nuns down there.

I knew that the purpose of the conversation was to try to find out if I had any interest in befriending him, which I did not, so I said reassuringly, "He hasn't been trying to get in with our group at all. He's been hanging out with Lansing and his crowd."

"Yes . . . Lansing . . . Of course . . . He's hardly here a week and he gets in with that crowd."

I was beginning to forget she was not a peer. My voice lowered conspiratorially, "I seen them together all the time."

She corrected me, "Saw. You saw them together. Unfortunately I've seen it before, boys going bad like that. He'll be in trouble right soon enough. If he isn't already."

She rose abruptly, and walked back around to her side of the desk. "I'm sure you'll do the right thing. You've got more sense than all the rest combined. I'm sure we can count on you to make the right judgments." She stuffed the last papers into her worn, black briefcase and snapped shut the brass clasp. "Now I want you to make me a promise. If you're ever in any doubts about anything at all you'll come and ask me. You'll do that for Sister, won't you? . . . The Church has so much wisdom to share – thousands of years of wisdom! If I've learned anything over these years it's that. You should thank God every day you're Catholic, one of the lucky ones born with faith, not some poor lost soul . . . " Her voice trailed off.

I supposed that she meant Tom, and not owing him any loyalty I said obsequiously, "Yes, Sister." I even added for good measure, perhaps showing off, perhaps a bit angry with Tom for threatening me on the road the day before; "I don't much like him. I think he's a real troublemaker. I hope that's not a sin. Judging him like that. I don't really know him, but I don't really like him. I'd just as soon stay away from him."

She smiled, and looked very pleased with me. "Well, like I said, you can always come and talk to me. I don't want you worrying about anything, anything at all, except maybe winning that trophy for us. Imagine Saint Cecilia's with their own champion diver. If God wills it you might even make it to the

Junior Olympics. Just imagine."

I said modestly, "I always try my best, Sister."

"I know you do. You're a fine boy, Daniel, a real credit to the school, and to your father."

While we were leaving the room together, as if we had somehow actually established a kind of equality in our conversation, she surprised me with a question, "I know you've said you don't like this new boy very much, but what do you think of him? I mean *really* think of him?" She had even turned her head and was looking directly at me.

I said spontaneously, "Oh, he's wild for sure. I mean, it's like he was born out in nature, not in a town or anything. You see his eyes? How long they are? Sort of like an animal or something you see out in the woods, like a fox but wide too, like a deer. And all summer he didn't wear any shoes. Which is strange, because he's not from a farm or anything but from a town, and Long Island no less. But once – I don't know – I was standing next to him in the post office – not talking to him or anything – just standing next to him – and he looked kind of – well, I don't know . . . "

She volunteered, " *Wicked*, maybe?"

I shrugged. I was actually going to say 'nice', but I hated that word, 'soft' perhaps, or 'kind', but the jolt of inappropriate words stopped me. I said instead something I was not in fact thinking, "My Italian grandmother use to say that shifty eyes are the sign of a shifty heart."

Sister laughed. "I certainly agree in this case."

I give myself credit for adding, "Maybe he's not shifty though. Maybe he's just, well, *original*. I guess that's all I can think of."

She looked a bit startled. "That sounds right to me . . . but there's no sense in our thinking too much about him now is there."

"Oh no, Sister."

"That's good."

At the end of the walk, as I was about to cross the street to the general store to buy myself a candy bar or a soda, and as she was about to walk the block or so to the convent behind the church, she paused for a moment and said, "Don't forget your promise. If you hear or see anything you'll let me know."

We parted. I crossed the street. But I surprised and a little angry because I had not promised her anything at all.

As the days and weeks progressed into October Tom and I continued to brush by each other in the post office or on the road, with a grunt or a nod, but without speaking to each other again – safe within the circles of our predetermined worlds. From the haven of my porch I would see him down at the corner of our yard talking to Lansing. Once, they pointed in my direction; Lansing squeezed Tom's shoulder reassuringly. But over what? He left the house for school earlier than I. His bus picked him up sharp at eight out at the corner and if I chose not to see him, I could wait inside until I heard the roar of the motor fading towards the highway. There was the appearance of our remaining inexorably apart. Even our futures seemed to point in different directions. Everyone took it for granted that the following year I would attend Saint Francis Academy, the boys' high school down the river in Poughkeepsie. My brother was already a senior there. He was going on to Fordham, as my father had, and as it was presumed I would: a steady march into an orderly Catholic future, not the criminal chaos predicted for Tom.

If it had not been for Richie I might not have thought about him at all. Richie kept feeding me gossip, which I did not discourage. We would be out in the playground during recess, leaning against the wire fence watching some of the smaller kids tussle with each other, our hands thrust into our pockets, kicking at stones near our feet, and Richie would say, his adolescent diffidence masking his avidity, "You want to hear the latest about Corrigan?"

We had been calling Tom by his last name for a couple of weeks. It seemed to make him less a person with whom we had to contend than a myth we might foster.

"Sure. Whatever," I said, cool, nonchalant; shrugging both shoulders.

"I hear he flunked sixth grade so he's only in ninth."

"So big deal. It figures don't it?"

"That's not the worst of it. Get this. You know when his birthday is? October 15th, 1952!"

I made a rapid mental calculation. If I was born in 1955, and would therefore be fourteen on January 22nd (I had been allowed to skip the fourth grade) that would make Tom precisely two years, three months and one week older.

Richie was irked. "Don't you get it?"

"Get what?"

"My birthday is October 12th," he exclaimed. "I mean, he's the same fucking sign as me!"

I said consolingly, "Yeah, but he's older, so it probably don't matter."

Although I hardly addressed one word to Tom, I seemed to encounter him everywhere. Coincidence piled on coincidence. Was he spying on me now? I'd be taking the garbage out to the end of our driveway and he would fly by on his bicycle, his head turned to look at me rather than gauging the hill down which he was precipitously about to plunge; I'd be walking into the village to take a parcel to the post office to be mailed for my father and he would drive by with his mother, his face glued against the window staring at me; I'd be standing in the general store talking to Eleanor or Mary; the bell would ring, I would turn my head, and it would be him; Richie and I would be standing in line at the movie theatre, and I would glance back to see him arriving with the same dark-haired boy my father had seen him with. It was weird, creepy. It made me superstitious.

By mid-October open aggression, the strategy of frustration, was in danger of breaking out between us. It almost came to a head one cold, rainy Saturday afternoon. I had been sitting by the soda fountain at the back of the general store talking to Eleanor and her grandfather, Max. She was mixing my double vanilla egg cream. I was whirling around on the stool closest to the door. A delivery man dressed in faded blue overalls was carrying in cases of soda. Cold wet gusts scattered leaves on the oiled wooden floor.

Eleanor was saying, "You sure you want an egg cream on a

day like this? I can make you some hot chocolate."

She wiped her wet hands on a flowered apron. Her cheeks were sunken and sallow, her eyes weighed with dark sacks. It was hard for me to believe that she was just a few years older than I, and a few months younger than my brother. Her pregnancy made her look in her late twenties. She lit a cigarette.

Her grandfather, the village curmudgeon, shook out his newspaper noisily and said sharply, "Put that out. I told you before not to smoke with the baby coming." He buried his nose again in the paper.

She snubbed out the cigarette, but not before taking a last, long drag. She pressed down the white plastic spout on the top of a large glass jar, squirting shimmering brown vanilla syrup into the bottom of a tall crystal glass.

Max folded the newspaper and laid it on the counter. I did not get along well with him. Hardly anyone did. He was too opinionated, too harsh in those opinions, too often wrong. I had seated myself as many stools away from him as I could.

He said to Eleanor, "So, did you talk to that counsellor or not?."

She said wearily, "You're not going to start in again are you, Grandpa?"

"You got to talk to someone. You're sure not going to talk to me or your mother."

"There's nothing to say." Her words were barely audible over the sound of jetting seltzer.

He raised his voice, though the sound had stopped before he spoke. "I don't know what good you think this is going to do, holding out on everyone like that. You're stubborn. Like your father."

That was meant as an insult. Her mother and father were divorced. He was a car salesman and had run off with another woman.

She did not say anything but stirred the mix too vigorously before sliding it across the counter to me. She wiped her hands on her apron. The delivery man was standing by the cash register tallying up a receipt. She walked away from us.

Her grandfather muttered. "Stubborn girl." I buried my

nose in my glass and drew the sickly sweet liquid through the waxed paper straw.

"What're they saying about it at school?"

I was not sure he was actually addressing me, so I ignored it.

"You. Danny. What're they saying about her at school? Someone must know who the father is."

I looked over at him and shrugged the way children do with grown-ups when they do not want to cooperate.

"So, what do you think? You got an opinion or you like all the rest gonna keep your mouth shut. Well? What have you got to say for yourself?"

I said, "She won't tell no one, so no one knows."

He muttered the words: half to himself, half to me. "She's got to talk to someone, maybe at least the school counsellor. No good going on like this. Her mother's worried sick about it. All she wants to know is if something bad is going on. Her imagination runs wild . . . not knowing anything for sure . . . "

I was going to bury my face in my glass but he asked, "So, what do you think? I hear you're a smart boy. You got any opinion or not?"

He intimidated me. I glanced over at Eleanor. She was just out of hearing, restocking the candy rack by the front window. I hardly glanced at him.

"Maybe she's angry."

He repeated my word, "Angry. What's she got to be angry about."

"You know. Over the divorce and stuff. Everyone's always hollering at her."

I looked over again in her direction, afraid that if she overheard she might think I was betraying her, the loyalty of peers.

He went back to his muttering. "She's angry and she shuts up . . . Is that what you think? Doesn't make any sense to me. What I think is she's spoiled. She's had it too easy all her life. Had things fed to her on a silver platter. We're the ones should be angry. Sneaking out at night and getting herself knocked up like that. Damned stupid. Now what? She's barely seventeen and going to be a mother. Hardly fit to be a mother."

I said, "Maybe she blames herself."

But he was not listening. He went on muttering, "not fit . . . not fit at all . . . what's the use . . . "

I tried to finish my drink as quickly as I could and make my escape. He was saying, "So what're we supposed to do? You. I mean you."

I shrugged. "Maybe she'd make a good mother."

"Sure. Pat her on the back. Tell her she did right and everything's fine."

"She just needs someone on her side."

I turned away from him. Eleanor had taken the clipboard from the delivery man and was signing the receipt. She did look nearly thirty. It didn't seem fair.

I went up the cash register to pay Eleanor for my drink and there was Tom lurking behind the comic book stand. I had not noticed him entering, but with the door propped open he could easily have slid in unnoticed.

I went outside. His bike was propped next to mine against the wall of the building. I waited until he came out, and asked him sharply, "You following me or something?"

He looked directly at me and asked calmly, "You really believe that stuff?"

"What stuff?"

"That she blames herself . . . and the rest what you said."

His question disarmed me but I did not want to explain myself to him. I was about to say that he should mind his own business, or that he was weird, but something in his expression, a genuine curiosity perhaps, stopped me. I pushed my bike a couple of feet to get it moving and jumped onto the seat, doing a turn around him before heading off towards my house. He was not watching me. He was adjusting his handbrake.

2. Spying

There were two ways to walk from my house to Tom's: around by the road, or the short cut through the woods. By the road, from our front door, I turned left, eastwards towards the village, and a hundred yards or so on, made another left at the corner of our property onto North Road, a quiet tree-lined lane winding leisurely through elegant horse farms and golf clubs to end in Manorton, five miles upriver and in another county. The right side for a full mile, all the way to the country club and golf course, was one continuous field of sweet corn, a Paul Bunyan-sized green stripe executed with geometric exactness. It was farmed by two brothers who would not sell to the developers, at least not until the late seventies when speculation drove the values up and it was wildly profitable to carve up the field into little plots of two-bedroom suburban houses. Thankfully, I was already in university by then.

On the left side, for the first few hundred feet, was our wild flower field. Father had it mown once a year to satisfy the village council. A low, eighteenth-century fieldstone wall marked the end of our property and the beginning of the Episcopal churchyard. Their property was several acres wide: a well-tended lawn, the church graveyard, a tree-lined driveway to the white-frame Victorian rectory set far back from the road, gray stone, neo-gothic church, an attached nursery school, another field, another stone wall, and Tom's yard and house. I could have walked by the road to his house at a brisk pace in three or four minutes.

The more direct route, one I would come always to take, was across our back yard through the six-foot high privet hedge and thick underbrush into the oak grove. In an enormous old tree, beside a gully, on a thick limb twenty feet above ground level, we had built our tree fort. The embankment of the gully was about six feet high and in wet weather slippery with mud and loose gravel. Except in spring or after a heavy rain, the stream bed never had more than a trickle of water meandering among the large rocks, enough for the occasional lone fox or the innumerable deer venturing out from their secret glade in the deep woods upriver. For one of our pioneering games we had hacked rough steps into the far bank so that we could clamber under-cover into the sumac and dogwood scrub. A trampled path skirted the back edge of the church property, although I could save a whole minute by crossing the churchyard in plain sight, if no one was about. Before I was born Dornbush had planted a stand of pines and the thick grove, like some giant green inkblot, marked the end of Tom's yard.

The village children thought of the woods as their own, though in actuality everything that was not our yard, Trinity's, or Tom's, was part of the riverfront property owned by a utopian commune. They took pains to guard the integrity of the forest. For example, they brought in state forestry advisers to mark diseased trees, and help them in the thinning of groves to allow for stronger growth. So long as we were not destructive they left us alone. A child's right to play in the woods was no doubt part of some natural law to them, one of the privileges of play, in contrast to the hunters in deer season who were in no uncertain terms told to go elsewhere and harangued about the ethics of killing. So long as no one ever chased us away, we thought the woods belonged to us.

Richie and I had mostly been responsible for building the tree fort. It was peaceful there, up among the branches. I could see, through the breaks in the leaves, collaged pieces of my world: the rounded peaks of the mountains westward; the smokestacks south blowing the stench of industry upriver; a corner of our blue shingled roof; the cross on the steeple of St. Cecilia's; a flash of the white siding of the school building; the water tank; the red chimney of Tom's house; Trinity's neo-gothic tower; the taller cross and angel headstones. As far around as I could see, best were the rustling green, quivering trees, and the thrill of birds flitting beneath me.

We had nailed five simple wooden slats to the trunk of the oak to serve as a ladder up to the first thick limb. Sawed-off stumps and solid branches provided us with hand-holds to climb twenty feet to the next elephant leg of a limb. The trap door in the floor of the fort was kept padlocked. Richie Mullen, Mickey Spellman, and I alone had keys. We could bolt the door from within as well, an impregnable eerie. Admission was by password. It changed week by week if not daily, or on a whim.

The fort had four sturdy walls and a leaking roof. We were permitted to stay overnight so long as we used battery torches and did not burn candles or gas lamps. Some children had been burned to death in such a tree fort about ten years before, when a kerosene lamp had exploded. The village never forgot the lesson.

I was sitting up there alone one Saturday, a warm late October morning, reading a comic book and waiting for Richie. He was never out of bed before twelve on weekends. The smell of crushed apples lingered in the air.

As I had been climbing the tree I had heard the low murmur of voices carried in waves on the breeze. I had not seen anyone through the still thick foliage. The sounds died down. I continued up into the hut; settled down on the floor with my back to the north wall, and opened the latest classic comic I had traded with Richie for one of my duplicates, *The Count of Monte Cristo* for *Robin Hood* .

What made me look down? The lingering suspicion that someone might be out there? A buried instinct that allows us to sense an approaching stranger? We had so many concealed spyholes and hidden look-out vantage points that it was easy to peer down on the boy who now stepped soundlessly out of the underbrush into clear view and came to the edge of the embankment. The gully was at the base of the tree that I was in. The opposite bank was higher than the near side, and created the optical illusion of making him taller, of bringing him closer. This was my first glimpse of Bobby, the boy that had been recently seen around with Tom. He wore a khaki army shirt, camouflage pants and torn sneakers; had jet black hair and eyes, tawny skin. He moved stealthily to the edge of the embankment without even cracking a twig, with great seriousness, utter attentiveness. I was dead certain that he knew I was there, though he never once glanced upwards. I pressed myself flat against the floor and glanced over my shoulder at the trap door. Yes, I had bolted it shut, and yes, the various defence weapons in our arsenal were piled against the opposite wall: the bucket of rocks, two thick limbs, several powerful slingshots made from the sealers of canning jars and a stack of acorns. The wind moaned around me. Had it concealed any sound I might have inadvertently made?

Tom's voice now, a loud, horse whisper, closer now, but

still lost in the underbrush, "Bobby . . . Hey, where are you? Shit, I'm stuck on some thorns . . . "

He emerged into the clearing, examining the edge of his torn red flannel shirt. "Fuck. I tore my shirt. Ma's going to kill me . . . "

Bobby jerked his thumb towards the tree hut but did not look up. He also kept his voice low. "That it? That the fort you're looking for?"

I could see them clearly through the slats in the floor.

Tom nodded, "Yeah, that's it all right."

"Don't look so hard to break into. Looks easy in fact." He pulled aside his shirt. He had a hatchet in a sheath attached to his belt.

Tom said, "I was up there a couple of days ago. The trap door's padlocked."

"No sweat, I can climb in over one of the walls by going up that side limb over there." I knew he was right. I used the limb myself whenever I forgot the key.

Tom shook his head. "Looks too dangerous."

"City boy. I can climb up and then maybe force the door from the inside and you can climb in."

Tom was prying up stones with the tip of his hiking boot. "How high you think it is?" He picked up a sizeable rock and weighed it in the palm of his hand. He eyed the tree and lobbed it over one of the walls. It fell near me; I shoved myself closer to the wall.

Bobby followed Tom's example. His rock, hurled with considerable more force, resoundingly struck the side of the fort precisely by my head.

"It wouldn't be such a bad place to hide out. With a little work here and there I can make it real nice. Shit. I use to live in less. You should see the last place. What's in it anyway?"

"Not much of anything. A few comic books and candles. Sissy shit like that." Tom poked around for another, perhaps larger rock, and added, "Anyway, I still think the little know-it-all shits need being taught a lesson and I still say we trash it."

"Maybe they got some dope hidden up there where you didn't find it."

"Not them little fairies. They're too square."

"We still should have a good look around. You never know what people hide."

"You chickening out or something? I thought you said you was going to help me trash it."

"I ain't chickening out. It's just kind of a shame. I mean, maybe we could capture it or something instead. Get our own lock. No one would ever find our stash if we put it like way up in the tree there." He pointed high above my head at the tree top. "See, there. No . . . way up there. Near that top branch. There's a hole. I can see it. Squirrel hole probably."

"Where? I don't see nothing."

"There. Almost at the top. Twenty, thirty feet above the hut. No cop is ever going to climb up there and look in some hole in a tree top. All we got to do is wrap it so it don't get wet. Or eaten. We don't want no squirrels getting stoned, falling out of there."

Tom laughed. "I see the advantage. Maybe we could do both. Like, trash it first to discourage them. No one would suspect us of using the same tree as a hiding place."

Tom shielded his eyes from the sun and again measured the distance to the fort. He threw his second rock and it too curved over the wall, but fell further from me. He wiped his hands against his pants and reached into his shirt pocket to pull out a joint.

Bobby asked, "Why you want to do it anyway?"

"I told you before. The other day . . . I'm in the locker room getting dressed after gym . . . " He patted his pockets for a match. " . . . in comes Wyant with his fag team, everyone all buddy-buddy, talking tough and grabbing each other's asses . . . and he like, pretends I don't exist, like I'm not even there and he can look right through me."

"Yeah, I been there. I know how that feels."

While Tom was pulling keys, coins, string, a red Swiss army knife out of his pants pocket, he continued, "And that coach . . . I hate his guts . . . he's a real mean bastard. Starts shouting at us to get out cause *his* boys got the room now and we little fairies have to clear out. So, get this, I get my stuff together and start to leave and I have to pass right by the little creep and just as I'm like two inches from him he whispers something to that Richie looking straight at me and starts laughing . . . so don't go asking why I got to get even . . . "

"Jesus, no wonder . . . "

"You got a match anyway?"

I felt a flash of anger. Richie and I had not been laughing at Tom at all. We had been laughing over a dirty joke Mickey had told us on the way in. Of course, as I had entered the dressing room, I had immediately noticed Tom sitting on a wooden bench at the far end of the row of olive-green lockers. But when I was with the swimming team, one of those protective circles within which I lived my life, I was in another sphere of reality altogether. Even if the Pope himself had walked into the locker room I might only have withdrawn further into the aura of the group. Didn't he know it was our hour to have the space? He hadn't even put his shoes and socks on. His body was lean and wiry. Someone had said that he had been on the wrestling team at his high school on Long Island but I had never believed it.

Bobby found a book of matches in his shirt pocket and handed them over to Tom. "Man, I'm like all sympathetic and shit but I still think we can kind of use the fort and maybe even so no one knows we even been there. You know, at night or something. Or I can come back during the day when everyone's in school."

Tom lit the joint. "Maybe you're right."

"Sure I'm right."

"I still think I got to get even with the little bastard somehow." He passed the joint to Bobby.

"You gotta do what you gotta do. Still . . . " He took a long, hard drag, and held it in for a few seconds without saying anything. " . . . I could sure use it as a hideout . . . sort of even live up there . . . without their knowing it." He passed it back to Tom.

"What about the crash pad? It ain't so bad there for you. I mean, you even got your own space up in the attic."

"It's okay, but it ain't well, free like this."

"That tree ain't so free. You're up there you got to worry

all the time. About one of those little creeps finding you by accident or something. I can see it now. One day, you're up there? Smoking a joint, feeling good, beating off and just by accident one of those little fag brats decides he's going to skip school and bang runs into you. Just like that. I mean, If I was you, I wouldn't want to worry about it."

Bobby took the stub back. "Maybe . . . "

The acrid smell had drifted up to me. Smoking pot was a major violation of the team code, and though practically everyone else had tried it I had not.

Bobby handed it back. Holding it cautiously Tom deftly managed a last hit before wetting two fingers, snubbing it out and downing it, the last ritual act.

Bobby said, "So, we gonna do anything or not? If we ain't we better get out of here."

"What do you think?"

"I say, don't worry about it man. You can get even with the little bastards any time. I mean next time you see them in the woods even. You'll have plenty of chances. So why worry about it now? Besides, I got to take a leak."

Bobby stepped to the edge of the embankment, and Tom followed suit. As they were diagonally beneath me, I had a clear view as they unzipped, and two streams of honey-colored piss arched over the weeds into the gully.

From back in the woods I heard a girl's voice shouting, "Hey, you two! Tom! Bobby! Where the fuck are you? I'm lost!"

Bobby shouted back over his shoulder, "We're over here Tara! This way."

A teenage girl emerged from the same berry thicket that had trapped Tom. She was very pregnant, and holding her stomach with both hands. Her face was flushed and covered in sweat. Continuing to hold her stomach with one hand, she lowered herself to the ground with the other.

"I gotta rest. You guys just deserted me. I couldn't go that fast. Man, I thought I'd have the baby right out here under the trees."

Tom zipped himself up and turned to her. "That wouldn't be such a bad idea, you know, having the baby out in nature. . . "

They lingered a few minutes more, before drifting off towards Tom's house.

I waited awhile until I was sure they were gone before scrambling down the tree. I had to tell Richie what had happened. What were we going to do if Bobby started using our fort as his hiding place? Who was he anyway? Probably some kind of runaway wanted by the police which was why he wanted to use the fort. Wait until he heard that Tom was now out to get both of us. Boy, that was news. I hurried through the woods out towards North Road and looked around cautiously before dashing across into the corn field, our back route to Richie's house. Not only that, the whole thing was a misunderstanding. I couldn't believe it. Just because he thought we were laughing at him. I had never done anything to him. He had even been mad because I had been talking to Mick. What *was* his problem? What did it have to do with him anyway? He was weird all right.

I barged into Richie's kitchen. I spent so much time there, and there were so many people coming and going in that household all the time, that no one would have expected me to knock. Richie's youngest brother was sitting at the kitchen table eating a bowl of cereal. It was nearly noon. Richie was still in bed. I took the stairs two at a time.

Richie came up with a plan, 'parallel lines of defence' as he called it. He would promise some of his oldest brother's *Playboy* magazines to Donny in exchange for any information he might overhear at Lansing's about a plot to ambush either of us. In the meantime he and I would stake out Tom's house starting that very evening. Tom's mother was working the night shift at the hospital, so if any funny business was going on over there, it would probably be when she was out.

It was overcast, murky gray, muggy with the threat of rain as we slipped out of the back door of Richie's house that evening at about seven thirty. We counted the number of seconds between the flashes of lightning and the low, distant rumble of thunder. Forty seconds; eight miles. The wind out of the west, in our faces. Perhaps half an hour before it rained.

We armed ourselves with flashlights, slingshots, and a straight oak branch that I weighed in my hand as walking stick and weapon, inspired by a picture I had seen in the traded comic book of Friar Tuck and Robin Hood duelling on a log bridge. We set out towards Tom's house by the back route, through Richie's yard and the school playground. The corn patch kept us hidden until we emerged on North Road opposite his house. All the lights were on downstairs and up. A two hundred foot obstacle course had to be overcome: drainage ditches, an amber lamp hung cantilevered out over the road precisely where we would have to make the exposed dash to the shelter of juniper shrubs at the left corner of the porch. We could hear music distinctly enough to identify it. A window was open somewhere.

Ricky whispered, "The Doors." He need not have lowered his voice.

I nodded. He had just bought the same record.

There was neither a car in the driveway, nor any coming along the road. We scurried across in a crouch, into the bushes. I was already familiar with the inside lay-out of the house. When it had been put up for sale a few months after old man Dornbush's death, father had taken his woman friend Clare to see it in the hopes that she would be tempted to buy it and move closer to him. I had gone along out of curiosity. The front door was at the far end of the porch away from where we crouched catching our breath. A dining-room window was just beyond us. The kitchen was at the back. We crept along the side and peered in.

The music was coming from the living room but there was no one in it, nor in the dining room. Stooping beneath the sills we scurried to the back of the house. I was excited but not frightened, confident that if someone had seen us we could make a dash into the pine grove at the back of Tom's yard and through the woods to the safety of my yard.

There were two kitchen windows, a low one and a high, long thin one over the sink. Richie scurried ahead first to the low window and pulled himself up by his fingertips to eye level, then quickly squatted down and gestured to me to keep down.

We leaned back against the house. Gusts of cold wet wind broke through the trees wetting our faces. My heart was pounding, more from adrenaline than fear. The window was open several inches at the top, and an inch or two at the bottom. In the lull between the gusts of wind, the smell of grass, the forlorn drone of Morrison drifted around us. I heard a cough, no doubt Tom just inside. I turned and carefully lifted myself up.

Tom was sitting at the kitchen counter, about ten feet away, his left side towards me, quietly reading a letter. The room did not at all fit my image of him. It was not only sparse, neat, and clean, but it was neater and cleaner than my own kitchen. Evidence of an organized female hand was everywhere, absent from our male domesticity. The dishes had been washed and carefully stacked. Nothing was out on any of the counter tops, as opposed to our moldering clutter. Near the window where I squatted there was a round oak table. A cut-glass fruit bowl stacked with bananas, apples and my favorite fruit, a ripe red pomegranate, was positioned precisely in the middle of a spotless, blue and white check tablecloth that drooped evenly on all sides. A peeled and quartered, uneaten apple lay at the edge of a cloth place-mat in front of Tom and on the tan Formica counter top to his left sat a small, open cardboard box. I could just glimpse an array of brightly colored postage stamps on one flap. The wrapping paper jutted up in jagged peaks on all sides, but I could not see what was inside.

Tom was wearing a black tee shirt and blue jeans, but no shoes or socks. He turned another page of what must have been ten.

Richie poked me and pulled himself up next to me. If we had sneezed, giggled, or even exhaled, or if Tom had suddenly on an instinct turned his head, we would certainly have been detected. Though the smell of grass lingered about us I could see no evidence of the smoldering joint, nor even an ash tray, pack of rolling papers, tweezers, or any of the paraphernalia of use, already hidden. Richie squeezed two fingers together and held them to his lips. I nodded. From the living room came the sound of a needle loudly scratching the surface of a record. The music was interrupted. Tom turned, though thankfully not towards us, and shouted, "Hey, watch it, will ya!"

A Beatles song replaced the Doors, " . . . take a sad song and make it better . . . " The boy I had seen him with earlier padded barefoot into the kitchen, wearing a plain white towel drooping down to his ankles. "Sorry 'bout that."

He went to the refrigerator, opened the door and squatted to get a better look inside. "Boy where did you get that stuff. I really am starved. Not to mention stoned. Can I have a piece of chicken?"

Tom said grumpily, "Yeah, sure, take anything you want." He went back to reading his letter,

"You want anything?"

"No."

Bobby slammed the door shut and walked towards Tom gnawing on a drumstick. "Delicious. Your mother's a great cook." He was thin but wiry; his skin taut, not an ounce of fat rounding the surfaces. He was going to put the gnawed bone down on the counter but Tom stopped him, "Not there. In the garbage can, under the sink."

He padded around the kitchen doing as he was told, garbage can to cupboard, cupboard to counter. He was saying, " . . . that's some letter you got. More like a book. How many pages is it anyway?"

Tom turned over another sheet but did not answer. Bobby leaned on his shoulder, "Fourteen, Boy, your father's some letter writer. My father'd never write me a letter, let alone one that long. He never even has that much to *say* to me." He peered over the edge of the open cardboard carton. "What'd he send you?"

Tom didn't answer and Bobby stretched out a hand to attempt to pull some of the wrapping paper aside to have a look within.

"Wait. Don't do that. I don't want no chicken grease all over everything. Wash your hands first."

Bobby pulled up one end of the towel and wiped his hands. Glancing at Tom he pulled aside the wrapping paper.

"What is it, a shirt?"

"No, dumbbell."

As Tom did not protest he pulled out a long, blue silk

kimono embossed with enamel white herons.

"A bathrobe. It looks like real silk."

"It's a silk kimono, from Japan."

"Is it your birthday or something?"

"No."

"Can I try it on?"

"You still wet? I don't want it wet."

"I'm not wet."

Tom did not say anything else for a few seconds, reading the last words of the letter. He wiped his eyes, as if the act of reading had clouded them, folded the letter carefully, and put it back into its envelope. He swung around on the swivel stool to face Bobby.

"At least you're clean . . . for a change."

"Nothing like a hot shower when you're stoned."

He slipped one arm through the ample, drooping sleeve, then the other; took off the towel. The wide sleeves hung as drapery from his thin extended arms. He spun quickly so that it billowed out.

"Feels great."

Tom looked inside the box and pulled out a wide sash.

"This goes with it."

He stood up and went over to Bobby, reached around him, brought the ends of the sash to the front and looped them, Bobby's arms still extended outward.

Richie slid down to the ground and tugged at my sleeve; I brushed his hand aside. He grabbed the edge of my jacket and half dragged me back to the cover of the juniper shrub, scurrying ahead of me across the road and back into the cornfield in the direction of his house. It had begun to rain. I was torn between following Richie, or returning secretly to Tom's, but by the time we had cleared the corn patch, I had decided instead to go home. Richie and I talked about everything. As soon as we were up in his room again, I was sure he would want to gossip about Tom, but I did not. I ran home through the rain, replaying the indelible images of Tom's arms encircling Bobby's waist and the snow-white towel crumbling in slow motion to the floor: upset, angry, and confused.

3. I SAY HELLO

I was tempted to sneak back to Tom's house alone, but did not. The opportunity presented itself a few evenings later. Father and Charlie were going to a career counselling meeting at St. Francis' leaving me home alone. I had homework to do; I had promised to phone Mickey after dinner to talk over team matters; it was cold and rainy; I could spy on him anytime I wanted; it did not have to be tonight. Perhaps it was also Coach's voice I heard. During practise he had shouted at me not to make the dive I was about to make because I was getting it 'all wrong' and might even hit the board. I tried to put Tom out of my mind, but did not entirely succeed.

The truth is that my image of him had radically changed. He had become more interesting, even intriguing, not for anything I might imagine, or any of the unusual reasons, but because the interior of his house represented something which had immense power over me: order informed by a maternal touch – the very thing missing from my own spaces, and which perhaps I tried to create internally. Our kitchen, though clean, was a perpetual mess. Father kept everything: piles of old magazines, newspapers, and scholarly journals were stacked in corners, on cupboards, on top of the refrigerator. He liked to say that our house was 'lived in'. In other words, everything was left where it fell, and not much was ever put away, unless Clare was about to visit. The cups, glasses, dishes, and silverware went from the kitchen table to the sink – where they might linger a day or so – from the sink to the drying rack – where they were air-dried 'naturally' – from the drying rack, one by one, to the kitchen table – to begin the cycle once again. But as we had scurried furtively past each of Tom's windows, each glance had revealed a freshly painted orderly domestic world: white rooms garnished with green plants and paintings, oriental carpets, arts and crafts furniture and lamps. The idea I had formed of him, and expected – colored candles flickering sinister shadows on walls hung with brightly patterned Indian cloths, pillows and mattresses on the floor though certainly no furniture, dirty plates with crusted reeking food, everything in turmoil – had been stood on its head as if Tom were some trickster playing with my sense of balance, or that odd Franciscan notion, turned on its head to reality. His world should not be the way I wanted my world to be. The opposites had been reversed; they did not belong to the right persons. It was threatening. It gave him allure.

If, because of our foray, I had formed an unexpectedly positive impression of Tom's home life, the rumors continued to fly, and his reputation as the village bad apple progressed apace. Reports were filtering in through Richie and my brother, like messages to minor potentates: that Tom had been seen bullying a couple of seventh-graders out of their lunch money; that Tom had been thrown out of class for talking back; that he had been caught behind the school smoking and was going to be suspended; that he was having an affair with the wife of the chemistry teacher. Father even added his bit. At the village board meeting Dr. Mason, still smarting from the incident of the overturned garbage cans, had wanted to discuss 'what was going to be done about the village miscreants' and had put forward a resolution to send someone to Tom's mother to tell her to control her son. The board decided that the next time something happened they would send Reggie, the village cop.

Thus, in the short time that Tom had been living in Madalin, from the beginning of July to the board meeting in the middle of October, he was well on his way to alienating himself in the village, apart from the very people who would only alienate him further from everyone else. He seemed to be receding ineluctably into a world of dumb, arrogant vandalism and rebellion, and possibly crime as well.

Our paths crossed frequently enough for him never to be far from my mind. Now that swimming season and practise had begun in earnest, I saw him around Jefferson High, though, still the superstitious child animist, I ascribed our frequent encounters to magic. Our village school was too small to have a gymnasium, still less a pool. The diocese had provided us with a bus and we were shuttled the ten miles from Madalin to Holland Corners three times a week for gym classes after which I stayed for swimming team practise. There were fleeting glimpses of him, not a word exchanged: once in a stairwell as our team crashed downstairs past him and he had to hug the wall, another time as I glimpsed him entering a classroom, and again at an assembly for a local politician, slumped down in his seat a few rows in front of me.

Scores of such encounters were usually accompanied by the same impression: that he was angry with me, not for anything I had ever done to him, because of course I had done nothing, but egregiously angry with my very existence. It made me a bit frightened of him, but curious of the passions of boyhood. I was not too young to understand that his anger at least proved that I incited some sort of emotional response, which I did not mind so long as he left me alone, or did not harm me. My obsession with swimming and the team had also given me a certain amount of body confidence, a physical edge over other boys my age. I remember saying to Richie that Tom had better not come after me but if he did I could out-run him any day.

We would be bussed to Jefferson at the end of the school day, and arrive there at about two thirty. The year before Mick and I had made the junior team. I was a very good diver. I had won a trophy the year before and had come close to setting a record for my age group, which this year I was determined to break. It was a serious commitment, not just as loyalty to the group, but as a personal test. There was for me something unbelievably exciting about climbing the ladder to the high board, walking slowly and carefully to the end, curling my toes over the edge, working myself another millimeter forward to the right position high above the glistening water, summoning all my resources to concentrate, the inhalations and exhalations in right rhythm as I bent my knees aware of the danger before the plunge.

There was also camaraderie – not the same as friendship, but important nonetheless. Mickey and I were never as close as I was with Richie, though he also lived in Madalin and was in our eighth-grade class. There was too much competition between us for us to have an easy intimacy. He had a crush on Jacqueline, and she was supposed to be my friend. She liked him; she said she even admired him, 'like a beautiful iceberg'.

He had a classical face: high forehead, aquiline nose and utterly clear skin. He was very tall for his age and had already formed the habit of standing right up against you and looking down on you imperiously. Someone had nicknamed him 'the Bishop'. He was emotionally diffident about almost everything; he kept himself apart from our village cliques. We both took the team very seriously, and work-outs and meets were for him a deadly earnest business to be treated with religious gravity and zeal. Competition is, after all, one of the sacred dogmas of an American boy's upbringing. I admired his deep voice – mine still mezzo if not quite soprano – and those long silken strands he already sported like some proud peacock; not much sprouted on me yet.

He and I would ride in the bus together . We would enter the locker room in high spirits, roughhousing, feeling a bit of an adrenaline rush before practise, flinging our gym bags on the wooden bench and sometimes, as a game, spinning the dials of our locks in unison to see who opened his first.

That afternoon he won, and said, "Jesus, we're late today. It's almost three. Coach is going to kill us."

No sooner had we entered the locker room than we were jarred into sport's reality and reminded of our discipline by Coach O'Malley's shrill whistle and foul insults. "Get your butts in the water you little faggots . . . come on don't just stand up there on that board you little queer . . . you do that one and a half again wrong and I'll come up there and kick your sweet ass . . . " He achieved results at least. Jefferson's team, including the junior, was almost always either at the top of the league or near it; and God help us when we were not. I don't think that the school board much noticed his verbal abuse, his sadistic overworking us, or cared if they did – part of a Spartan toughening, as they might very well have called it.

"He's on Stanley's case again, poor little fuck." Mickey said, pulling off his shirt and throwing it onto the shelf.

"No wonder. He can't ever get anything right. He pulls the whole team down."

Half or more of the lights had already been turned off, the section where we were still lit but the back area in semi-darkness, to remind any stragglers that they had to get out. The locker room was usually deserted by the time the two of us were changing, but today as we entered there were still some older boys lingering at the back of the room, Tom among them, and of course I had noticed him immediately.

Mickey jerked his head back in their direction. "What're they up to? Jesus! Drugs it looks like. Let's get out of here fast."

I counted four, including Tom.

One of them said loudly, "Where do you get off charging that much? I don't care what kind of shit it is."

Tom answered, "You want it, you pay the price."

Another boy said, "Okay, okay. Come on, you guys, just divvy up. We hammered this all out before."

There were mumblings from the others but I saw one of them handing something over to Tom. The three of them passed us on their way out, but Tom lingered.

Mickey and I had been discussing a new dive, a backward flip, that we had been practising together. Mickey had long, lithe legs and was thinking maybe he could put them to use in the back flip, like long weights, to give him more spin.

"I really fucked it up yesterday," he said.

"Yeah, well, today's today," I said philosophically.

"Jesus, you're slow. You ain't even got your shirt off." He slammed the metal door shut. "Come on, hurry up. I'll wait for you."

"I got this fucking knot in my shoe. You better go on ahead."

He shrugged and walked off. The locker room reverberated with echoed sounds, but everything in the room itself was still. Tom and I remained at opposite ends. He was not looking in my direction. Should I say hello? Undo the false impression he had before? He was about thirty feet away, so that would have been awkward. I knew I had to hurry or Coach would make me do laps and I wanted to get in as many practise dives as I could that afternoon. I undid my belt and glanced over. He had reached into his locker to get his jacket and was putting his left arm through the sleeve. I hastily removed the rest of my clothes and put on my black and gold striped trunks. I clicked the lock shut and spun the dial. He was walking towards me; his lips clenched tight, a dark menacing look furrowing his brow.

I turned to face him, forced a smile, and said, "Hey, Tom? How're you today?"

He raised his eyes in surprise; opened his mouth to say something; thought better of it; shrugged his shoulders, and hurried by without a word.

4. Speaking words of wisdom

From this point on I can begin to date more precisely the various events that marked the evolution of my friendship with Tom. Halloween fell on a Thursday that year. Our school party was Saturday the 26th. My diary only begins a month later in November, but the impression Tom made on me the evening of the party still lingers: of someone who did not belong, not just out of place, but whose whole being was an anomaly.

Jacqueline was head of the entertainment committee; she had signed up Professor Matthews, artist in residence at father's college, whose hobby, as 'The Great Callisto', was performing magic tricks at children's parties and women's garden clubs. He owned a splendid yellow and white Victorian house in the village which had once belonged to a famous novelist. I cut his lawn during the summer vacation period for extra spending money, so I knew him a bit better than I did some of the other professors.

There would be, as usual, a competition for the best costume. A local man who owned the appliance store in Holland Corners was providing an expensive FM radio as first prize. I did not have a radio. I wanted a radio, especially one as nice as this, but I could not decide what I wanted to be. I went through various costume books in the college library, and even convinced Father to drive me across the river to a party shop. After browsing through the racks for hours, nothing much captured my imagination.

Perhaps inspired by our spying on Tom, Richie was thinking of going as Sherlock Holmes, but I pointed out to him that this idea had already won the first prize two or three years back and, therefore, had no chance of winning again so soon. He wanted me to go as Watson. Together we'd stand a better chance of winning.

I did not much like being second fiddle, and put forth sound arguments. What could Watson look like? Sherlock Holmes had his cloak, funny hat with flaps, a pipe, and even a violin, but what did Watson have that made everyone know he was Watson, *just by looking at him*? Richie suggested that I carry a black bag, and hang a stethoscope around my neck.

"Don't be funny," I said.

"So you come up with an idea."

I rattled off a list. If we went together as a pair: Uncas and the Deerslayer, Batman and Robin, the Two Musketeers; if alone: George Washington with an axe, Houdini, a ghost, a skeleton, a pirate with a patch – none of which captured either of our imaginations.

My brother had offered some sarcasms when I whined about it at the dinner table one evening: The Incredible Shrinking Boy; a giant cockroach; an albatross around his neck, the village idiot. I had mentioned to father that Jacqueline and Mickey were going as Dorothy and the Wizard of Oz. His offering was the Lion or Tin Man, but these too would mean being upstaged. I knew at least that I did not want to be anyone who could only be recognized by the character they were with.

I had been harboring all along a secret wish. That past summer at the county fair my palm had been read by a gypsy woman wearing long silver ear-rings and an ankle-length florid dress. A gypsy boy was standing at a podium at the entrance to the tent selling tickets, wearing a gold braided vest and baggy Sindbad pants. I had been with Jacqueline and she had said something about his looking "foxy". I also remembered that one day during the past summer, while helping Matthews to clean out his studio, he had pulled out a theater trunk with various bits and pieces of costumes, including an Arab robe and a white silk turban. I phoned him and asked if I could use them. Of course I could borrow the 'Abu Nuwas outfit', he said, thus suggesting a name, and adding a few descriptive possibilities: 'Fortune Teller

Supreme?' 'The Magnificent Magi?'

When I called Richie to tell him that I would not go as Watson, he said he had decided after all not to go as Holmes. He would rather be a modern detective. With the help of a fedora, some papier maché, and paint, he had decided to go as Sam Spade, with a black falcon pinned to his shoulder.

My paternal grandfather once told me, "Every place has the largest or oddest something." Madalin had St. Cecilia's, one of those few Catholic village grade schools. By the time I graduated high school, some four and a half years later, it had been sadly closed down and amalgamated with the new school at Holland Corners. The population in the Valley was by then expanding. A new tract of houses was being built in the village, and a new street was even added. The school was too small to contain the growth. Our eighth grade class had fifteen, but the smaller first-grade room was overcrowded with twenty-six, the first signal of change..

The Franciscan Order ran both St. Cecilia's church and the school, begun in the 1880s as a mission chapel, rapidly expanded by the turn of the century into a parish for the wealthy Catholic gentry, as well as the Irish and Italian laborers that had migrated into the valley to work in the orchards and vineyards, or to service the railroad. Perhaps the Church also thought it needed a counterforce to the solid Episcopal presence, or a political toe-hold among the influential.

The clapboard school building was donated to the order by an eccentric Catholic millionaire in the early 1920s, before the crash and his own bankruptcy. It was an imposing structure, and in fact a color photograph of it was used for the cover of a book entitled *Hudson Valley Gothic*. It stood squarely in the middle of the village, divided from the street by a wide front lawn cut precisely down the middle by a brick walk. I was told that there had even been a picket fence, rose arbor and gate, but these were gone by the time I started school. The path had been widened to accommodate the children. It might have seemed odd to enter school each day via a cake-box facade, elegant front porch, wide double doors with etched glass panes, an Italian marble foyer, but if this is the way things are from the beginning, children think it is normal.

The building seemed to me an endless series of interconnecting rooms that once had been kitchens and pantries, studies, sitting, and sewing rooms, and now were classrooms and storage closets. The property was large enough to contain its own full-sized baseball diamond, and – unwisely one might say – just beyond outfield behind a low hedge, a garden where the nuns tried to grow some of their own vegetables. I saw them often, wearing gray aprons, hoeing rows, as if the Church might revert to its medieval instincts given any rural chance. They lived on the upper floors, a spotless, cleansed realm to which I only once had limited access.

The library occupied two levels of the west wing tower. The loft area had a low ceiling, and oak bookshelves that were only shoulder high. An open stairway and rod-iron railing afforded a view of the lower room. I had decided to ensconce myself under the large bay windows, and had been allowed to clear away the chairs and spread the array of pillows Jacqueline and I had covered with remnants of cheap Indian silk. The sisters read to us there. I can still hear the late autumn wind rattling the glass; or the scatter-shot of hail, driving us further into the romance: *Kidnapped, Treasure Island.* What would it might be like to be Hawkins at that moment, sitting beneath waving palms, or eavesdropping on Long John Silver's treachery? The late autumn gales tore the leaves from the trees; the early spring rain washed the winter dirt from the glass.

For the party we had dimmed the lights and placed candles and carved pumpkins on the window sills and on top of bookcases. Orange and black streamers and paper skulls dangled from lamps. Fake cobwebs had been stretched across doorways. Corn stalks and dried ears of corn were piled in corners. Jacqueline had brought a sound effects record. Cats' screeches, cackles of witches' laughter, maidens' screams, and the hoots of midnight owls drifted in the eerie air through the building. A strange place for Abu Nuwas, though he might have liked the air of skulduggery.

I had made a sign out of a piece of white matting board. Along the top edge I poked two holes, threaded a piece of white string, and hung it from a brass wall lamp above my head:

THE GREAT ABU NUWAS
PALM READER EXTRAORDINAIRE
DARE TO LEARN YOUR DARKEST SECRETS
25¢ DONATION TO THE BOOK FUND

For the contributions, I had covered a shoe box in green crepe paper and pasted on various sized gold stars. It sat on a table to my right.

The high room was noisy and stuffy. My legs were getting cramped. I had taken a break to see Matthews's magic act, take a piss, count the $3.95 cents I had already earned, wondering who had under or over paid. Charlie had shown up with his latest girl-friend. Even father had poked his head in to see how I was doing and take the requisite snapshots.

It was not that there were no other high-school students in the room, even from Jefferson, or adults for that matter, that made Tom seem so out of place. Perhaps the atmosphere was too childish. Several second-graders were sitting around me playing jacks; throwing candy at each other, erupting into fights. A small girl was crying because someone had spilled cider on her dress. Perhaps the room rustled with too many Catholic habits. The village fire brigade in full fire gear might have been too small-town.

As I leaned over the rod-iron railing looking down on the milling and crowding I thought how strange he looked standing by himself near the door. I do not even know why I say standing by himself because he was being jostled and pushed as people squeezed to go in and out. It was clear he did not belong. Not there, not to anything in that room. Why had he even come? He was not self-conscious, or nervous; awkward, bothered, or tense. Was it simple? Did he stand out because he was taller than the small children around him? Or something he wore? The white colonial shirt with ruffled sleeves and pearl buttons; the deerskin vest? Had he stepped out of the eighteenth century, time-travelled to be there? Perhaps it was even more simply that everything in the room was within the circle of my world, except him. His arms were folded. He was looking around. I was sure he had not seen me but I suddenly thought, with great clarity and certainty, that he was looking *for* me. I jerked back from the railing out of view.

I sat down cross-legged on the cushions again, and put my turban back on. Even before he emerged up the spiral staircase I knew that the metallic ring of the treads would be him. He paused at the top of the stairs, eyeing me, my sign. Matthews was still doing his last tricks so everyone else was downstairs. He walked over, fished in his pocket for the requisite quarter, and sat down next to me without asking.

Another of his incongruities – his nails were meticulously clean and trimmed as if recently manicured. His fingers and hand were long and tapered, graceful. We had brushed by each other before; his elbow once jabbing me as we both tried to take the same comic book off the rack in the general store. We had literally run into each other in the hall at Jefferson, and once did a soft-shoe shuffle in the stairwell: together to the right, together to the left. He had taken me by the arms, and shoved me aside to pass. There was always some irritation or impatience on his part to mark those encounters.

I glanced quickly at his face. He did not look hostile. His forehead was high and clear of the slightest line or blemish. His eyes were elongated, feral, so dark blue I had mistaken them for black. He was turned a bit sideways. The ponytail was half way down his back, the ends curled and waved, his ears hidden. His nose was thin and refined, not pug like mine; his mouth long and sensual with full, drooping, indulgent lower lip. The mask he projected out in public, on the street, vanished in proximity. I did not find him so threatening, sullen, macho, tough, stubborn, stupid. As we leaned together I realized he smelled of spice, reminding me of sailing ships but nothing modern or of my life.

He held out his hand, and said, "Do you want to read it?"

I leaned over it but did not dare to touch it. A bead of cold sweat ran down my side, surprising me. I said, "You have a lot of triangles in your hand."

"Is that good or bad?"

"I don't know if it's either one."

"So what does it mean."

"It sort of means fate. Like you've got a fate or something."

"Destiny."

"Or it can mean you're going to be an artist. Or you're an artist already."

He looked up in surprise. I pointed to the middle of the three main lines, even daring now to run my finger over it, our heads together over his hand.

"This line is real heavy which means you'll be famous. See how it crosses the money line? That means fame'll bring you fortune. But lots of criss-crossing lines that those mean danger too. And see how this line breaks the other? This one here is your love line and these two lines and this one mean you'll have maybe two marriages but only one kid. Those lines are pretty thick too, which means they're important." I dared to glance up. He had let me take hold of his hand. He looked relaxed, even peaceful. "Hey, look here, at this, this break means you had an accident when you were small, maybe about three and that it was very serious, and you were probably even in the hospital."

That startled him, and he said quickly, "I was hit by a car when I was three and had to go to the hospital. How did you know that?"

"It's in your hand," I said. I am still not sure how I knew that. I don't think I had heard about it from anyone.

I continued, "You were sick for many months, but an old person took care of you. Not your mother."

"My grandfather," he said.

"Your life was in danger but he helped you get over it, and then here, he helps you again, sort of when you're about ten or so."

He nodded again.

"But you have a long life," I continued, "At least I think so because there are funny crossing lines which can mean there's lots of trouble ahead."

"Like what?"

"Sort of big violent events, or maybe just obstacles to over-come."

"You mean more accidents?"

"No . . . " I bent closer again. Our heads were almost touching. "More like bad influences. All around you. I can see in your hand all these . . . sort of animal faces . . . you know . . . looking at you from trees and bushes and things . . . but not friendly at all . . . sort of weird . . . but they're all enclosed in triangles which means you overcome them."

He pulled his hand away. "I don't think you can see that in my hand. I mean, I never heard that before. Someone else read my hand once, but they never saw no animals."

"So?"

He was not being hostile in any way. In fact, he seemed surprisingly together.

He ended it abruptly. "Anyway, thanks. It was worth the quarter." He stood up. I was going to say that I was not finished, that I had seen other things, but he turned and left. "Catch you around. Maybe," I heard as he descended the stairs.

No sooner did he leave than I had one of those attacks of conflict that he was so good at causing. Had he been there to make a fool of me? To tell Lansing and that crowd that I was doing all these fairy things and spouting mumbo-jumbo? Was he just curious? Gate-crashing? Taking stock?

Someone had put on a Pete Seeger record and a very loud sing-a-long was in progress. Jacqueline poked her head upstairs to tell me that the judging of the costumes was in five minutes. I did not want to be Abu Nuwas any longer. I took off the turban and went downstairs to join the others.

It was a foregone conclusion that Jacqueline and Mickey would win for Dorothy and the Wizard. I was hardly even listening as Sister called out their names. I looked around for Tom, but did not see him. Richie was working his way through the crowd towards me. There was clapping. Jackie and Mick were walking to the front of the room to get their radio. I felt withdrawn, hardly participating, glad that I had not been singled out. Richie would have seen Tom coming up to the loft. I knew why he was coming over, but I did not want to gossip. Before he could reach me I made my departure the opposite way and went home.

5. PURSUED

A spell of wet and windy, early November weather followed, which either matched or made my mood: on edge, pent-up, grouchy, jittery. I snapped at my father, brother, Richie, Jacqueline, the cat. Uncharacteristically, I immediately went to my room after dinner, and when I had no homework, stretched out on the bed and read science fiction. I had joined a science fiction book club. Stacks of books would arrive, the collected works of Arthur C. Clarke and Robert Heinlein, devoured within days. The brass wall lamp over my left shoulder cast a direct light upon the book. My knees were drawn up. I had a blanket thrown over me like an old man withdrawn from the world.

One evening Father poked his head in the door.

"You okay?"

I looked up from my book, frowned and nodded.

"Not sick, I hope?"

I shook my head. "No."

My brother was passing. His head appeared. "You in a mood again?"

I shrugged.

He tried to push past into my room but Father blocked him. "Leave him alone. He's okay. Sure you don't need anything?"

"No."

"If you want something you call me, you hear?"

I nodded. "I'm fine."

He pulled the door almost closed, leaving it open a crack so he could peek in again. It annoyed me; I got out of bed and closed it completely, then lost myself again in a world where different colored stars illuminated the night sky and a young man dreamed of freedom.

I did not see much of Tom but I was thinking about him all the time, even entertaining the occasional dream, one in which I floated through his bedroom window and hovered over his sleeping form. I awoke, unsettled. 2:23 a.m. The house was cold. I stood at the bedroom window. The bright moon illuminated the bleak back field, the trees blown clean by autumn winds. The lights in Tom's house were still on, probably his mother just returning from work. I wanted to go over, not so much to spy again as to confirm that everything was still as orderly as I had first seen it.

Of course I did not go back, and when I did see Tom again after the party, friends of his or mine were around and I did not even say hello, nor did he. I also discovered a formula, which was perhaps one of the true signs of ending childhood, of transition and change: if I consciously tried to run into him I ran into him; but if I consciously tried not to run into him I still ran into him. In other words, contrary to the thoughts and imaginings of the child within, I was not the cause of everything that was occurring between us. Something else was causing our encounters. I was still young enough, however, to think that this was due to an exterior if not an interior magic. Was I secretly willing our meetings without knowing it? The more I tried to think of other things, the more I thought of him. Which led me to another thought. One day as I was taking out my bike to go into the village I closed my eyes, strained my mind as hard as I could, and willed Tom to appear. I went into the store, stopped by the post office and rode home slowly, even pausing at the corner of North Road to see if he was in front of his house, or coming my way. He was not, and I went home. He had his own power. I could not cause his actions. It made me angry.

Being a good Catholic boy, I came up with another reason for my inability to affect events. God was determining our meetings and I was not worthy. I began to pray and make promises. "Lord, if you let me see Tom today I'll sacrifice my dessert to You." Answered Catholic prayers always needed a sacrifice. When this did not work I thought I might be displeasing Him in some way, perhaps because I was masturbating too much, or because I was snapping at father. If I was losing the mystical ability to control things, then I might still be able to influence God in order to get my way. Was I morally unworthy? Was I being bad? Was my faith not strong enough? I resolved to be obsequiously nice to Father, and to study harder than usual even though I was either first or second in the class depending on Jacqueline's moods and efforts.

More disturbing to me, my attitude towards the team began to change. I can see now that the shift might have been triggered by the incident at Tom's house – the pressure of unconscious or suppressed feelings, or part of the process of a boy's maturation. It happened automatically; one moment I felt one way, the next moment another. One moment I took everything, including my body, for granted; the next moment anything could make me self-conscious.

There was a lot of sex talk on our team, especially when we were changing or in the showers. I had been more than willing to add my bit. And I had also seen scores of boys naked, and paraded naked in front of them. Undressing had been something of a natural act, commonplace. A white Turkish towel had never signified what I began to see it signifying, the sign of a sexual ritual. Our obscenity satisfied our male egos; it had an expected quality to it; boys who engaged in sports were supposed to be obscene.

Team sex came in many forms. Sometimes, at the start of a swimming meet, as we stood with our toes curled around the edge of the pool and bent waiting for the gun or whistle, we would get erections. I am sure that is why so many girls pushed and shoved each other to be able to sit in the front rows to watch us. A good number of things besides sex can cause an erection in a boy: anxiety or outright fear, excitement, or strenuous competition. It happened to me a couple of times as I stood on the high diving board ready to do a backwards flip. There was nothing you could do about it except block it out of your mind, and concentrate on the dive. Comments inevitably followed. The most common was, "Hey, Wyant, didn't you get enough last night?" Sometimes, however, they would be couched in more risky terms. Once I heard, "Hey Danny, was that me you were thinkin' of – or your dog?"

In the locker room or showers too the thing would stiffen of its own accord. I had seen enough of them to know they could even be classified: long and thin, short and thick, straight, tapered, and most of them circumcised – as with most American males at that time. Some boys draped towels over it, or pushed it down impatiently as if it were their unruly child. Some ignored it; let it do its thing. You were only supposed to comment on it when someone was drawing attention to it for some reason, brandishing it aggressively or making an obscene remark or gesture. Humor is a useful tool for defusing desire.

Team sex was superficial; it only engaged the surface world. I never openly witnessed the sexual desire of one boy for another; I knew of no crushes, love affairs, or sexual obsessions, though certainly some mutual masturbating went on, some groping and grabbing, a lot of flaunting, but these were physical acts that did not imply an emotional engagement.

In that atmosphere of nudity, hard-ons, comments on girls' anatomies, macho camaraderie and obscene banter, it might be aggressive but it was never tender. "Hey, you fag." Or, "What're you staring at you little fag, your next meal?" Not only was there no mystery, but mystery, or affection for that matter, was impossible. Sex was just sex. The penis was just a penis. All sorts of stratagems were used to objectify it, but which really served to prevent it from becoming an object of desire. It was given nicknames: cocks, dicks, joy-sticks, tools, peters. Some would refer to theirs by name. 'Dickey' and 'dickey bird' was perhaps the most common, and one of my team-mates, accused of rubbing it too much, had his named 'Lamp' for him, after Aladdin, which was a bit more inventive.

Sex talk was as much a part of team life as sports talk or exercise. Being in the youngest category I was given a good deal of information about how to jerk off, jack off, pull my puck, trot the mouse, treadle my dinkum (was that nineteenth century?), and one of my favorites that I hardly heard anywhere other than in Madalin, 'choke your chicken'. Someone in the showers would say, "Hey, Danny boy your dong's a bit red. Been choking the chicken?" This would be followed by cackling that somehow managed to sound like orgasm.

If I had been writing it all down I might have compiled from what the older boys told me, a Kama Sutra of boy masturbation techniques. There were obviously a lot of taboos, rules, and regulations governing it. If you gripped it solidly in your fist that was manly. Rubbing it delicately, playing with it tenderly, in any way getting sentimental, was 'fag stuff' – threatening. Bringing yourself off as fast as you could, especially if you were doing it with someone else, scored you high points. You could use oil, cream, or maybe do it with soap when you were showering. You could also rub into a pillow, or against the sheets, but that would prove messy. There were jokes about handkerchiefs, socks and Kleenex.

Stories were told. The most common was 'the outrageous circumstance' tale: someone jerking off in the movie theatre with his girlfriend, or rubbing off on the carpet watching television, right under the eyes of his parents who would of course choose not to notice that their son's gyrations meant he was coming in his pyjamas. It was a matter of banter and competition, though I do recall Coach warning us on a number of occasions, especially if we had lost a match, about "you girls beating off too much – save it for the enemy" – aggression and suppressed sexuality as cause and effect. There were very hush-hush rumors around about a couple of boys, also a rumor about a very pretty boy and the team physiotherapist, but I had no personal knowledge of either. Mostly the talk was about solitary pleasures, or roles. The older boy in our banter was always the active partner, the younger boy passive. "Hey Danny, you bending over for me?" My ass was patted and slapped, towels flicked against it; praised for its roundness, firmness, tightness. There was no seduction in this. I never felt threatened by it, because I was not being singled out.

I might call all of this sex, but certainly not desire, and most certainly not the desire of one male for another. That would have engaged the emotions in a way I did not experience as part of that reality of adolescent braggadocio – boys strutting their wares. Can it even be called sex? Sex should signify itself, but all of this 'sex' usually signified something else: prowess, power, even humor, or any of a number of gender traits American boys were conditioned to act out: aggression, a certain militancy. Sex for pleasure, or for pleasure with another boy, was too stigmatized, scorned, even criminalized to become sexual desire.

At its most positive one can interpret all this banter and sex talk as being an education in American manhood roles. My team mates and I were being good citizens, genuflecting to a sexual materialism. We might have revelled in the physical responses of our bodies, but with each other this was only to distance ourselves from emotions and attachments. It was never to allow sex to become merely sex. In other words, our American gender role was a denial of the reality of the real, full personhood of the other, not to mention ourselves as well. Another male's emotions would never be our responsibility.

The first sense of something changing for me was that I now began to feel shy about undressing. I laid this down to a biological fact, an embarrassment. I was getting on to fourteen by then, but had no visible pubic hair. It must have been some remark someone made ("Jesus, I shot right over my shoulder last night") or Mickey's growth being praised by one of the older boys, though he was only a month or two older than I ("Don't let your girlfriend get her braces stuck in your bush"). Even the closest examination did not reveal even the suggestion of a follicle. Was I a freak? I became self-conscious at parading back and forth nude to the showers and began to hide myself, but I also began to crack fewer jokes, be embarrassed by Mickey's hard-on, not wanting to shower at all.

I doubt if I can ascribe the new self-consciousness entirely to Tom. Surely it must as much have been the workings of a complex of internal responses. In fact, for days Tom would quite disappear from sight, if not mind. Had he run away? Moved away? Huddled down in my mackinaw, my cap pulled around my ears against the raw November wind and icy stinging rain I would nevertheless keep my eyes peeled for him as I sprinted across the windswept main street to the store, the few hundred yards down the road to the warm stillness of my home, or dashed from the school door to the bus waiting to take me to practise. As I gradually ceded to him and God more power, I began to believe that in the dark shadows of a dreary autumn afternoon or evening he lurked somewhere hardly as an embodied person, but as a shadow that could at will materialize into form.

Quite suddenly the weather turned calm and warm and I was back in the woods again. It was warm enough to be in shirt sleeves, a last exposure before those dark months buried in cloth. There had been fierce winds and I took to cleaning away the debris deposited on the tree-house floor, nailing back some boards blown off by a violent gust. I found bits and pieces of splintered and sodden shingles torn from the roof all over the woods. One of the side walls was yanked off as if by one sharp pull. My hammer fell too hard on the water-softened plank, gouging a deep groove into which moisture immediately seeped.

Some pieces had broken too badly to use again, but there was a woodpile out behind the Anglican church and the Reverend Edgewater had given me permission to use some of the blackened, discarded boards. The woodpile was at the very back edge of the church yard. Beyond it was the commune woods and a path to the main commune house. To my left there was the path that led down into the gully and up to the oak tree in which our tree house perched, and the beginning of my back yard. To my right the path continued to the end border of Tom's yard.

I was rifling through the woodpile when Tom, Lansing, and Bobby appeared at the edge of Tom's yard. They were carrying air rifles. Lansing had spotted me by the woodpile. He started shouting and waving his gun.

"Hey, there's that little fag. Look he's stealing from the woodpile." He brandished a fist as well, and shouted in my direction, "Hey you little shit. What the fuck are you doing in our woods? Come on you guys let's get him. Come on Tom, here's our chance. Let's beat the shit out of him!"

I found it hard to breathe. My palms went cold and damp. I felt like a fool, caught red-handed and alone. Had they been in Tom's back yard all along? Or had they seen me from one of Tom's windows and decided to sneak up on me. They began to advance out of his yard, but were still fifty or even a hundred feet away. I glanced around to take in my advantages or disadvantages. There was enough yard and overgrown field still separating us. With forced nonchalance I pretended to continue to pull boards out of the pile. I could not find the boards I wanted. Everything was too wet, caked with dirt or tar, too thin, too split, or too large to carry. I kicked at the pile, glanced up at them. They seemed to be huddled in some kind of discussion but were too far away for me to hear anything. I shoved my hands in my jacket pocket and started to saunter away. I heard Bobby say clearly, "Hey, he's getting away." Lansing cried, "Come on. I tell you he's alone and it ain't no trap. Let's get 'im and teach the little fairy a lesson. Come on Tom! You go get him!"

There was the crashing of a body into the underbrush. I glanced back. Tom was running through some young sumacs towards me; the other two were close behind and goading him on, "Go get 'im Tom! Beat his ass! Kill him! Get 'em!"

I had been walking, but now I dashed forward. Tom was gaining, but there was a good distance between us and I was a confident and fast runner. It could not have been more than two or three hundred yards to the gully, and the same again to my yard. I knew precisely where I could leap down the slope and up the other side without slipping, which would easily bring me to safety. I was running now at full tilt, and glanced back once to see that I was not only maintaining the distance between myself and Tom but lengthening it.

I heard shouting, mostly Lansing's maniacal tones. "Hey, he's gettin' away. Come on Tom! Get 'im. Get 'im! Faster. Faster!"

I had almost reached the gully when I looked back again. It was clear that I had such a good head start that I could get clean away. I could already see the back door of my house. I was very angry. As I ran, I was thinking to myself, "These are my woods as much as theirs. They don't have any right to chase me out of them. I mean, who do they think they are? I'm not scared of them. I'm not going to let them chase me." And just as I reached the gully, before I even leapt down the embankment to the safety of the oak tree where I could have scrambled up into the tree house or made it to my yard, I suddenly stopped dead in my tracks and turned, my hands hanging at my side and waited for Tom to catch up with me.

Bobby was close on Tom's heals. He might have out-stripped Tom but it seemed as if they had a design to allow Tom to get to me first. Lansing was huffing and puffing yards behind. I waited. Tom slowed down to a trot. Bobby caught up with him. I did not move. Tom walked towards me. He had pushed Bobby behind him. Lansing had stopped and was bent over in a crouch trying to catch his breath. Tom was only a few yards away now, looking at me suspiciously. Perhaps he thought I had a knife or a gun or something. I stood my ground: calmly, as one can be in a state of suppressed rage.

Tom came to within a few feet of me. Lansing started shout-ing again, "Come on, Tom. Sock him in the jaw. Beat the shit out of 'im!" He was stumbling under his huge weight, close enough now for me to hear his wheezing.

Tom approached me cautiously, ten feet, five, closer still. I stared him in the eyes and made no move at all. I could see he was puzzled.

In his hesitation, I burst out, "You guys don't have any rights over these woods! I mean I was born here in these woods and you ain't got no right to chase me out of here and I ain't runnin' away from you and I ain't scared of you because they don't belong to you and who do you guys think you are any-way?"

In spite of my words I must have been frightened. Lansing and Bobby were now even with Tom; the three of them stand-ing menacingly in front of me. Lansing's thick face was contorted with hatred. He pushed Tom from behind, propelling him a foot closer to me. "Hit the little fucker. You can take 'im. He's a little chicken shit." Bobby kept still. Tom lurched closer a couple of steps, took a couple more on his own. He was now at most only a foot from me, close enough to smell him.

I said angrily, but softly, "All you've been doing since you moved in here is start trouble. Who the hell do you think you are? Lansing's little lackey or something? I ain't afraid of you and you ain't gonna chase me out of these woods. They're my woods, not your woods. You don't know anything. You're just a stupid little shit."

I really don't think that Tom intended to hit me. He was

looking at me in utter astonishment, his mouth open, blinking, as if I were some extraterrestrial creature suddenly materialized in his path.

There we were, in a stand-off, and for a second or two, even longer I think, none of us, not even Lansing said a word. It must have made an odd sight, three boys faced off against the one.

And then, well, I simply turned and leapt down the gully embankment and up the other slope. Without even looking back I walked the distance to the dividing hedges and just before I squeezed through the opening into my yard I did turn around and look back again. The three of them were moving off towards the road. I don't remember throughout the incident Tom having said one word.

6. TOM APOLOGIZES

The weather continued warm and dry. Late the following afternoon, when I went back to the church woodpile to finish the task interrupted the day before, I heard a metal lawn rake being scraped too vigorously over the hard ground and caught a glimpse of Tom, alone in his back yard, gathering leaves. He did not see me; at least I did not think he saw me. I paused for a moment watching him with unfeigned curiosity before stepping out of sight behind the woodpile to gather boards.

Finding solid planks proved a more difficult and time-consuming task than I had expected. It was necessary to shift a good part of the pile in order to reach the bottom layers. Several clean lengths were finally set aside; the disordered stack reassembled.

The entire task had taken perhaps half an hour. As I was ready to leave, I peeked around again to see what Tom was up to and whether he was heading in my direction. He was gathering up an armful of leaves and grass cuttings, and started towards the compost heap out in the woods behind the church yard. Someone from the commune must have asked him to contribute to the pile for their organic garden. It took him directly across my path, not twenty feet away, but he did not even glance in my direction. Surely, he must have seen me.

I lingered in a conflict. Even if he was ignoring me, should I say something to him? Should I simply pick up the boards and leave? He turned and started back towards his yard. This time he passed even closer to me, not ten feet away, looking directly ahead.

As he drew even I said, "So, you going to say something?"

He stopped, and turned to face me, brushing flakes of grass and leaves off his green and black check wool shirt. "You want me to?"

"That depends."

He turned to leave. "If you're going to play a game . . . "

I said angrily, "Me play a game! You're the one playing the game. That was pretty stupid yesterday . . . you and Lansing . . . I mean . . do you really think that Lansing is your friend or something? All he's looking for is someone to do his dirty work. That's sure a friend a guy needs. You really got taste in people, don't you? What are you? Doing everything Lansing tells you to do?"

He thrust his hands into his pockets. "What if I am? What's it to you?"

I replied angrily, "What's it to me? I'll tell you what it's to me. You or no one's got no right to chase me out of these woods. I mean I was *born* in these woods and here you are hardly here a couple of months and trying to take things over like you got some rights or something. You ought to dump Lansing. Or maybe you should just go back to Long Island where this kind of crap happens all the time but not here because with friends like Lansing you don't need no enemies because you're going to be in all the trouble you need before you know it. Why you in with them anyway? What's your problem? I mean, Lansing thinks he can go anywhere he wants and bully anyone just because he's like eight hundred pounds and mean as shit. You don't even know anything about him. He's the biggest trouble-maker in the whole fucking U S of A? And Jesus he's even been in jail, which is probably where he'll drag you down to along with him."

"You don't know what it's all about. It's not what you

think it is. You think you know but you don't."

"So, try me. What's it all about?"

"What's the use? You've already judged me like the rest. Anyway, maybe it's better you don't know."

"That's a cop-out if I ever heard one."

He shook his head. "Don't push it . . . "

My mother's Sicilian blood got the best of me again.

"Me don't push it. As if there was any mystery here! I know all about you . . . I mean *everyone* knows *everything* about you even if you're too stupid to know that everyone in a village like this would know everything about everyone. I mean do you think for even one second that people don't know all about you? I heard all the stories about all the trouble you been in since you was living in Long Island – with drugs and shit and being the big man – and then, here you are, you move in and got the chance to make a clean start and five seconds later the first dumb-ass thing you go and do is get in with the worst crowd of them all. Talk about childish! Christ, turning over garbage cans on Mason's porch! I haven't even wanted to do anything like that since I was five no less do it! So what's next? Breaking and entry? Robbing the Holland Corner's First National Bank? Lansing doesn't give a shit about you or what kind of trouble he gets you into. He's just out for himself and hey – guess what – if you happen to get in the way or get into trouble – well too bad for you because he's gonna look out for numero uno and walk the other way. Guarantee it."

Tom was staring at me wide-eyed but not threateningly. It helped calm me down.

He replied, "You don't know half as much as you think you know. And anyway, you and your friends – you're all so lily white. Jesus! You're the perfect-student-big-trophy-winner-altar-boy-debating-team something or other and what are you? Twelve? Thirteen? What could you really know about me? Christ, I mean you're even the *flag raiser*."

"So? What's the point? A guy's gotta survive in a place like Madalin. You can say all you want but when push comes to shove and you're like in real trouble I'd be willing to bet a million dollars Lansing and his crowd would shaft you faster than they can spit and Richie wouldn't do that to me or me to him I can tell you because we never did and we've had our times too."

Tom shrugged, "Lansing was the only one that would talk to me when I moved in. Not you. Or Richie. You wouldn't even give me the time of day. So why should I listen to you now? It's not like I was welcome here or anything and I had all these choices and made a bad one or that I was good enough for this precious little fucking middle-class village."

"That's stupid. You're such a stupid shit. I don't even know why I'm talking to you. I never seen you go out of your way to give me the time of day but you were sure ready to give the elbow in the hallway plenty of times. I mean, Lansing just wanted your drugs. Everyone knew about it. Acapulco Gold. What else do you think he's after?"

"So, why do you give a fuck? Maybe I never went out of my way but you're in so thick with your crowd you never much gave me the time of day either."

"Who gave me the chance?"

"And?"

I said more calmly, "I don't think you're like Lansing. I don't think you're like that. Not really. You got more to you than that . . . something . . . well . . . more than you think. I don't think you're mean like him just because you want to act tough. Not really. Lansing's a lost cause. But I don't think you're a lost cause. There's something else. I don't know. You're worth more. Worth something."

He shook his head. A suppressed laugh suddenly escaped, "You're something. You pretend to go around knowing everything . . . You're really something. So what are you saying? . . . You offering me something?"

I spit on the ground. "You go to hell. You just go to hell."

He suddenly looked upset, and said, "Wait. Hold on. Don't get angry. I didn't mean it the way it sounded."

"You fucking go to hell. You did mean it. And you can just go to hell. I'm wrong! I'm dead wrong! You're a waste of time. A fucking waste of time."

A slight breeze was detaching some of the remaining leaves. They drifted slowly across our path. The morning sun was still warm, as if winter were very far away. Birds in distant trees, the chatter of a squirrel somewhere should have reassured me. Was everything normal? I turned and stomped off in a rage.

Several hours went by. I repaired the tree house; helped Richie finish another model. At five o'clock I was in our kitchen. It was late enough in the year to have all the lights on. The room was warm; smelled of the chocolate chip cookies that Clare had baked earlier. I was sitting at the round oak kitchen table doing some math homework. There was a knock at the back door. I jumped up and slid over to the door on stocking feet, expecting to find Richie or Mickey, but it was Tom.

As I opened the door a draft of cold wet wind blew in. The weather had turned. There were drops of water on his face. He had on a thin jacket and was hugging himself and stomping around. "Look," he said right out. "I just came over to say I'm sorry. I didn't want the conversation to end like that so . . . well . . . I'm sorry." He hugged his arms tighter, and tucked in his chin. "I guess that's all," he said.

I gaped at him and finally managed to say, "So, is this peace or something?"

He shrugged, "If that's what you want."

I held open the storm door wider. "Guess you better come in. You're freezing out there."

He brushed past me into the kitchen.

PART TWO: COURTED BUT NOT SEDUCED

1. SECRETS AND LIES

For the first few weeks of our friendship, no one knew that Tom was coming around to see me. The empty woods provided a convenient cover. By that time of year the lone bird-watcher, or one of the commune poets dreaming Arcadian verse, would be unlikely to notice someone skulking along the fringe of trees. He would knock on the kitchen door a few minutes after I had returned from school or practise, if he was not waiting there already. He managed to leave before either Father or Charlie arrived.

He started bringing me things. Bags of dried apricots, raisins, pineapple; carob-covered dates or muesli-and-honey wafer bars would be produced from the cornucopia of his pockets. A health food store had recently opened in Woodstock and he was hitchhiking there on weekends. Sometimes it was two apples, or a pear he would cut in half. He always waited until I took the first bite. Fruit became a colored wrist band, an extra one woven for me, he said. It was attached to my wrist as solemnly as one might bestow the sacred Brahmanic thread; wrapped twice, the ends woven together, not tied. He turned my wrist this way and that, very pleased with his handiwork; and me. Later, ready to lie about where it had come from, I even brandished it under Father's and Charlie's noses, but they never noticed. At diving practise the next day Coach made me take it off.

These token objects represented a progression, from sharing, to bestowal; from studied curiosity to risk. We were sitting at my kitchen table one late afternoon. My brother was due home about five. Tom was about to leave. He had been anxious, distracted that day. I had even asked him if everything was all right. With some trepidation, he pulled out of his shirt pocket a small packet wrapped in white tissue.

"Here. This is for you," he said nervously. "My father sent it."

I hesitated. Everything else that he had either given me, or that we had shared, had both been offered and accepted naturally.

"How come? It's not my birthday."

"It's . . . well . . . for the swimming match."

He meant the regionals, but they were not until January. I unwrapped it. Inside was a gold amulet two inches high and one inch wide of a woman holding a lotus.

"What is it?"

"It's Lakshmi. The Indian goddess of fortune. It's for luck."

"It looks like real gold."

"It is. My father said it's more than a hundred years old."

"I can't take this, Tom. He sent it to you. Besides, Coach doesn't let us wear anything around our necks when we're diving."

"You don't have to. You can pin it to the back of your locker door. It just has to be some place near you."

"Where did it come from?"

"He bought it in Bangkok, I think. When he was on shore leave."

"You should keep it for yourself. I mean, he sent it to you and maybe he'd be pissed if he knew you gave it away."

"No. You don't understand. You're supposed to give it away."

I continued to protest. He looked frustrated and said impatiently, "Here. I'll read you." He fished a letter out of his back pocket. I wondered if this were the same letter I had seen him reading in his kitchen that night. He leafed through it, reading only the relevant passages.

Dearest Son . . .
. . . so, I thought you might like this. It's a hundred years old, or more and I bought it at an antique

70

store in Bangkok when I was on leave in September. The man said it was 1850s, Northern Indian . . . 24 carat gold . . . Lakshmi, goddess of good fortune . . . She brings you good luck . . . The way it works is that you have to keep it safe for ever, or give it away to someone you care about, but if you lose it it's bad luck, so don't ever lose it . . .

I turned the tiny figure over in my hand. A declaration of feeling had come along with it, even if given obliquely in someone else's words. Perhaps that is what confused me. The shared objects had become not just gifts, like a pair of socks given at Christmas by a distant aunt. They had become objects of desire accompanied by veiled messages, a little dangerous.

As with the gifts, so with the secrecy of his visits. At first it was all a game, not to mention convenient. I never mentioned he had been at the house because that might have meant explaining, or being teased. Perhaps I was not all that sure yet about him. Perhaps the power of childhood still had me in its grip and I could not so easily shift into another reality. One thing was certain – in the hot-house reality of Madalin, secrets and lies were revelations waiting to be made.

Of course, if we were meeting secretly I also continued to run into him around the village and at Jefferson. By tacit agreement, we passed without speaking, publicly unrecognized intimacies being one of the great oddities of boyhood.

One late afternoon as Richie and I were walking from his house into the village we spotted him coming out of the laundromat. Richie grabbed me by the arm and pulled me behind a tree.

"Quick! Behind here. There's Corrigan."

Tom had stepped into the road and was peeling open a candy wrapper. If he had seen us he did not let on. Without turning to look in our direction he walked away towards his house. Richie gave a sigh of relief.

"Boy, that was a close call . . . I wonder where his pals are?" he added sarcastically.

"I don't know. I haven't seen them together for a few days."

"Me neither. I wonder what's going on."

"Probably they just got fed up with each other."

"Maybe they had a fight or something."

"Nah. I doubt it. We would have heard about it from blab-ber-mouth Donny."

"Guess you're right. Hey, wait a minute. Come to think of it I did see them passing each other in the street the other day without even saying hello. I bet something *is* going on."

I did not like the drift of the conversation. Richie, after all, could ferret out the most buried morsel and present it for our delectation. If he were now to turn his snooping nose upon Tom, like a dog to a truffle, it could lead him to me.

I said uneasily, "Jesus, who cares. I got better things to do than go around poking my nose in Lansing's business."

He said hesitantly, "Yeah, who cares." But he added, "But I bet you a million bucks Donny knows something he's not telling."

I left Richie at his house. When I walked into the house, Charlie was on the telephone talking to one of his girlfriends. Father was still not home from his office at the college. Dinner would not be for an hour.

I went upstairs to my room. Lights were on all over Tom's house. If Bobby was not there he would be alone. His mother's night shift ran for another two months. I changed into what my father called my 'old clothes' – jeans, sweat shirt and sneakers – grabbed an apple from the refrigerator, made sure not to let Charlie see me when I went out, and cut across the backyard and woods to his house without even bothering to throw on a jacket. It was a cold evening, snow flurries and a light wind; the frozen blades of grass crunched underfoot.

I scurried to the back door. Shading my eyes, I peered through the glass. No signs of anyone. Directly in front of me was a long hallway that did not quite divide the house into two equal halves. At the far end to the right I could see the edge of a long window I knew was next to the front door; I could not see the door itself. Tom's green and black wool jacket and a gray-green thermal coat were hanging alongside a woman's dark brown cloak; two pairs of boots, rubbers, Tom's muddy work shoes, an umbrella, a woollen cap fallen from the shelf above, lay scattered along the floor. It did not look like Bobby was there.

I had to finish the apple before he opened the door. Or else what? I would freeze to death? He would be dead? It was one of those superstitious games I invented for myself at that age. I knocked again more loudly, hugging my shoulders and stomping around. Now I really was getting cold; his fault. I could see a corner of the kitchen through a doorway to my immediate left: bright, freshly painted, inviting. I threw away the apple core. He was taking too long. The game did not count unless I wolfed down the last bit as he approached. If he didn't open up pretty quick I was going to freeze to death.

I was worried about what might be happening between him and Lansing. Or rather, about what I had said that afternoon to Tom about being friends with Lansing. I was going to let him have it as soon as I saw him. He was going to have to keep his mouth shut about what I'd said because if the creep ever found out I'd been talking about him behind his back my ass was grass. Especially if he found out he'd been dropped like a hot potato and Tom was hanging out now with *me*. At least until today, because if he didn't hurry up he'd find a frozen stiff on his doorstep. Not only that, if Tom had dropped him because of all those things I had said, well, that was his choice, and not Lansing or anyone could hold me to blame because it was a free world, wasn't it? And that was only half the story. There was still this business about him sneaking off every day – that's right, sneaking off – before Father got home as if he had timed it so perfectly that Father could be walking in the front door and he'd be walking out the back door. What was he? Trying to pretend he was psychic, or something? Probably he had cased the joint with a stopwatch. Jesus! I was starting to sound like Richie. I banged again.

I heard him coming downstairs with great thumps and thuds, taking the steps two or three at a time. He used the brass bulb decoration at the bottom of the banister to spin himself around into the hall, a game he might have been playing for years, though they had only been in the house a few months.

73

He walked towards me, buttoning up his flannel shirt, hanging loose outside his beltless pants. He was barefoot.

He turned on the outside light and flung open the door, genuinely surprised to see me; his face lit up with pleasure. "Hey, come on in, I was just gonna take a shower. Where's your jacket? You must be fucking freezing."

I brushed past him into the hall. "I gotta talk to you."

The house was warm, much warmer than we kept ours, scented appetizingly: nutmeg, cheese; fish perhaps?

"What's up?"

I went ahead of him into the kitchen, my shoulders hunched, my head lowered like a bull for the charge. I turned and faced him. Hardly paying any attention to me, he walked over to the oven and peered in; to the refrigerator where he loaded in his arms a quart of milk, a melon, a carton of eggs; to a shelf for bananas and a vat of farm honey. He carried it all precariously to the counter and set it down, watching me all the time out of the corner of his eye.

"You want something to drink? I was going to make a milk shake for myself. Why don't you stay for dinner? My mother made enough casserole for ten armies." He skipped back over to the oven and peered in again. "It'll be ready in about an hour." He glanced at his watch. "Half."

The counter divided the sink area from the rest of the kitchen and was between us. His long hair when hanging loose fell over his shoulders like a gilt shawl. With both hands, he gathered it behind his head, as women do, then let it loose again. "I forgot to tell you, you got to take your shoes off." His mother was a stickler for order and cleanliness because she had to work so hard. He pointed to a stool on my side of the counter.

I had intended to say what I had to say and leave, but I meekly took off my shoes and slid up onto the wicker seat.

As he was preparing the mix he was saying, "Hey I saw you at school today going into the gym. I was on my way to detention. All I was doing was passing someone a stick of gum and the teacher probably thought it was uppers or downers or something 'cause he comes rushing down the aisle grabs it from me and tears it open. Spearmint. Everybody started laughing so he gives me detention. Which is where I was going when I seen you."

"Boy, that's rough."

The blender whirred. He added a container of milk, holding the top with his hand. When he went to the cupboard to get glasses I noticed that the dishes were neatly stacked by size, the glasses aligned in straight rows. Watercolors of fruit hung perfectly centered on the walls, a hand-woven rug lay in front of the sink, an enormous, healthy bright green fern hung by the window. He turned the blender off, poured the frothy pink mixture into two glasses and slid one over to me. I wound my legs around the legs of the stool.

My room was the way his mother kept his house, everything always in order, and clean. His house was an extension of my room, or of me; I felt at home, as if a burden had been lifted. Perhaps that was why I was now tongue-tied.

Tom said, "I just got a new Beatles record. You want to hear it?"

"Sure."

We went into the living room. A large oil painting hung over the sofa. At that age I did not notice things like art work on the walls of houses. Tom had to point it out; he was proud of it. It measured about ten feet square. He invited me to go closer. The paint was laid on in thin, quick, long brush strokes, red and yellow predominating. Collaged bits of newspaper headlines, magazine headings, original photographs about the Kennedy assassination, were pasted here and there with gruesome order and logic. At one point, for example, a gob of red paint with great force had been thrown against the canvas so that it exploded into a violent burst, and while the paint was still wet a cut-out of Oswald's face had been pressed into the wet blob. What seemed like dried brown blood spattered *carte de visite* of Lincoln. Masks from Goya's 'Disasters of War' were sketched in red ink, Breughelesque distortions, twisted forms crowded behind the warehouse windows. It was signed bottom right, 'Ray Silvers, 1965', and beneath it in tiny letters the inscription, 'for Tom'. He pointed again. In the center of the picture there was a sunburst aura, whites and pale yellows, and a two-inch square photograph of Tom with ironic angel's wings sketched in black ink with quick strokes.

Silvers was his grandfather. "My mother's father," he added. "His name is really Silverstein."

"It's pretty wild."

His mother had nursed her father for the last year, after his cancer operation, he explained. It was in remission now. She decided they needed a change because he was always in trouble anyway in the town where they were living. The job at Northern Dutchess Hospital was her opportunity.

He put on the new album. It was still only about five thirty; I did not have to be home for awhile. I settled into a worn easy chair. An enormous palm ficus stood in the corner, a hanging begonia by the window, a fern on the coffee table, against one wall a three-cushion sofa covered with a brightly flowered slip cover. The center of the hardwood floor was covered by a crimson Persian carpet intricately figured with a tree of life, the border teeming with vines, plants and animal life. The off-white drapes were embossed with idealized pointed leaves. The television set was encased in a wooden cabinet with doors. He handed me the jacket album and settled down on the floor next to my chair, his arms around his knees.

Take a sad song . . . It was just about everyone's favorite song that autumn. I hardly heard anything else on the radio, or being hummed or whistled in the school halls. Still, I had never actually read through the words before, and did not own the record myself, although we also had a record player in our living room.

The song played its way through to the end, and then automatically started over again. Tom had his head resting on his raised knees. I do not know what possessed me but I noticed that, in the haste of putting on his shirt when I knocked, the collar was turned inward. He was sitting at arm's length. I reached down, turned it out, and smoothed it down. He reached back with his left hand and grazed the surface of my skin, his hand warm and dry, lingering. I had a good deal of physical energy, was jittery and even at times a bit manic. His hand calmed me, made me feel peaceful and secure, as if engrossed in a meditation. The record played through for the third time.

I ran the few hundred yards to our door. It was a little after six. Father was sitting at the kitchen table reading his newspaper, filling the room with pipe smoke. He had on a navy blue wool sweater; the house was chilly. No one had started to cook yet. Everything was completely messy. I wished I had stayed at Tom's to eat. Father looked over the top of his newspaper, shook it out and folded it. He was annoyed.

"Where've you been in this weather with no coat?"

Without missing a beat I said, "Just out to the tree house. I left my pocket knife up there and I needed it to finish a model."

He looked at his watch, but did not set aside his paper. "I've been sitting here fifteen minutes."

"I forgot to bring a flashlight so I had a hard time finding it."

"I don't want you catching flu. You put on a coat in this weather. And aren't you supposed to be cooking us pancakes tonight?"

"Oh shit, I forgot. Sorry."

"Just because you started training again doesn't mean you can go around with a bad macho mouth. Even Clare's started complaining about your swearing."

"Sorry. Won't happen again."

He muttered something and raised the paper.

2. THE ROBBERY

I did not see Tom for a number of days; I had extra training for the first of the out-of-town meets in which I was scheduled to dive. Away meets utterly absorbed and overexcited me, made me lose sleep. The newspaper clipping in my scrap-book gives me one good line, "Youngster Dan Wyant, a newcomer with real promise, executed his forward one and half somersault in tuck position with pike-out from the one meter not just with perfect form but with flair . . . " Diving was not just a sport to me, nor a passion. It was a language unto itself, as if it had nationality, borders, and was only understandable to the naturalized, the initiated. Somehow, to me, sex was also close to language, and there might not have been as much distance as I thought between my diving and my still unarticulated feelings for Tom.

As I had climbed the ladder, and paused to collect myself at the beginning of the approach, I could hear Coach O'Malley's constant admonition resounding at the back of my mind, "Get the alignment right, Wyant, and everything else will flow. Alignment, alignment, alignment . . . " As I came out, and went into entry, I had a visceral sense that it had all worked together. Everything was right. Perfection of poise; balance. Diving was a Buddhist exercise.

My sense of satisfaction, the calm I felt after a successful meet, did not last very long. I was walking to school that Monday morning when Richie came careening towards me, pedalling furiously. I was a little late, having slept in a bit, my muscles aching from the extra exertion. It was my morning to be patrol boy at the cross walk in front of school. I thought he was on his way to warn me that Sister Francesca was going to reprimand me for being tardy and not taking my responsibilities seriously. What if one of the first-graders had an accident because I was not on duty? I could already hear her moral imperatives.

He skidded to a halt. "Jesus, I tried to phone you at least ten times this morning. The line was busy."

"Dad was on the phone talking to Clare. You know how it is."

"You're late. I wanted to catch you before you got to school."

"I know I'm late. I slept in. Man I'm aching all over. What's up?"

"Jesus. You haven't even *heard*? Where you been, man! Someone broke in the liquor store last night. That's what. Robbed it blind too. Reggie told me they got quite a haul. Two or three thousand." Reggie the cop was Richie's brother-in-law.

"Two or three *thousand* ."

The store was directly across the street from the laundromat, on the opposite corner, attached to a small Italian grocery, both owned by Dante Gennaro. If you wanted something in one store he had to close the other. He tended to treat me a bit better than the other village boys because he and my mother's family were from the same area of Sicily. He would add a few extra pieces of candy to my bag, or make sure I had the freshest donuts. Rather unfairly, I disliked him because every time I went in to buy something he would say, "That'll be fifty dollars," instead of fifty cents, or "two hundred" instead of "two". The repetition of what never was a joke to me, week after week, year after year, drove me crazy. I thought he was greedy; mad.

I asked, "How did they get in?"

At the back of the building there was a small, high window leading into a toilet. A rod-iron grate and screen were bolted over it and the thieves had pried them off with a crowbar, broken the glass, unlatched the frame, and crawled through.

Richie added, " . . . and get this! They like put tape over the glass – you know so no one would hear them breaking it? And they must have known the old screen over the window was all rusted 'cause Reggie said the shingles were so crumbly you could practically pull the nails out with your hand."

"Figures. The old miser would never fix anything like that."

"That's not the point."

"So what's the point?"

"The point is they knew what they were doing. They had to be *professionals*! Outsiders I bet."

I wasn't convinced. Why would any thief worth his weight in stolen property, I argued, waste his time on anything in Madalin? I could see robbing the bank in Kingston or even in Holland Corners. But Gennaro's?

Richie made a good case for it though. Not only had the thieves known which window to go through, but they had known that Gennaro kept his money in a secret hiding place behind a portion of shelving. A hinged section swung out to reveal a niche. That meant they had cased the joint, and explained why the shop was not ransacked. They had gone straight to the hiding place. Nor had they left any fingerprints. Gennaro had only discovered the theft at six the next morning, when he went downstairs to get his morning paper. He had called Reggie at

6:05.

Outsiders still seemed far-fetched. Everything he had said could still mean that it was an inside job. Gennaro was quite capable of robbing himself for the insurance money, I said unkindly. Or his daughter. She was as greedy as he was. Or his wife. Or even Lansing for that matter. There were enough candidates right around here.

Lansing was out, Richie thought, because the window opening was too small to admit his huge body. Most of his crowd were older teens, thickened with too much beer, except for Donny. Everyone knew he was too stupid, and too much of a blabbermouth, to be included in a 'major' crime. Richie thought it was less likely to be Lansing's crowd than one of the teenage gangs, the Black Hawks for instance, who were responsible for the wave of car thefts in the Valley the year before, and who might be on the loose again.

Just as we reached the school walk – the first bell went and I knew I would definitely be reprimanded – he said he had almost forgotten to tell me that the crooks had walked off with about thirty cases of imported Scotch whiskey. Gennaro ordered it for the bank for their Christmas gifts every year. At twenty-five dollars a bottle that was also a pretty penny, and they would have needed a small truck to haul that kind of loot, or a van. Maybe it was also a clue. He would let me know more later after training that afternoon, when he had a chance to talk to Reggie.

In fact, I can begin to date events more accurately from that day onwards because of the robbery. It was easy to put together copies of the articles that appeared in the local papers. Most of them did not add much to the details Richie had supplied:

MADALIN STORE ROBBED
Tuesday, Nov. 19, 1968. Holland Corners
On Monday, Nov. 18, at approximately 4:00 a.m.
a robbery occurred at the premises of Madalin Liquor Store, Madalin, New York . . . The owner Dante Gennaro said that the thieves got away with one week's gross and 60 cases of expensive imported

whiskey special ordered for the Holland Corners
First National Bank . . . Madalin Chief of Police
Reginald Morse reassured us that there was already
a suspect and expected an early arrest.

After practise, about five o'clock, as I was walking past
Richie's house, he came running out to intercept me. Struggling
to get an arm through his jacket sleeve he shouted, "Hey! Wait
up! I got news . . . " An important clue had indeed been found at
the crime site: a small piece of green and black wool cloth torn
off a wool shirt or lumber jacket. The fibers were attached to a
corner of the wire mesh by the window, no doubt pulled off as
the thief squeezed through. Reggie had taken it to the police lab
in Poughkeepsie for analysis.

I said, "It's not much to go on. There must be millions of
jackets around like that. My father use to have one. So does
your brother, don't he? Hey, yeah, your brother!"

"And who else?" He answered it for me, rather triumphantly. "Corrigan. That's who. And he's the only one regularly
wears it."

I said immediately that Corrigan had to be too tall to fit
through the opening, maybe not as big as Lansing but big nonetheless. I reminded him that he was the one who had hit the
baseball through that very window, which was why Gennaro
had put the grating and the wire up in the first place. When he
tried to squeeze through to get the baseball before Gennaro could
find out even he had a hard time squeezing through, so how
could Tom?

We were walking down the middle of the main street, im-
aginatively named Broadway, towards my house. The few cars
were going around us. Richie argued, "If *you* remember right,
the reason I couldn't get through the window was because there
were crates or something on the inside blocking it, not because
it was too small. I still think Corrigan could squeeze through
the space and tear his jacket without noticing. Or maybe it was
that other kid. He's small enough to squeeze through."

"Bobby?"

"Sure. Why not? Maybe they were in it together."

"I can't see that skinny kid picking up all those heavy cases. What would either of them want with all that liquor anyway. And how did they get them out. No one answered that yet. I still think the best bet is Gennaro himself."

We had reached the intersection by the laundromat and Richie stopped. "Anyway Reggie's not back from the lab yet, so I'm going to hang out over at my sister's until he gets home. You want to come?"

"No. I have to get some homework in before dinner."

"Do it over at her house."

"With her kids making all that racket? I'd never get anything done. Besides, what can they tell from a few old threads?"

"A lot – what kind of dirt's on it, where it came from, even what brand of laundry soap it was washed in. Come on. He said he'd be home by six. Then you and me would be the first to know."

"No, I can't. Just phone me when you know something."

Richie turned left to his sister's house, and I continued on. I could have phoned Tom from home but if Charlie was there and heard me talking to him he'd force me to tell him why I might be warning Tom of all people. I started up our driveway, a decoy so everyone would think I was going home, but continued around to the back of the house and jogged the distance through the woods to Tom's. The green plaid wool jacket was hanging innocently on a hook in plain sight. I could not see any tears. The weather had been warm enough for him to have worn it instead of his parka. If he knew it was torn, or even if he didn't know it was torn but had been wearing it, why would he be leaving it right out there in plain sight? What if he had lent it to Bobby? That was what I was more worried about.

He was in the kitchen and came to the door immediately. I brushed past him in my usual brusque way. "You hear about the robbery?" I did not remove my coat or shoes.

"Course I heard. Everybody's heard."

"I bet you haven't heard the latest about what they found on the window."

"No. I haven't heard. You going to take your jacket off?"

I blurted out what I had just learned, glancing compulsively at the jacket hanging right there next to my shoulder.

He frowned and bit his lower lip. "I suppose that means that everybody thinks I did it?"

"I don't. Richie didn't exactly say you did it either."

"Well, for the record I didn't."

"I know you didn't."

He suddenly shook his head and whistled, as if the significance of that patch of wool had just washed over him. "Man. It's weird though. I don't know. I got to think about it, but I just bet everybody is going to say I did."

"I don't give a shit. Don't let it bother you. You got nothing to worry about."

He said cynically, "Yeah sure . . . Anyway, you staying or going?"

"No, I've been running late the whole day and got a shit load of homework to do still." A thought struck me. My hand already on the doorknob, I turned and asked, "Are you Quaker?"

"Quaker?"

"That's what I heard some people saying the other day in the post office. That you were Quaker, some kind of radical free-thinker pacifist."

"Jesus, I don't know how people find out these sorts of things, but Mom was going to this Quaker meeting on Long Island for awhile and I went a couple of times with her. But Grandpa Silvers is as Jewish as a bagel, Russian and Ukrainian, and Dad's family is Irish and Scots and who knows what else. So I guess I'm about as mongrel as you can get. Maybe the description fits though. Why do you ask?"

"No reason. I mean, I'm a Catholic and all, but Quaker is okay too."

"Thanks."

I wanted to be back by the time Richie called with more news and ran home. I was already convinced of Tom's innocence, in that magical way that boys think. When I had told Tom about the clue he had not even glanced at his jacket, still less tried to block my view or snatch it off the hook to hide it. That proved his innocence more than any verbal assurance. I was ready to forget about it all.

After dinner, as I was sitting at my desk studying and still waiting for Richie to call, my brother poked his head in my door, and said, "You studying? Can I come in?"

"What does it look like? No, you can't come in. I've got to finish this history quiz."

He looked back over his shoulder down the hallway and came into my room anyway, pushing the door partly closed, keeping his voice low. "Listen, I got to ask you something."

"You want to borrow money again, the answer is no."

"I don't want to borrow money. This is serious this time. Brother to brother stuff."

He was not giving off any of the signals I knew meant he was teasing or being sarcastic: the curling at the corner of the mouth, the raised eyebrows, the folded arms, the head pulled back, the questioning tone. He glanced back nervously over his shoulder. "I've seen you a few times coming home late through the woods. Hold your horses! I wasn't spying or anything. I just happened to see it."

"Sure. Just happened."

"Believe me or don't believe me, that isn't the point. The point is, you're not coming from your fort, are you. You're coming from Tom's house."

"What's it to you?"

"What's it to me is you're being so sneaky. I bet you're smoking dope with him. Ain't you? He's getting you stoned. I hear he's got terrific shit."

"I suppose you want some. Sorry to disappoint you, not that it's your business in the first place, but just for the record, I never smoked even one joint . . . *ever*."

"So why you hanging out with him?"

"Who said I was? You said I was. I didn't say I was. So what even if I was?"

"Keep your voice down. You want Dad coming in? Maybe I heard a few things you haven't heard, and I wouldn't want to start hearing them about you."

"Like what?"

"He got into some pretty deep shit on the Island and Ron and the guys are saying he's got to be behind Gennaro's."

"I know for a fact that he had nothing to do with it. I mean, Jesus, he's Quaker."

"Come on, get real! As if there weren't any rotten apple Quakers . . . You're hopeless. Just remember, when the shit hits the fan I gave you your chance."

Richie phoned me about eight. To warn me, as it turned out. Reggie had just left his house and was on his way over to question *me.*

"Me!"

"He said he saw you and Tom together down by the river the other day and the two of you were acting pretty suspicious."

"All I was doing was walking along the tracks and we just met by accident."

"Reggie said you gave Tom what looked like a joint."

"What was he, up on the cliff again with those binoculars your sister got him for his birthday? That was the worst thing she could have done for us. All it was was a stick of gum."

Tom and I had been taking a walk along the tracks. When Reggie saw us I really was giving him a stick of gum, but I was upset nonetheless, because for some reason something I said to Tom must have really struck him because he suddenly put his arm around me and squeezed me. Reggie must have seen that too. Tom and I had talked for a few minutes and gone separate ways. Reggie must have been parked at the cliff-side above us the whole time. I might have to embellish the story: we had met by accident, I had been looking for objects to put in a school project; I had handed him the whole pack of gum. And about that squeeze, well, Tom liked to pretend he was European and they were more physical. I know it must have looked weird, but that was the way he was sometimes.

I brought my homework downstairs to the kitchen table to wait. By all appearances nothing was going on, therefore there was nothing to say to either Father or Charlie.

It was about half an hour later when the front doorbell rang.

"I'll get it," I shouted.

Reggie was in full regalia: badge, cap, and gun.

I asked him in and said, "Hi. You must be here to see Dad. I'll go get him." He was in his study, and came out to see who was ringing at that hour. They shook hands. Reggie put his cap under his arm, and unzipped his brown leather jacket. His puffed, pink neck was too large for his starched shirt. He looked drawn, haggard. He was always having trouble with his wife. They would have terrible fights after which he would drive too fast through the village in his new police car. Everyone knew about their arguments. The neighbors heard them screaming at each other doors away. His eyes were puffy, black bags weighed them down making him look somnambulant. He said he was making the rounds to see if anyone had seen or heard anything that might throw some light on the robbery. Just a routine call.

Father nodded, but looked puzzled. "Why don't we go into the living room? Would you like some coffee."

"Thanks anyway but this'll only take a couple of minutes and I have quite a few people to see. I'm questioning a lot of the kids and I just thought maybe Dan here might have heard or seen something around school or picked up something from one of the other kids." He pulled a small notepad out of the breast pocket of his blue shirt, extracted a pencil from the spiral binding and licked the tip of it. He turned to me. "Now I'm just going to ask you a couple of routine questions . . . Let's see now. Dan . . . Daniel Wyant. Any middle name?"

"Bradford."

He said everything as he wrote it. "Dan . .iel . . Brad ford Wy. . . ant." He wrote that at the top of a fresh page. "Date of birth?"

"January 22nd, 1956."

He looked at his wristwatch. "Eight thirty-four p.m. November 19th, 1968." He licked the pencil again. "Heard from Coach O'Malley the other day that you had those new dives down almost perfect. He thought you were almost ready for the big try-outs. There's going to be some pretty stiff competition up there in Albany in January. Especially what's his name from Syracuse."

"Jim Spruce. He's good. Coach is working us pretty hard."

"So he said. I got a lot of confidence in you. More than

confidence. You promise not to tell anybody, I'll let you in on a little secret. A few of us bet money on you that you were going to win the regionals. I personally got a bit of money riding on you."

I was surprised, as no one had ever bet anything on me before, but I said with trained modesty, "I'll do my best."

"Course you will! We're counting on it. Now, Danny, I got to ask you a few questions here, not that I'm accusing you or anything, so hear me out first. You see, just by accident the other day, about a week ago today, I was out in the woods behind the churchyard – the folks over in the community said some hunters were in the woods – in other words, doing my job, not nosing around anybody's business. That clear?" I nodded. "That's how I came to see you and that Corrigan boy out playing with some kind of bow and arrow, looking real friendly to me. Enjoying yourself too. So then, a few days later I see the two of you walking along down North Road together heading towards his house. So I said to myself, Reggie, you better talk to Danny because if he's becoming friends with Corrigan he doesn't know what he's getting himself into. But – I got to admit it – I just forgot all about it. Went right out of my head." The sweat was now gathering at his sideburns and upper lip. "Until a couple of days ago. There I am parked up at the cliff having my coffee and donut and making sure none of them bums are getting under any trains, and along the path there comes you and this Corrigan laughing and talking away and then sure as I'm standing here what do you do, you reach in your jacket and pull out this stick of something which sure looks suspicious. So I said to myself the first opportunity I got to ask Danny what this is the two of them were doing there. Unofficial of course. And now there's this robbery, and tell you the truth, well Tom's a suspect like my blabbermouth brother-in-law probably told you already, so it's as good a time as any to ask you . . . " His pencil poised, waiting for an explanation.

I tried to sound blasé. "We weren't doing nothing really. I was just out collecting some stuff for a school project and happened to run into him, and was giving him some bubble gum, you know the flat kind with the baseball cards. Guess that's what you saw."

"The box looked to me about a couple of inches square and a couple of inches high, not like any gum wrapper I ever seen, so you sure you want to stick to that story?"

"Sure. It was just gum."

Reggie wrote it all in his notebook, put the pencil back into the spiral binding, closed the notebook and stuffed it into his shirt pocket again. "The rest we can just let be unofficial, between you and me and your dad here . . . If you know anything at all, even something you think isn't important, about Tom and the robbery, now is the time to say it. Don't answer too fast. Just take you time."

"I don't know anything more than Richie does, but I don't think Tom had anything to do with it."

"Now why would that be?"

"Cause he just didn't. I mean, for one thing he's way to tall to fit through that little window."

Instead of commenting on that, Reggie said, "If you knew something you'd tell me now wouldn't you?"

"Sure. Why not?"

"I got your promise on that."

Tom had told me he had not done it, and that was good enough for me, so I readily gave my word. "No. There's nothing. I just don't think Tom had anything to do with it."

"Well, we got lots of clues besides the patch, you know. But that ain't the point, the point is I don't want to be finding out later that you knew something all along and didn't say so when you had the chance because that would make you an accessory and I'd be real sorry about that."

I shrugged but did not say anything further.

Reggie added for good measure, "That Corrigan's a trouble-maker and you ought to stay clear of him unless you want to get into his kind of trouble. A piece of friendly advice. You keep hanging out with him, no good will come of it, and I'd hate to see that. I seen kids like him come and go. Bad news. He's a mean s.o.b. all right. I've read his record: fights, break-ins, drugs. You name it. It sure ain't pretty "

I snapped, "I heard his record wasn't all that bad. Breaking into someone's house. I know all about that. All the kids do."

Father said sternly, "Don't you use that tone with Officer Morse."

"It's okay, Henry. Danny here might be a little upset. Breaking into a house isn't even a fraction of it, not one tenth. I can't go into it. The files are confidential. And I'm not going to argue with you. I just got one last thing to say. You hear anything you come to me. Okay?"

"I already said I would."

He reached into his shirt pocket again, but this time pulled out a business card. He handed it across and I stuffed it into my shirt pocket. He hit my shoulder lightly with his closed fist. "Okay buddy, you remember I got a tenner riding on you. You hear anything you let me know?" He actually winked at me.

No sooner had the door closed than Father said angrily, "What was that all about?"

"Nothing."

"What do you mean nothing! I want to talk to you."

He would have shoved me into the living room had I not gone in there on my own. "What's all this about you and Tom and drugs? I want the truth now."

Used to being the center of attention, if not adulation, I was frightened enough now to defend myself shrilly. "Nothing is going on! Nothing! It's just like I said. I was walking on the tracks looking for stuff for a school project and bumped into Tom and gave him some fucking gum and Reggie thought it was drugs or something. I mean what's he doing spying on people in the first place!"

"Don't you use language like that. That can't be all. What about the other time, when he saw you in Tom's yard?"

'I don't know. I was probably just out back and saw him shooting at things and went over to see what it was. I mean it's no crime to shoot a couple of arrows at a cardboard box."

"I don't know, none of this sounds right to me."

"Reggie is a jackass. He's even a big fat fucking liar. He wasn't telling you why he really came over here and why he thinks that Tom is the thief. Richie called and told me the whole story so I know everything that's going on."

"I told you, I don't want you using that language. So, how about starting from the beginning and telling me. I seem to be the last one around here who finds out anything."

I told him about the plaid wool clue found on the window grate and its alleged connection to Tom. Father looked surprised.

I added, "Reggie's trying to invent a whole case against Tom and he's trying to drag me into it too. But it's all crazy. They don't have any proof. They won't have the tests back yet for a couple of days. What if he has a hunting jacket – like nine-tenths of the village has the same kind of wool jacket not to mention half the Valley – and even you had one, so why doesn't everyone suspect you! Right away he's got to accuse Tom be-cause Tom's got a record and he's an outsider. I hate this fucking village. Why do they have to pick on him?"

"Calm down. And stop swearing." Father raised a hand, palm outward to me, "Okay, okay, I see what you're saying. So long as you give me your word you're not hiding anything from me."

"What do you mean hiding? I told you what I know!"

"Okay, calm down. Enough for now." Father was pale and upset. I knew that the first thing he would do would be to lock himself in his study and call Clare from his extension. He said, "Let's make some hot chocolate. Both of us need to calm down."

I nodded. But later, as I was going up to my room Charlie intercepted me in the hallway. I cut him short with a fierce hiss. "Don't you start! I warn you. Don't start. I'm not talking to you." He was attempting to block the door to my room, but backed off.

I paced around my room like a caged panther, wanting to telephone Tom or rush out the back door to his house again, knowing that I could do neither. I wish I could say that this was the last of it for that evening, but it was not. A few minutes later the phone rang. Richie again. I had quite forgotten to call him back after his brother-in-law's visit, as I had promised.

"Why didn't you call me? What happened? Was Reggie there or not?"

"Yeah, he just left."

"So?"

"So, he asked the usual dumb questions. It's just like I thought. He's trying to pin it all on Tom and he hasn't got a thing to go on."

That was not the latest. The latest was that after Reggie left our house he had gone over to Tom's and when Tom had shown him his jacket Reggie had noticed a small piece missing from the hem. It was enough to take him in for questioning.

Richie added, for good measure, "I just bet they find enough to book him."

"I bet they don't. Like they don't have the tests yet, do they? Well, I bet the pieces don't match."

"You're on."

Feeling powerless, I could not sleep that night, anxious and angry. I arose several times to go to the window. It was raining. The lights never came on in Tom's house.

3. TOM'S ROOM AND HIS MOTHER

With sullen, stubborn persistence, but without hesitation, I trudged over to Tom's house before school the next day. The sun was already out, melting the snow fallen during the night, still deep in shaded patches. I rapped on the back door; smelled coffee and toast. The air was damp, penetratingly cold; I shivered and hugged myself, stamping around in the same spot and knocking the back of my boots against the cement foundation to dislodge the mud and slush.

Tom's mother came to open the door. Because of her hospital schedule, we had not yet met; I had seen her only from a distance: through the car window as they drove through the village, or coming out of the cinema with Tom. She was wearing a quilted dressing gown, decorated with blue irises and gold birds, pulled tight around her waist by a tan braided cord. Her long dark, gray-streaked hair was hanging loose about her shoulders. She pressed a steaming cup of coffee between her hands. An imposing, matronly person, stocky but not obese, five feet ten perhaps – tall for an American woman in those years. Her blue eyes were sharp and lively, not dark, long and oriental like Tom's. I knew that she only returned home at about two a.m., usually sleeping until late morning, so I was surprised to see her. A charcoal-gray, tumultuous cloud bank was already gathering on the western horizon. She gathered the robe tighter at her neck with her left hand, as if shielding herself not only from the impending weather but from winter, from troubles.

"Hello. You're Daniel. Come in. Tom's not up yet ."

They had not kept him overnight! I was surprised, elated. I politely removed my knitted wool cap, even remembered that she wanted shoes removed. I had a few minutes to spare before the first bell.

"Do you want some coffee? It's made."

"No thank you. I don't drink coffee; I had my breakfast already."

"You're out early. What time does your school start?"

"Eight thirty."

"Tom likes to sleep until the last possible minute. He's not going to school today though. We have an appointment with the lawyer at ten." We entered the familiar kitchen. "I can make you some hot chocolate if you like?"

I unzipped my jacket and slipped onto a stool. I said politely if not formally, "Thank you. I only have a few minutes though." I held my wool cap with both hands, twisting it round and round, following her every action, afraid to blink. She stooped over to get a small kettle from a bottom shelf, took out the same cups, set them down on the same mats, in more or less the same place on the counter, as I had had seen Tom do any number of times. Would the repetition and imitation of acts reveal some underlying mystery? Patterns of mother-son connection?

"Tom said you were an excellent diver?"

She had noticed I was carrying a gym bag.

"I won a junior trophy last year. Just the county though. Coach said I wasn't ready for the regionals until this year."

"I wish Tom would take up a sport again at his new school. He doesn't seem interested in anything here. Maybe you can influence him. He used to be on the wrestling team in his old

92

school where we lived out on the Island. For two straight years."

"He never told me that."

"He wasn't as good at it as you are at diving. He didn't win any trophies – which is maybe why he didn't say anything to you about it – but he took it seriously enough."

"The wrestling team always needs new people. It's probably not as good as the one on Long Island though. Our swimming team is the best team in the school."

"He's thinks he's not good enough so he says there's no use doing it. Silly really. There are all sorts of reasons why you do something, but he won't listen to me. Maybe you can talk some sense into him."

Her face was haggard from too little sleep, or over-working. She seemed old to be Tom's mother; I found out later that she was forty, that is younger than my father, whose face was not as old to me as hers. I liked her face; there was something kind and intelligent in it; her gaze was direct. Her fur-lined slippers clacked against the linoleum floor.

I asked her suddenly. "Do you like being a nurse?"

"I do like it. I've always liked it, right from the first day, when I was still at nursing school. I feel lucky to have found something I could do to support us that I like doing. It's hard work. Sometimes too much. Especially this night shift. I don't like leaving Tom alone nights. They would only give me the job if I agreed to do the night shift for six months. You would think, for a hospital they'd understand about raising a teenager. But someone has to do it . . . Do you know what you want to be?"

"Everyone says I should be a doctor or a psychiatrist."

"Is that what you want?"

"I don't know. They make a lot of money, but I don't know yet. I think I might like to be an archeologist or anthropologist and go to Europe to live. My Italian aunt and uncle said I could go live with them in Sicily."

"It's beautiful there. You've quite a while before you have to decide. Tom has to start thinking about it now."

"What does he say he wants to be?"

"An artist, like his grandfather. My father. Who's become quite successful now. But it was a struggle when I was growing up. Did Tom show you the paintings in the living room?"

I nodded. "He didn't tell me he wanted to be an artist."

"Oh yes. He makes very nice drawings. His grandfather started him drawing when he was three or four. He's quite good . . . " She added bitterly, "He won't even work at that now. I don't know what's gotten into him. I guess I don't feel very kindly towards him this morning."

"How come they didn't keep him?"

"They kept his coat, for tests. They shouldn't have questioned him in the first place. Just a few threads like that. It was nothing. Now everyone will think he did it. It's not so easy to turn around people's impressions once they're formed." The kettle whistled for my drink. She went over to shut it off. "I wanted him to make a fresh start . . . "

"I know he didn't do it. I really don't think he did."

"I can see you're a good friend. Real friends are rare. I hope he realizes it. As for those others . . . " She did not finish; she mixed the chocolate for me.

I glanced at the wall clock. "I have to go soon or I'll be late."

"Why don't you go wake him for me; bring him his coffee. I'll give you a tray. He needs to get up now anyway. We have to leave soon to be at the lawyer's on time. It's about an hour's drive at least."

Even though I had been at Tom's house four or five times, I had never been in his room. In fact, as there was an extra toilet on the ground floor, I had not even been upstairs. We usually played a game together at the kitchen table or sprawled on the living-room floor and listened to music. I knew exactly where his room lay in proportion to the upstairs – at the back left corner of the second floor, because I could see his window from mine. I was suddenly shy. Wouldn't he be mad if I woke him up? I didn't like it when someone did that to me. She wouldn't hear it. He wouldn't mind, and if I didn't she would have to do it herself.

The upstairs hall was dim and still. A worn, wine-red oriental runner, the soft light through the vitrage covering the west window at the opposite end, back-lighting the Christmas cactus in blood-red bloom, the space heavy and thick as if walking down the aisle of a claustrophobic chapel; the smell of coffee and toast drifting up. I carried the tray precariously. His door was closed. I nudged it open with my foot.

If Tom's house was diametrically opposite to our house – all order and neatness while ours was clutter and disarray – Tom's room was the diametric opposite of not just his house but my own room. It was not just messy; it was Chaos. I kept my room compulsively neat and clean, perhaps as compensation for the general mess, and perhaps Tom was compensating too. I do not think he could have made the space any messier than it was. Not just a physical confusion, a disorder of the senses, an amorphous jumble that they say can spin off inspiration within the matrix of creativity. Most of us internalize chaos, within our feelings, within the emotional intensity of our reactions. Tom was externalizing his. From the looks of it he could not ever have thrown anything out. At least, what he avowed, when much later I said something about helping him to clean it all up, was that everything he kept had some small or large significance to him, objects that accumulated from confusion to jumble, jumble to clutter, clutter mess, mess to shambles and if finally pushed far enough over the edge – a gift few people had – shambles to chaos, or a kind of return to the edge of meaning. Pushing things to their limit so that they threatened going over the edge – one of Tom's characteristics, as I was to learn – risks reason.

I set the tray down on the floor. The room was dark. A forest-green windowshade was held up with thumb-tacks. How did he hold it open? None of the over-stuffed dresser drawers trailing ends of variously colored clothing was completely closed. There was an enormous black cabinet with glass doors along one wall, the visible shelves crammed with the bric-a-brac of hoarded childhood pastimes: airplanes and ships with missing parts; broken sea shells; half painted and unpainted plaster molds; a school microscope; some flat plastic cases displaying badly preserved butterflies and beetles; a pair of cheap binoculars; a plastic statue of wrestlers; an empty aquarium, the motor and filters resting idly at the bottom; mugs from various vacation places; an eighteenth-century Thai Buddha I found out later had real value. But what was real value in that room?

The walls were even cluttered. Morrison and Stones posters; a Navy destroyer calendar; a snapshot of his father stuck directly to the wall with tacks rather than neatly framed in silver as I had done with the photograph of my mother, and carefully centered on my dresser top; his mother and he on a beach, a man I did not know with his arm around Tom's neck whom I took to be his grandfather – balding head and a trim athletic body wearing for who knows what reason those old-fashioned woollen swimming trunks that I still don't think anyone in their right mind would choose to put in contact with human skin; a Tibetan thangka. He had painted an enormous sky blue peace symbol on the wall above the head of his bed. I could not imagine Father giving me permission to do such a thing. The other drawings were on sheets of brown grocery wrapping paper jaggedly torn: of a cat with its fur on end, and on the ceiling an enormous pterodactyl; but also huge – some three feet across –expressive, charcoal sketches of body parts: an eye, a foot, a finger. The room, the drawings, even Tom perhaps, were all wild displays of pure energy.

I had consciously intended to rush in and cheerfully tell him to wake up. But the darkened room, the surprise of chaos, his sleeping form, subdued me. His bed was a mattress flat on the floor. He lay on his stomach hugging a pillow; the tree-of-life quilt had slipped down to the small of his back, like a moth wriggled half free of its chrysalis. I sat down on the edge and shook him. His back was sweaty, as if he had been working or running in his dreams. His eyes flickered; he rolled over, and stretched, blinked.

"Hey. Danny . . . what are you doing here?"

"Your morning coffee, sire." I fetched it dutifully from the tray and presented it, handle towards him, with a flourish.

"What time is it?"

"8:15. I have to go in five minutes."

He sat up and took the cup. His face puffy, his right cheek red and creased from lying on it.

"Shit. We have to go to the fucking lawyer's this morning."

"I know. Your mother told me."

He held the cup between both hands just as I had seen his mother doing earlier, blew on the surface though it was not too hot. He set it on the floor next to him and fumbled among the clothing, pulling out of the heap a pair of plain white boxer shorts which he put on under the cover. He struggled out of the tangle and went to the window, fixing the corner of the shade to a nail sticking out of the frame.

"It snowed last night. Yuk. Last night. What a night. I feel like I've got a hangover." He yanked at the end of something sticking out of a half-closed drawer, and drew out a thermal undershirt. "How cold is it?"

"Freezing." I looked at my watch. "I really have to go. What happened anyway?"

"I can tell you everything in a nutshell. They asked lots of stupid questions and let me go because they didn't have squat."

"Sounds like Reggie Rent-a-Cop. He's a real jackass. Always hassling us. The village doesn't really need a cop. He just makes up things so they won't find out they're wasting taxpayer's money paying him."

"In the meantime I got to get myself a lawyer. And it's going to cost a lot of money, which we'll have to get from my grandfather, who'll throw a fit and threaten to put me in reform school."

"That bad, huh?"

"Yeah, that bad."

4. FATHER INTERVENES

It is late afternoon, perhaps a few days later. I am riding with Father in the front seat of the car, on our way over to Kingston to buy some new gym shoes for me, and stationery supplies for him. We are already thinking of Thanksgiving, so this might be the week before. Clare will be coming to help with the cooking. Should we buy a frozen turkey this year, save us a trip when the shops are crowded? He is going to drop me off at the mall first, and pick me up later. I also need a duffel bag, and shorts. The wind rocks the car, and howls through the metal cables as we drive west over the bridge.

The mall is spartan in comparison to the one-stop, enclosed monoliths that now dominate the Valley and have eviscerated the urban centers. A single line of stores at the far side of a vast parking lot; pale orange fog lamps at the tops of high poles casting a diffuse, shadowless light on the wet metal of hundreds of cars, their colorful finishes patinated with dull gray from the early evening mist and rain.

We are crawling along bumper to bumper in an endless file, before us as far as I can see and behind us to the bridge. The windshield wipers squeak annoyingly across the glass. We are not talking. I have turned on the light inside the car to read a comic book, but Father reaches up and turns it off. He says it distracts him from his driving and is probably illegal anyway except in an emergency. He is still annoyed with me for Reggie's visit. We are not talking much. We have another mile to go. Father taps on the steering wheel with the palm of his hand, accompanying a melody he does not hum. He is looking out of his window. But what is there to see? On his side of the road there is a new car dealership, lumber yard, gas station, and a farmhouse crammed between the fast food restaurants. He has commented on the anachronism several times: machine and garden; the garden will disappear, squeezed out with no more feeling than if it were a pimple. It is hard for me to see through the streams of water running down my window. It fogs over. I wipe it with my sleeve. I catch a glimpse of an open field with new construction in it, the cement foundation blocks of another mall already laid.

We move forward a few feet more. Father stops his drumming. He tries to make conversation with a question I have already answered days before.

"What does Coach say about the regionals?"

"He says it's going to be pretty stiff competition."

"Does he think you're ready?"

"I guess."

"Sounds like he's not sure. Or is this just you?"

"I don't know. I think I am."

"You don't sound very confident. He wouldn't let you do it if he didn't think you had more than a good chance of winning, would he?"

"Guess not."

"Well, he held you back last year when you wanted to compete and you ended up thinking he was right."

I imitated Coach's voice sarcastically, "All he ever says is, 'Better try harder Wyant, work out more, do a zillion push-ups.' Stuff like that."

"Well, that's how he is."

"I know," I wearily agreed.

"He wants you to believe in yourself, not depend on flattery."

"But it would be nice once in a while."

"Same old doubting Dan, eh? I haven't heard his voice for awhile. Thought the coach had knocked him out of you."

I turned towards him. "This Donovan? From Syracuse? He's really good. And six months older than me. That's like a whole half year's practise and competitions ahead of me."

"Oh come on now. Think of it as a challenge. What do you think sports are anyway? Do you think you can beat him?"

"I don't know. I got a few things down better than him."

"That new dive O'Malley's been harping on? How is it going?"

"Pretty good . . . "

At practise the day before I had finally managed to get it right, though I was not sure I could repeat it. I had just stepped onto the board, my hands still grasping the sides of the ladder. And froze. I could not let go or take the next step along the board. My mind went blank. For a second or two I hardly knew where I was.

Coach shouted up at me, "Come on Wyant! Get out there and just do it. We haven't got all day. What the fuck are you waiting for? Your girlfriend to spread 'em?"

He had been warned several times by the school authorities to clean up his language. He seemed to think it was part of the job.

I was dizzy, and did not trust myself to take the next step.

I could not focus on anything, either thought or action. I had closed my eyes, but was registering everything around me.

Coach was muttering under his breath, "Christ, what's his problem. He freezing up on me? Am I going to have to send someone up after him? He never did that before. Hey, Mickey, come over here!" He shouted up again at me, "Come on Wyant. What do I have to do, come up there and kick your little butt?"

I let go of the ladder, did the breathing exercise the coach had recommended, pulled down the edges of my suit, wiggled my hands to loosen up, shifted the center of balance to the balls of my feet, mentally rehearsing the walk in the approach, the five precise steps forward, arm swing correct, into the forward and upward lift. I was doing a simple forward dive that day but as I took off I knew that it was right, sensed a silence and expectation around me, my arms spread, coming together for entry. As my head shot up and I shook it free, I saw Coach standing at the edge of the pool with one hand on his hip, nodding his head with surprise.

"Christ, Wyant! You finally got it right."

He extended a hand to pull me out of the water. "You do that good in Albany and, well, we'll see won't we."

Mickey came over, shaking his head. "Fucking perfect. I can't believe it. Abso-fucking-lutely perfect."

He had brought my towel and draped it around my shoulders, a team-mate solicitation.

I finished telling Father the story, and he commented, "It makes sense to me. You were focused one hundred percent on what you had to do. One hundred percent concentrated. Which is the way to do it. So, why all the doubts?"

"What if I can't do it again?"

He laughed. "You are a Doubting Thomas. Look, there's a couple of months yet before the competition so you'll just have to do it perfect a few times more to prove it to yourself. Do you know why you froze?"

"No, I don't know. It never happened before."

"What were you thinking about?"

"Nothing really. I wasn't afraid or anything. My mind just went blank. It was weird."

Father fell silent, mulling it over. What had paralyzed me, even made me dizzy, was the enormous energy I had been expending to suppress everything bothering me. But all Father finally said was, "Odd."

He dropped me off at the curb, by the shoe store. It was raining hard; I ducked under the overhang. I had seen the shoes I wanted a couple of weeks before, and the store still had them: just the right spring, just the right purple stripe; the ones everyone else had or wanted. It was more difficult to find the right bag; I had to go to two or three stores for that. Dark blue, or dark green, so it would look a little different, set a bit of a trend, but fit in. I settled for something black with mustard yellow stripes, a bit classy, but maybe that's what I needed for Albany.

I left the store, the shoe box in a plastic bag, the duffel bag in my right hand. Father was waiting for me in front of the stationery store. He nodded and smiled. I held the bag open so he could see the shoes; I handed him the change. He had to go back inside; he forgot the typewriter ribbon; maybe I can help him choose a new pen? When he has writer's block he blames it on the pen. If he switches ink colors, black to blue or blue to black again, ball point to fountain pen, or pen to pencils – Hemingway used pencils, he says – it helps unblock him. I can choose a new book if I want, another science fiction novel to keep up with Richie.

It is getting on towards closing time when we decide to head home. The wind is blowing harder now. We have to stay against the shop windows to keep dry. The temperature has dropped. Wet snow as large as chunks of paper is settling into slush, changing into rain, back into snow.

It is dark by now. The sidewalk is crowded. Father wants some coffee, I want a piece of pie. We halt under the overhang. There is a fast food restaurant fifty or a hundred feet across open, unprotected space. I pull up my collar. Is it worth getting wet?

He nudges me, points. "That Tom over there?" I had seen him, but had hoped Father would not.

I nod, and mutter more to myself, "And Lansing."

They are huddled against the wall, under the wide eaves of the restaurant, a light directly above them, not just Lansing and

Tom but Bobby, the pregnant girl who was with them in the woods, and another boy who has his back to me. Lansing is waving a finger close to Tom's face. Bawling him out? Warning him? Tom knocks the hand aside, and Lansing shoves him. It looks as if Tom might lose his balance but Bobby steadies him, steps in front of him, and pushes Lansing's shoulder back. I am surprised that Lansing does not punch Bobby in the face. Instead he brandishes a fist over Bobby's shoulder, shouting at Tom, though it is impossible to decipher what through the wind and rain. Lansing points at the other boy, now turned half way towards us. I am sure I have not seen him before. White skin, sensual mouth, almost too impeccably dressed in a white cashmere turtleneck sweater and charcoal-gray corduroys. A bit older than me but younger than Tom. Tom thrusts him protectively behind his back with his left arm. Bobby grabs Tom's free arm, thus preventing him from hitting Lansing. Or trying to drag Tom away?

Father says, "I don't like the looks of that." He walks to the end of the overhang. The gusts of wet snow fall on the front of his coat. My God, is he going to go over there!

Lansing shoves Bobby away, and grabs Tom by his coat collar. His open palm is already pulled back to strike. Father mutters something I cannot hear; Bobby shouts. Tom's arm shoots up to his face to protect himself, but too late. The force of Lansing's slap pitches Tom's head to the side. The boy Tom is shielding runs away, around the side of the building.

Father exclaims, "Shit! That bastard!" He hardly ever swears, especially within my hearing. Suddenly he cups his mouth and shouts, "Hey Tom! You coming or not? We haven't got all day!"

Heads jerk around towards us. Father waves vigorously to him and shouts even louder, "Come on! I told you to meet us at nine and it's quarter past! We can't wait all day!"

The girl grabs Bobby's coat sleeve and pulls him away. Lansing has Tom's collar in both hands now, glancing back and forth between him and us. He thrusts Tom away, against the wall of the building and ambles off.

Tom is left standing alone. He hesitates, unsure whether

to join us, or go his own way.

To my amazement, Father shouts again, "Come on! You get yourself over here right now!"

But Tom does not. He pulls up his collar against the wet clots of snow and rain and walks off in the opposite direction across the open car park.

Father mutters something to himself I cannot hear. he shakes his head, smiles and says to me, "Well . . . I tried, didn't I?"

5. THE CASE SO FAR

The forensic tests showed that the threads recovered from the crime scene did not match Tom's jacket and he was eventually given it back.

Although there was no evidence to link him to the robbery, doubts about his innocence persisted, despite the fact that Dr. Mason himself had spoken up for him at one of the village meetings, 'in all fairness'. Sometime between one and one fifteen on the night of the robbery, or about the time the police thought the crime had taken place, he was driving by Tom's house on a emergency call and had seen him looking out of the living-room window. But even that was construed as further proof of his guilt: the police had not pinpointed the time of the robbery that precisely; hearing a car, Tom could have rushed to the window to establish an alibi. Why else would he be up at that hour? If he was home at one fifteen, and again at two, when his mother returned from her night shift, he would have had to pull off the whole job within forty-five minutes, which seemed unlikely even to some of the die-hard sceptics. Or, as Richie summed it up, "Yeah, well, he may not have broken into the liquor store himself but I bet you a million dollars he masterminded the whole thing."

"Yeah, guilty until proven innocent," I protested to no avail.

Richie threw himself into the task of gathering together all of the known facts and molding them into a theory. He bought himself a large manila folder into which he gathered the newspaper clippings from the local papers, and the photocopy of the forensic report that he had sneaked from his brother-in-law's desk. On the outside of the folder he printed in large letters, CASE OF THE MADALIN CAPER, a kind of Hardy Boys mystery. He proceeded to list all the facts and theories he had so far constructed.

Whoever did it, he deduced, knew too many significant details for it to have been anything other than either an inside or a professional job. The screen and bars over the back window were rusted or loose enough to be removed without too much effort or noise. Looking in from the outside, the brass window lock looked closed, but it was in fact broken; the window could just be slid up. The side windows, on the other hand, were properly locked; Gennaro had even nailed their frames shut. The bathroom window had to open for ventilation.

How many people could have known about the swinging panel and niche? Not many. More interesting was why the thieves had not tried to conceal the fact that they knew. Were they worried about risking discovery by taking the time to mess things up a bit?

Gennaro could have been clever enough to think he could throw the police off the scent by making it look like the robbers had inside information. His wife, we thought with some unkindness, was greedy enough to engineer such a stunt for the insurance money. It was also well known that there was bad feeling between him and his daughter. She had won the high school beauty contest the year before, and it had gone to her head. She was running a bit wild with some senior Jefferson boy. Her father did not approve and she resented his possessive control.

The hiding place and cash box, in fact, presented several possibilities. It might have been discovered accidentally by someone in the shop buying something; Gennaro might have been careless, leaving the panel open a crack, or he might have been caught closing it when someone entered, or might not have pulled the shade on the front window one night, or not pulled it all the way thinking he had, and someone driving or walking by might have seen him. A regular customer, therefore, or a local. On the other hand Tom had been seen hanging around the shop when he first moved in, probably trying to buy beer with a fake ID before people found out how old he really was. He could have stumbled in one evening when Gennaro was stashing away the day's take.

Whoever broke in was small. The opening through which they had to squeeze was about a foot and a half square. I might fit through it, but not Lansing or Tom, especially with a jacket. Which brought up the matter of the green and black wool threads and presented Richie with another possibility. The crooks might have wanted everyone to think that Tom had done it by planting the threads on the corner of the screen. Lansing was quite capable of setting up the robbery to make it look like Tom did it in order to deflect suspicion from himself, or possibly to get even with Tom for not selling him any more grass or taking over some of his territory – which is what Donny thought. Lansing knew the village well enough to realize that just by leaving behind a few simple clues he could get everyone to believe that Tom did it, taking the heat off himself and sending a warning to Tom not to meddle with him. Did Tom owe Lansing money? Or vice versa? Did Tom have too much on Lansing, and was this his way of keeping Tom quiet? The robbery might have been a show of control.

The opening was too small for Tom, and Dr. Mason had seen him standing by the front window about the time he was supposed to be pulling the job, but that was not conclusive for Richie, or the village. Richie had another explanation. Tom had glanced out of the window because he had been waiting for an accomplice or accomplices, maybe that Indian boy. He was small enough. He could have wearing the same kind of jacket; maybe they even planned it that way. Once Tom's jacket was in the clear it would take the heat off him, at least with the police, if not with the skeptical villagers.

The matter of the prints in the flower-bed under the window was harder to explain. The ground was soft that night; the thief had tried to cover over his traces by scraping the area with a stick but had missed a heel mark from a well-known make of sneakers. No mud had been found inside but the thief could have removed his shoes before he dropped inside, not to leave marks or simply to make less noise.

The police had also found the stick used to scrape the ground; it had a few particles of leaves from the flower-bed stuck to it. Near where it was lying were also two sets of boot marks, pointing away from the store. One set belonged to a small person, about a hundred pounds and five four or five, and the other to a large person, six feet or more and a couple of hundred pounds. They might have been lighter and carrying the heavy cases of whiskey. Donny and Lansing? Tom and Bobby? An unknown third? There were no traces of a vehicle at all, no tire treads from a van, truck, or car, or even a wheelbarrow. The thieves must have walked quite a way with the cases, risking being seen, which was also another odd point about the whole affair. Fifty cases were missing, but where had they parked the get-away car or van? No one had heard or seen it. Richie wondered if he was back to Gennaro again? Was Gennaro his own thief? None of the above?

There were still a lot of loose ends. How much had actually been stolen? Gennaro had calculated from the receipts that it must have been about two and a half thousand dollars. It had been a busy weekend, the holiday coming up soon, and he was planning to go to the bank first thing that Monday morning. That seemed to Richie like a lot of money for a Friday and Saturday in Madalin. What if he was hiding money from the tax people and decided to claim it after the theft? He could easily have faked receipts; they were handwritten on a pad with a carbon. There had also been money in the cash register, about forty hundred and fifty dollars, he claimed.

Black paint traces had also been found around the window sill and frame and again on the cash box. The police said it was probably from the handle of a wide-blade knife, perhaps army issue, which had been used to pry open the box. They were common enough, however, and you could buy one at either the army-navy surplus store in Kingston or Poughkeepsie.

There were no fingerprints around the window, on the cash register drawer or cash box; except for Gennaro's, his wife's and daughter's.

There were traces of marijuana ash in the fibres of the piece of cloth the police retrieved from the screen, and hay dust as well. Had the person wearing it been sleeping in a barn? The police were following through on that. Did this mean that it was one of the road bums we saw wandering along the railroad tracks?

At this stage there were simply too many suspects: Gennaro, his wife, his daughter, Tom, Bobby, Lansing, Donny, tramps, gypsies, locals, every gang in the Valley. How could anyone possibly narrow it down?

Part Three: Seduced But Not Married

1. Out in the open

An unseasonably fierce blizzard on the Monday after Thanksgiving preoccupied the village. Twelve inches of snow fell overnight, a record for the end of November. School was cancelled, and we set ourselves to digging out. Two days later it rained, turning everything to slush. The sun came out driving the temperature up to fifty degrees. We shed clothes and the ground was clear again.

The village was busy with other problems. It did not much want to bother any more with Gennaro's complaints and cries for justice, so long as nothing further was happening – to him or them. The results of the forensic test, the return of Tom's jacket, and the inability of the police to produce a suspect in the robbery did not entirely allay the suspicions against him, but for awhile no one much talked about it.

I had been avoiding Tom in the corridors at Jefferson or on the streets of Madalin: dodging into classrooms, crossing the street not to be seen talking to him. A few times, when he passed me or surprised me in a doorway, he would look confused or stare questioningly into my eyes about to say something before I would turn away and continue on my way. Once, in the laundromat, we actually brushed shoulders without exchanging so much as a word, perhaps recognizing in the secret, silent code of boys the need for public distance.

After Reggie's visit to our house, word spread that I had been seen around with Tom and might know more about things than I was letting on. Which, of course, I did not. If everyone knew we were friendly, why not be friendly openly? Had the motivation for avoiding him vanished?

That Wednesday afternoon in the week after the holiday, as I entered the front doors of Jefferson on my way to practise, I saw him standing by the main lockers in an alcove to the right of the entrance having difficulties opening an old, rusty padlock, yanking at it, muttering, frowning, slamming it against the metal door. I took him by surprise.

"It won't open that way. Want some help?"

"This thing's a piece of shit."

He moved aside to make room for me, smelling visceral, his body electric, mine shy, awkward, nervous, alert.

"Sure you got the combination right?"

"Of course I've got the combination right! It's just rusted."

"What an antique. Where did you pick it up? Must be a hundred years old. Probably just needs some oil."

He turned the dial again, too quickly, with similar results, cursed and slammed it again. "Jesus F. Christ!"

"Come on, let me try."

I put my books down on the floor. He handed me a dirty, crumpled piece of paper on which the combination was written in faded pencil. I whirled the dial – right four, left past zero once to seven, around twice to five, back to one – and stopped it very carefully, making sure that the faded black dot aligned exactly at each digit. It opened smoothly.

I huffed on my fingernails, and rubbed them on my jacket.

"Takes a pro. All you need is a little patience."

"Thanks. I'll remember that." He put a couple of books in, took a couple of books out. "You coming or going?" he asked.

"Coming. You know, training. You?"

"I've got one more period . . . social studies . . . and detention."

"Again! What did you do now?"

"I just took a couple of photographs in English class."

"Which teacher you got?"

"Mulder. He's an ass."

"Tell me about it. My brother had him. So what was so interesting in *his* class you had to photograph it?"

"Nothing much. Just Mulder himself."

"Just! No wonder! I mean, what did he do? Sneeze and wipe it on his sleeve or something?"

"He was shouting at this kid, for nothing really. I mean, in a real rage, waving his arms around and everything. And this kid had his head down looking mad and scared."

"Mulder to a tee," I said. A box camera was sitting on the shelf of the locker. "Can I see it?"

He took it down off the shelf and handed it to me.

"Looks expensive," I said.

He had mentioned that his grandfather had given him a twin lens camera for his birthday in October, a black, rectangular, flat-bottomed box which could stand securely on a flat surface, such as a school desk. I had not seen it before, perhaps because he was keeping it here in his locker. He put the black leather strap over my head and opened the lid for me.

"You have to look down into the viewer there."

"Everything's upside down. How can you take a picture like that?"

"It's easy once you get used to it."

I turned the camera slowly side to side: classmates walking by, turning to stare at us, muttering to each other, a finger raised here and there.

"So, then, how did you get caught?"

The camera had been sitting on his knee but the noise of the shutter unreeling on a long exposure had given him away. Mulder had warned him that if he caught him again next time he'd confiscate the camera.

I looked down into the viewer again. A pretty girl was bending over the water fountain, her right hand holding her hair back. Just beyond two senior boys were watching her and whispering to each other. One hitched up his crotch and with his elbow poked the other in the ribs. From the opposite end of the corridor a junior high boy was walking towards us, blowing an enormous bubble. A tall boy on the basketball team walked past him and pricked it. The pink, distended ball burst in his face and, flushed red with anger, he started picking the pieces of wet gum from his cheek.

I swung around towards Tom and pressed the shutter.

"Okay, wise guy, hand it back and I'll take one of you."

I slipped the strap over my head. He took it quickly, hardly looking into the viewer.

"You were too close. You're not going to see anything except my nostrils."

I am wearing my team jacket, unzipped. The requisite Catholic school tie has already come off. The shirt is open a few buttons; gold chain on a finely sculpted neck, the coy smile – am I affecting a pubescent Byronic rebellion, or signals of an erotic dare? I could never judge my own looks, but once, on a bus with my father when I was six or seven – where could we have been going in a bus and not in our car? – a woman came over to tell my father that he had a beautiful son, a word, like nice or cute, I did not at all like. For me my forehead was too high, my brown eyes too large, my mouth too thick and sensual – 'dangerous', one of the nuns had called it, which secretly pleased me. I inspected my clear skin daily, lest it misbehave.

Tom has on a black turtleneck shirt, unusual wear. There is a gold stud in his right ear, which somehow I had forgotten. This also was unusual in that era, or at least at Jefferson. It makes me notice that his ears have just the suggestion of points, like some wild creature stepped out of a Poussin landscape. His left eyebrow is raised; he scrutinizes me as I scrutinize him. Who is the subject of the photograph? I have ready adjectives for his looks: sharp, for example, aware. The photograph does not show that his eyes were in perpetual motion, a sign of a high IQ I had read somewhere, sometimes darting over the surface of my face and ruffling it, as a bird rushing to fly disturbs the surface of a pond. Other words too: different, unique. I saw my looks reflected in someone else's face; Tom's I never saw in anyone else. Fierce? Thin lines fan from the sides of his eyes. Tired? Anxious? A deep vertical line at the bridge of his nose divides left side from right. Intense? Had he managed to crowd more into his life in the same number of years than all the rest of us? Odd; mysterious; complex. In the black and white print his eyebrows and hair are white, on shades of gray; the burnished gold, the highlighting of red neutralized.

Coach O'Malley suddenly appeared in the landing of the

gym stairwell, saw me and shouted.

"Come on Wyant. Playtime's over. Put the toys away and get yourself changed. Williams is down from Albany to check us out and maybe give us a few pointers so move your ass."

I handed the camera back to Tom and he put it on the shelf of the locker.

"Got to go. What time's your detention over?"

"Four thirty . . . five."

"You going straight home? My father's picking me up about five, five thirty. You want a ride?"

"I don't know. I might finish the work I have to do in detention by four."

"You can wait around for an hour can't you?"

" I suppose . . . "

He hesitated. I was impatient, not wanting the coach to holler at me in front of everyone, in the main hallway.

"How do you usually get home when you're late?"

"I just hitch a ride. There's always someone going at least to the highway."

We were walking down the hall together towards the west stairwell. He was going upstairs to the third floor and I downstairs to the connecting underground passage into the new gymnasium wing. People brushed by us. Perhaps, self-conscious as I was, I imagined that they glanced or stared at us. I held myself rigidly straight and pretended not to look around.

I added some cajoling. "You can go to the library and do some homework. You'd only have to do it later at home anyway, wouldn't you?"

We had edged onto the landing by then. The bell had gone off, that last minute before the classroom doors closed, the din of pounding feet, the maddening rush. We were jostled aside. It was harder to hear him above the two-octave din of half-broken voices. Still, we lingered. I would catch hell from Coach and Tom would be late.

He suddenly said, "Okay. Where shall I meet you?"

"By the locker room door or out by the car park. We got a blue Peugeot. It's French . . . "

"I know," he interrupted. "I'll see you later then."

"Great!"

He went upstairs. I lingered a moment, watching his back recede, thinking that, as Richie had said, he was strange all right, out of place here, as he would have been at any high school, like an adult who decides to finish his diploma when he is forty or a recently arrived immigrant with a language and manners all his own. I ran downstairs. I was happy.

Coach O'Malley greeted me at the locker room door and pulled me aside. Tom was in one of his gym classes. He had heard that he'd been on the wrestling team at his old school and that he was good, 'real good'. He had asked him about joining our team but he had said no. Was there anything I could do about it? I didn't think so.

"Maybe you can work on him. Except, I heard he's pretty into the drug scene. You know anything about that?"

"No, not really."

"Kids into drugs is tragic. Thank God we've got no problems like that on this team. That's all we'd need. Right?"

"Right."

"Okay, okay. So get a move on. I don't want any laggards keeping Williams waiting."

He patted my ass as I walked by.

Mickey had the locker next to mine but was already changed and about to go to the pool. I opened my locker and began undressing. Mickey sat down on the bench to wait for me, stretching out his long legs. He was only six months older than I, but a head taller; thin, lithe, more short-distance speed, too unsure of his gangly limbs to exceed at diving. We criticized each other's performances; it worked out well. Because of my success he drove himself further, and this in turn demanded more of me. He would almost certainly qualify for the try-outs.

I said, "My father's picking me up about five. You need a ride home?" He lived in Madalin, on South Road near the waterfall.

"Jackie and her father are picking me up. Why don't you come over to her place? That chick Linda from Mercy is going to be there. They're doing some kind of science project together. Jackie says Linda thinks you're a real fox."

"I already got it arranged with my father."

"So call him up."

"I don't know. I got a lot of work to do. Maybe some other time."

"Ah. Come on. Fuck the work. You never know, you might get lucky."

"No. I got to do that English paper yet."

"Where's your priorities, man? Believe me this Linda's got the hots for you. You won't even have to work at it. You got it made. Take my word. She's hot all right for sure. All you got to do is sort of sit close and let your hand accidentally hit her knee and . . . bingo! Open sesame. I might be able to set it up so it's just the two of you in the living room. Ask Jackie to show me her stamp collection or something so the two of you are alone. What do you say? English you can do anytime but tits like that you got to sacrifice."

I responded with a question. "What are you doing your paper on?"

"Shit. I don't know yet. 'My future hopes.' What a dumb topic. Man, those nuns sometimes. Like I'm supposed to know or something. What about you?"

"I don't know I thought I'd write about diving or coaching, or maybe archeology."

"You still on that jag?"

The idea had come to me the summer I had been visiting my relatives in Sicily. My uncle taught classical history and had taken me to see the major temple sights.

"Francesca will have a conniption fit if you don't say you want to be Pope or at least a cardinal. They all think you're going to be a priest like you're the last great white hope for the church or something."

I threw my underwear in the locker and took my bathing suit off the hook. My lack of hair made me self-conscious in front of hirsute Mickey and I turned aside.

He said, "Pope Danny the Innocent. Doesn't sound too bad."

"Clam it up will you."

I slipped on my suit and changed the subject. "Coach said

there's some hot shot down from Albany to look us over."

"Williams. From the State U. I met him just now. He coached a couple of Olympic gold-medalists. You know not just good, real good. He takes you on and you're *in*."

As we were walking out of the locker room he suddenly asked me again, "You sure you don't want to come over to Jackie's? You're not mad at me or anything are you?"

"No. Nothing like that. Just want to finish my work. Maybe next time . . . "

I did not mention meeting Tom.

The two coaches were standing by the diving board. I was uncomfortable about meeting someone new and important, in my bathing suit. Williams towered over me. He would have been at least six feet four and two hundred and fifty pounds, solid and tough, more like a cattle rancher than a swimming coach. My hand disappeared in his. His eyes were small and shrewd. He had a nasal, John Wayne drawl.

"You gonna show me your stuff today, kid?"

"I'll do my best."

"O'Malley here says you got promise."

He had never said that to me and I blushed.

O'Malley wanted me to do a few simple dives – reverse dive straight, forward dive with half twist – before trying the more complicated inward one a half with pike we had been working on. I knew that Father was right, that the secret of diving successfully was to acquire the ability to focus on nothing except the dive itself, block out everything, let go of thought, allow my reflexes to take over. It was not until my third or fourth attempt that I felt that narrowing of the field of consciousness, that funnelling of energy into one point, a palpable feeling in the pit of the body that I had it right, for me one of the sensual pleasures of diving. I broke the surface with geometric precision.

Williams himself extended his hand to pull me effortlessly out of the pool.

"Not bad, kid. Pretty good I'd even say. Plenty of room for improvement maybe but something to work with there for sure."

116

Several of the team were hovering about to hear what he said and I took in their envious looks with pleasure.

O'Malley said, "What did I tell you Bob? The kid's got talent don't you think?"

"Give me a few weeks with him first then we'll see." He asked me, "What do you think? You willing to come up to Albany every Saturday crack of dawn to work out?"

"I guess."

Williams looked miffed. "What do you mean you guess?"

"I'll have to ask my father."

"I'll talk to him. Don't you worry about that. Even if I have to drive you there myself."

"Well you guys work it out. So, let's say I'll see you Saturday at seven sharp unless I hear different from Coach here. Okay?"

My hand was still wet. I had nowhere to wipe it. I put it sheepishly in his.

"Thank you, sir," I said with proper Catholic school manners.

As I was heading for the showers, O'Malley signalled for me to wait. He was talking to another boy on the team, and I waited until they were through. He had a small notebook in which he scribbled down with just the stub of a pencil his criticisms of our performance. It never seemed to occur to him to note anything good and so, as I stood there and he squinted at the small page, and flipped to another, knowing the routine well enough I wondered how much further he would have me push myself, take on just how much more pain for the few days of toning that it would take to add just that much more of an edge to a dive?

"That was okay today but I want you to do more leg bends and sit-ups at home. You're still not getting enough leverage, and you got to put a little more into it yet. I mean that last one was okay but everything else was either off or mediocre. You look tired today. What about your diet? You watching your diet? You look peaked. Sure nothing's worrying you? . . . You got that exercise mat home I told you to get, didn't you? You using it regularly? . . . Okay. So, let's see . . . " He was crossing things off as he went along. He closed the notebook, stuffed it into his back pocket. "You're still too uneven. Some days you got everything right and some days you can't get anything right. Plus ten to minus ten. That's too uneven Wyant. It's too like a mood swing and you know what I think of mood swimmers. Join the girls' team . . . Let me have a look . . . Yeah, you do look tired. Dark circles even. Everything okay at home? Not jerking off too much are you kid?" I forced a laugh, out of duty. "Get some extra sleep tonight will you? Keep it zipped up a few days will yah. I guarantee it'll make a difference. Do it for me Wyant, for the team. For your sore pecker. Give it a rest. Plenty of time for that . . . "

He was right. My diving was moody, either on or off. The warning bells had already been going off in my own head. Mood divers could be good, even great, but that is not what I wanted to be. I had set myself the private goal of being the best and even, despite whatever I was feeling. Like never crying after my mother died. Like never crying.

Down in the showers I let the water run hot to extra hot, then abruptly to cold. I did the same thing at home. I had the idea, gleaned from who knows where, that this would prevent me from getting a cold. Most athletes believe some old wives' tales.

I wrapped the thin frayed towel around my waist. It molded itself to my wet body in a familiar way. I padded back to the scratched and dented matt-black locker. There was a long aisle dividing two rows of lockers: wooden benches in front of a line of ten, a break, another ten, a break, and again ten; three aisles in all, two hundred and forty lockers. Mine was number 93 in the second row. Over the aisles were bare fluorescent lights, each unit about a yard long. The ceiling was a mass array of chrome heating and ventilation conduits, blue plastic piping and water pipes, hissing, clanging, echoing. The background was painted black. When the room was filled the pale, dirty yellow, cement block walls reverberated deafeningly. The pungency of still lingering stale sweat mixed with acrid chlorine. The empty room obliquely echoed sounds, the shrill whistle or thud of a basketball from the gym in one direction, splashes, shouts, the thump of the released board from another, or even the din of running steps and classroom bells descending the stairwell out beyond the tiled rooms and corridors of the gym.

Only the aisle I was in was lit. My socks were turned inside out, my shirt crumpled, my jeans in a roll, my underpants twisted up. I took the towel off, hung it on a hook on the inside of the door and started to untangle it all. I was alone. Mickey was gone. Tom? A chill blew through the room raising goose bumps along my arms and legs, intimations of vulnerability. They seemed to me the fleshy product of my sleek, delayed pubescence, like hives from allergies. I slipped on the frayed gray jockey shorts. I did not like to be there alone, transported, trapped inside some desolate Hopperesque, alienated world.

I found Tom at the top of the stairs leaning against the wall just inside the back entrance still reading his book. When I asked him what it was he said, "*Siddhartha*, only the most important book I've ever read, that's what", because Hesse knew that to be free you always had to be ready. I said I wasn't sure what he meant and he said he would lend it to me when he was finished, but he wanted it back because it was the kind of book you had to read ten or eleven times. He put it inside his khaki, army surplus knapsack, tightened the straps and slung it over his shoulders.

Powdered snow swept across the deserted parking lot. Father had not yet arrived.

2. INNOCENT ACTS

The snow whirled dervish circles around us. I suggested that we go across the street to the diner to wait for Father. I would phone him at his office. The welcome smell of freshly brewed coffee, frying onions, eggs, toast, butter, and the communality of popular song. I took off my blue wool cap and shook the snow from my collar. Tom wiped his wet forehead with a clean, white handkerchief. A couple of the team were sitting with their girlfriends at the other end of the room. Nodded exchanges.

We slid into a red leather booth. The waitress came over:

thin, fortyish, plain, with a perpetually stern expression, her weapon, or defence, against our adolescent nonsense. Her name tag read 'Violet', a bit like her perpetual mood. She took a pencil from behind her ear and said impatiently, "So whad'ya you two want?" I ordered a strawberry shake, and Tom coffee.

I immediately slid out of the booth to call Father at his office. He answered on the first ring.

"Thank God you had the sense to call. You must have been freezing waiting for me. I bet you thought I forgot you but I couldn't get the car started. Must be that blasted carburetor again. I knew I should have had it fixed weeks ago when it started acting up. I'm stuck here waiting for the mechanic. Where are you calling from?"

"Across the street at the diner. How much longer you going to be?"

"I don't know. I phoned almost an hour ago and he still isn't here. Probably he's got a lot of calls because of the weather." He added defensively, "He's the only one I can call. No one else around here understands foreign cars."

"It's starting to snow really hard. Maybe I better hitch a ride."

"You know I don't like you hitching. Especially in this weather."

"I'll be careful."

"I'd rather you waited."

"But right now there's a lot of cars going in that direction. If I wait too long the roads'll really be bad and I might not get home at all. I don't want to get stranded here."

"Maybe you're right. But promise to keep well off the road. It's pretty slippery out there. And use some judgment. Don't go taking a ride with just anyone. Go straight home . . . You listening to me?"

"I'm listening. I'll call you as soon as you're home. Charlie home yet?"

"I just tried and there was no answer. He's probably having trouble too, like the rest of us." He added impatiently, "Anyway, I'd better get off."

"Hey, wait! Don't hang up. I got something to ask you."

"Can't it wait until later? I'm trying to keep the line free in case Charlie or the mechanic calls."

"It'll only take a second."

I told him about Coach Williams's offer and the Saturdays in Albany.

"He must have thought you were pretty good to make such a generous offer of his time. It sounds like a real opportunity. But we have to discuss it when I get home."

"So, can I then?"

"I said we have to discuss it. You should be having a social life weekends too, not just alternating between school work and the team all the time. Not to mention doing things with us as a family. I'm concerned about that."

"We still got Sundays together."

"I said we'd discuss it. Period. End of sentence. And then I'll have to think about it for awhile. Maybe I should even go and see O'Malley myself . . . "

I hated it when he began to intellectualize decisions that had to do with me, but I also knew when to back off.

The snow was coming down harder. Despite, or because of it, we caught a ride almost immediately, with an elderly man dressed in hunting clothes and driving a twenty-year-old pick-up truck. The long visor of his red hunting cap hid his face. A shot-gun was fixed to a rack in the rear window. Behind the seat were waders, a twenty-two, several boxes of shells, next to him on the plastic seat a wicker basket. That, and the floor stick shift, took up a full space. I leaned against Tom.

I was in high spirits and babbled on to the driver. Did he know about hunting in the commune woods and that when they caught someone shooting deer or pheasants on their property they gave them a choice of either calling the police or going to one of their community meetings where they would preach to them about being kind to the wild life and not killing things, which I had heard was way worse than getting arrested or paying a fine, but, of course, I never had to go to any of their meetings and maybe, because they protected the animals the woods were full of deer and I had even seen a fox more than once as if they all knew they could live there and be safe. Which was pretty nice for me because I could see them from our yard or from up in our tree fort. Glancing at me, he asked me too aggressively where this Eden was. I caught a glimpse of a bulbous scarred nose, and a twisted, badly mended jaw; I was evasive.

He dropped us off in front of Tom's house. It wasn't any trouble because he could continue along North Road to Manorton and rejoin the highway there to Stuyvesant, where he lived. It was the least he could do in this weather. We thanked him as we descended. The wind had died down, the snow falling straight, the flakes so large that each one that landed on my sleeve could be studied in its own mathematical purity, like Islamic tile patterns. We dashed up onto Tom's front porch. I rubbed my hands together and stomped the snow off my shoes as he fumbled in his pocket for the keys. A gust of invitingly warm air welcomed us in.

He asked, "You wanna go straight in?"

"I don't know. What do you want to do?"

"Smoke a joint first. But we got to go out back, so it don't smell up the place."

"You want to?"

"Sure. You?"

"Sure, if you want to."

"I have to get the stuff inside – up in my room. Better come in but take your shoes off so we don't get the hall wet."

The stairs were just in front of us; he took them two at a time. I closed and locked the front door. My shoes in my hand I padded down the dark, quiet hallway to the back vestibule, my heart racing, excited by fear and anticipation. What if it made me crazy or weird like in those stories I had heard from the priests, the coach and some of the other kids. What if I freaked out and starting tearing my hair? What if I got hooked on it?

Less than a minute seemed to go by before he bounded downstairs, smiling and holding up two joints. We went out back. A protective portico sheltered us from the snow. He lit up, took a deep drag, and held it out to me. Even if I had not smoked a joint before, I knew enough from hearsay about the mechanisms of smoking to carry off my side without coughing, or otherwise making a fool of myself. I passed it back.

"Great stuff," I said, through a mouthful. "Real smooth."

"The best there is. Acapulco Gold. No one's got such great shit as this. I only got a couple of joints left. For special occasions. But, you'll see, it's intense; one's gonna be enough."

"Thanks for sharing . . . "

"Hey, what are friends for?"

When we were down to the stub he held it out to me.

"Yours."

I said, "It's okay, you can have it."

He shook his head. "The first time I smoke with someone I always give them the last bit. The best part. Sort of a ritual with me."

I held out my hand to catch some snow, watching the flakes dissolve into cold water before rubbing it on my cheek. I could have stayed outside the whole night. The storm was so peaceful, everything was so quiet. But we went in. He did not turn the lights on. I hung my jacket next to his, very deliberately, even pulling the cuff out of the sleeve to make sure it hung straight. Lingering. The general silence amplified each sound: the refrigerator motor, the cracks and snaps of expanding and contracting wood, the furnace beneath us, although in the world around all sounds were muffled by the still, descending snow. I took off my shoes.

"You okay?"

I nodded. "Fine. Why not? Phew. I mean . . . excellent . . . weird . . . "

"You want to listen to some music? I got the new Doors record."

"Yeah, great. Mickey just got it too and says it's cool, but I ain't had a chance to hear it yet."

Were my words slurred? I was amazed that I could formulate a sentence, or stand for that matter. I was feeling dizzy. Even the hairs on my arms were extensions of feeling. We were in the kitchen. He took a pitcher of fresh orange juice out of the refrigerator and handed me two glasses from the cabinet. I thought he was going into the living room but he headed up the stairs.

"Record player's in my room now. My mother doesn't like most of what I play."

I tagged after him into his room. He lit a thick, rainbow-colored candle sitting in a crystal ashtray on his dresser. It smelled faintly of rose water and Arab palaces.

"You want some of this o.j.?"

"Sure."

I held out both glasses as he poured. We clicked. It took him a moment or two to find the right record amid the piles strewn over the floor, the bed, the bentwood rocking chair. He kept the volume low, the lights off. I was still standing by the door. He came over and took the empty glass out of my hand.

I wandered over to the window. I could see tiny patches of our house through the barren trees. How odd, I thought, a light was on in my bedroom. I had not left a light on in my bedroom. Why was it on? Was I there also? Bilocating? Sometimes Charlie went in to use my encyclopedia, or try to steal some of the money I hoarded away in various nooks and crannies. Was he home? Should I leave? He wouldn't find any treasures today.

Tom came over and stood next to me.

"Snow is great, isn't it? We didn't have this kind of view out on the Island. Just back yards with garbage cans and shit. Nothing like this. Awesome. I hope we never move again. It's a real drag."

"Look at that. A light's on in my room. I didn't know you could see my window. I mean, I can see yours so I should have figured you could see mine. But I didn't. Weird, isn't it? Like it must mean something, don't you think?"

"Everything does."

"Look at that, I just saw a shadow. Must be my rat-fink brother trying to steal the money I saved. But I got it good and hidden this time. He'll never find . . . Look at that will yah, the light just went out. He probably gave up. I bet he's pissed right now. Not finding anything . . . Hey. I know. We could send signals back and forth. Morse code. With a flashlight."

"Or just thoughts."

"Yeah! Like, psychic shit."

"Shall we try it."

"You mean now?"

"Sure."

124

"So, what am I thinking?"

I closed my eyes and pressed my finger tips to my temples in mock imitation of a medium. I turned towards him so as to better direct the energy, my brow furrowed in deep concentration. I thought with all my strength, 'tree hut', and formulated a picture. Everything was so still around us. The mood of the falling snow had extended its circumference around the two of us, enwrapped us in a mantle of stillness. He was standing close: smelling of grass and musk, alerted again by the feral scent, something wild, or old, like history. He took a step – to close the circle, I thought, or to get inside my thoughts and images, to merge our body heat, as if we were both wearing one set of clothes. My hands were still pressed to my forehead. He gently removed them, and leaned forward until his forehead touched mine, squeezing my hands in his.

When he opened his mouth to speak, his warm breath poured gently over my face, What were his exact words at that moment, were they born of some understanding he naturally had, rather than some psychic gift? I began to shake violently.

He said, very quietly, "it's okay. It's okay."

Sweat trickled down my side. I put my hands on his waist to steady myself. He lightly kissed the side of my face below the ear, my neck, a breeze over blades of grass.

"No, don't. Please . . . " I said.

"It's all right, Danny."

He had given a name to his desire.

The telephone was ringing. We must have dozed off. I looked at my watch; five minutes to seven. I somehow knew it must be my father. Tom started to get up.

He said anxiously, "Jesus. Who's that now? Must be my mother. She calls at least once every night from work."

He struggled naked out of the sleeping-bag. The phone continued to ring, eight, nine, ten. A second later he called up to me.

"Dan. It's your father."

I bounded downstairs. He handed me the phone and went back up. I heard the bathroom door opening, and water running in the sink.

"Why didn't you tell me you were going over there? I mean I've just been phoning everyone under the sun and thought for sure something terrible had happened to you in the storm."

"We were listening to music and couldn't hear the phone. I thought it might be you. You home?"

"Yeah . . . at last. The stupid fool didn't come to get me started until half an hour ago. The roads are awful. I could hardly make it back. Guess you got a ride all right."

"Yeah. Tom was in the diner so we decided to team up, like you said, so it was safer. We got a ride with some old guy in a pick-up truck, from Stuyvesant. Man the roads were really bad."

"I was half sick to death. Don't ever do that again. I called Charlie about half an hour after talking to you and he said you weren't home yet."

"Sorry 'bout that. Man, you got to hear the new album Tom's got. I'll see if I can borrow it."

"You should have at least called your brother."

"I tried phoning him but the line was always busy and once no one answered. He was probably talking to *Gloria*."

"You could have phoned me at the office . . . anyway, we're eating in a few minutes."

"I was going to eat here."

"Charlie made a big pot of sauce. Why don't the two of you come here? Where's Tom? I'll ask him if you like."

The phone was hanging on the kitchen wall by the doorway. There was an extra long cord, and I was prancing about, stretching it as far as the window so that I could watch the still falling snow.

"His mother left a casserole. Macaroni and cheese. It's already in the oven," I lied. "It's almost ready. There's enough for an army. Anyway, I don't think he'd want to come over today. Not in this snow. He'd have to bring all the stuff we're using to do his project. I'm helping him and we got about another hour to do. Jesus. Look at it come down. There must be six inches already. No way we'll have school tomorrow."

"You know I don't like your eating over any of your

friends' without their parent's permission."

"But his mother knows I *might*. She made enough for me just in case I would. I'm sure it's okay."

"Still you should ask her."

"She's at work. I can't go calling the hospital and I promised Tom I'd help him finish this science thing he's doing. And he's going to show me a few things in math that he knows way better than me. You know me and math. I'd only have to come back here after I eat. In all the snow. I mean, can you believe it? I hope it keeps up all night even. I'll bet you we don't have any school tomorrow. So? Can I? Can I?"

He began to hesitate . . . well . . . he just didn't know . . . which I knew invariably led to refusals. I slumped down on a straight back chair under the telephone, hardly listening, looking down at my flat expanse of stomach. A white crust and flakes had formed around the navel. I peeled a bit away and held it up to smell it.

"I'll leave her a thank you note, so she doesn't think I'm taking advantage or anything. Tom told me she likes me. She thinks I'm very polite. It's just a meal, after all. It's almost made."

"Is this going to be a habit?" I heard Charlie in the background saying something. Father paused, then continued impatiently, "Oh all right, but next time Tom comes here. And I want you to say in your note that I'll call her tomorrow at noon to thank her myself."

"Fair enough."

"And you be home by eight thirty. You hear? Not a minute later."

"I promise, I promise. Cross my heart." But I added in such a matter-of-fact way that it made Father laugh, "You're really strict with me, you know. I mean, it's not like I'm on the other side of the world or anything and could get stranded. I'm practically in our own back yard."

"That's not the point."

"Yeah, I know, you don't want me taking advantage of Mrs. Corrigan's hospitality."

"Exactly."

I did not press the point, not wanting to risk an argument

just then so I said quickly, "Okay, eight thirty."

I reached up to put the phone in its cradle. Tom was standing naked in the doorway, erect, like some satyr stepped off the side of a Greek vase. I had not heard him come back downstairs. His body surprised me: compact, wiry, his stomach muscled, his waist narrow, the base of his long, curved cock accented by dancing tongues of wispy orange flame. Had he been standing there long?

I had replaced the receiver in the cradle but my hand was still raised holding it. Was I frightened? The grass had begun to wear off. There was nothing to hide behind.

"That your father?" He walked over to me.

I nodded. "He says I can stay until eight thirty."

"I know. I heard. You all right?"

"Sure. Why wouldn't I be?"

He was standing so close that his legs touched my knees. He reached down and slipped the gold chain off my neck and put it on the counter next to us; slid off my wrist watch and put it next to the chain. I was nervously clenching and squeezing my arms, biting my lower lip; he unclenched my hands. He was wearing three plastic multicolored bands on his left wrist which he had braided himself. He took them off and laid them beside my things; he also wore a gold chain and a wrist watch and he took these off too. I knew his little ritual meant that, being completely naked, nothing was between us. I was hard and excited but not trembling. He knelt on the floor before me and pushed my legs apart, kissing the insides of my thighs, slowly moving higher. I sank lower in the chair, caressing his hair, and did not resist.

Tom is curled on his side faced away from me. I extricate myself from the sleeping-bag. I have to piss. It is eight fifteen, I have to be home in a few minutes. I am hungry but know I cannot ask for anything to eat there.

His mother's bedroom door is open. As I enter her room I have the tangible sense that I am being wrapped in the lingering scent of that day's cologne. I walk to the dressing table, turn over the mother-of-pearl hairbrush in my hand. Long hairs stick to the bristles, dark brown and gray; I brush back a lock from my forehead. The closet door is ajar. Everything hangs so neatly according to kind, all the fronts facing in the same direction: the blouses together; several jackets in a row slightly separated from each other; a long cream-colored cotton nightgown decorated with white lace; a silk slip I take off its hanger. It looks expensive, breathes the scents of Italian hill towns, is embroidered with blue anemones. It is cool as it passes over my shoulders and falls over my hips. The strap falls from my left shoulder exposing my chest, but I do not slide it back. There is a full length mirror on the back of the door. I turn this way and that, touch a dark red, sensitive spot on my lower lip, study the red mark above my nipple. The silk billows: Narcissus Erect. The strong arch of a bridge span; it can support weight. On the night table a nail file, an emery stick; on the floor by a rocking chair pink fur slippers set evenly together; a pink satin bedspread; chintz curtains. None of this, not even its mood, exists anywhere in my house. Atop the dresser I slide my hand over the silver box in which there are lace handkerchiefs; a round, ormolu music box atop which the figure of a ballerina. It plays a Schubert rondo. Tom has come up silently behind me. He puts his hands on my hips, presses his face into my hair. The girl spins and turns. He pushes the slip up out of the way and wants to enter me. I am frightened, push him away, and remove the slip.

3. FATHER VOICES DOUBT

The snow ended before dawn, more than enough to close roads and cancel school. At about two I heard the giant plow rumbling by the house on its way downhill, pushing the snow into high banks on both sides of the road and further blocking our driveway, already cleared once. I came outside just as it roared by again in first gear on its return uphill from the riverside, spewing sand and rock salt behind it like some sick, groaning, diarrhetic elephant. The sun was shining; the air still. I tried to blow vapor rings in the cold air.

Father poked his head out the front door. "Tom's on the

phone!"

"Tell him I'll call him back in five minutes. I'm almost finished."

I scooped up the last chunks and threw them onto the mound I had made to one side of the drive with the thought that perhaps I would ice it over and make an igloo later.

I caught a glimpse of myself in the hallway mirror as I passed, my cheeks and the tip of my nose bright red. Father was in his study typing. He had left the door ajar. I went upstairs to phone Tom back on the hallway extension. My hands were numb from working without gloves. It was hard to dial his number.

We had made plans the evening before that I would go there at noon. He had grown impatient and wanted to know if I was still coming. His mother had left early for work so she could do some shopping. She had liked my note. I was such a 'nice boy' and could stay for dinner any time I wanted. She had even made enough chicken this morning for me to eat over there. If I was still coming. If I wanted to.

I wasn't sure that eating over two nights in a row was such a good idea. I would have to ask Father, and he would probably say no. Why not try? he insisted. I would see. Actually, I was a bit peeved with him for phoning in the first place. I had intended on going over there, but without telling anyone. Tom suddenly said in that nervous, hurried way that people have of intruding something into a conversation that they are reluctant or embarrassed to say, "I got one more joint of the good stuff left. You want to share it later?"

"I don't know. It made me pretty dizzy."

"It might not this time."

"I don't know, it might."

"So what if it does. You want to or not?"

"I don't know. I got to think about it."

"You coming over now?"

"The snow's pretty deep. I'll have to come around by the road."

"So?"

"Give me a few minutes . . . "

Father was still typing when I passed his door again. He

called out, "Danny, is that you? Will you come in here a minute?"

I pushed open the door but did not enter. He finished the line he was on before looking up.

"You going to Tom's or Richie's?"

"Tom's."

"I want to talk to you about that. Will you close the door."

"I told him I'd be right over."

"Well, he can wait."

I closed the door sullenly but did not sit down.

He pointed to an old easy chair opposite his desk, which my brother referred to as the hot seat. Only dire matters were discussed there.

The room was large enough to contain his oak desk, a table and even an old sofa, all stacked with papers, magazines folded back to certain articles, a book upside down piled upon another book upside down. The walls were lined with oak bookcases, the shelves crammed two layers deep and overflowing. Our house was a house of books. There were stacks of them everywhere: on the coffee table in wobbly piles, on the fireplace mantel, on end tables, and library caddies bought at country house sales; stacked in corners, in closets, in the attic in boxes and trunks, or loose on the floor, in the garage and a shed behind the house, in the basement, back seat of the car, in a basket by the toilet; lying by the bath-tub on a stand, on top of the refrigerator, in the spare room and in his room, in my brother's room, and even at the back of my closet. It was not just a hodgepodge either of anything and everything amassed by compulsion. Father was an avid but discriminating collector of American and English poetry first editions. The collection came to me after he died in the mid nineties. He was scrutinizing me over the top of his Franklin glasses. I hated that because it seemed like a false air, a role.

"Why are you going to Tom's again today and not Richie's?"

"We didn't finish his project yesterday. We got a couple more hours work on it."

"Well, I don't know if I like that. Your getting in too thick with Tom. Neglecting your other friends."

My temper flared. "What are you talking about? I'm not neglecting anybody. What do you mean?"

"What I'm saying is that Richie called you ten times today, and you never called him back now, but Tom calls you once and you phone him right away."

"So? So what? I mean, so . . . what?"

"Lower your voice, will you. I'm just concerned about you neglecting Richie and your other friends and hanging out too much with Tom. It's not like you, to be disloyal . . . "

"Disloyal! Neglect! What are you talking about? I don't know what you're talking about!"

"Yes you do."

"No I don't. I don't know! I never did anything bad to Richie! You can ask him yourself. I don't have to return every call he makes. I never have. He doesn't expect it. You can ask him if you don't believe me. I see Richie every fucking day at school. I mean, you forget he sits right smack next to me. What did he say? What did he say to you?"

"Calm down will you, and don't shout at me. And for God's sake watch your mouth. He didn't say anything to me."

"Then why are you bringing all this up? I know why. It's because you don't like Tom. I've hardly been over there even once and you're already telling me I can't go over. You hate him."

"I didn't say you couldn't go, and you're wrong, I don't hate Tom, or even Lansing for that matter, who he's hanging out with by the way, as you saw with our own eyes. And why you would still want to get mixed up with him when he's thick with Lansing well, that's anybody's guess."

"Yeah right, like arguing and fighting is in thick. I saw it all right . . . You're just making all this stuff up because you *do* hate him. Everyone does. Even Charlie. You can't convince me different."

"Well, I'll say it again. I have nothing against him personally, but you know as well as I do what his reputation is around here and I don't want it rubbing off on you. Tom is trouble with a capital T."

I pouted, and slumped down in the chair. "What's the use. Now you're forbidding me to go see people. Why don't you just throw away the key?"

"I didn't say I was forbidding you, but if you keep going on like this I will . . . Richie used to be over here every day, or you were over there. But I haven't seen him for weeks. From the two of you calling each other all the time. you're not calling him at all. Feast or famine. We never had any of this trouble when you were going over to Richie's."

"Trouble! What do you mean trouble? I don't know what you're talking about."

"Yes you do. You're the one should be the lawyer, not your brother."

"Ha ha. Very funny."

"You better watch your mouth young man, or I really will send you to your room."

"It's your fault. You said you'd call his mother and you never did. I asked him and he said you didn't. If you had called her she would have told you about my note and how I was welcome any time but you wouldn't even do that."

He looked startled, as if an arrow had grazed, if not struck, him. He took his glasses off, wiped his eyes and squeezed his temples.

He said half to me and half to himself, "Well . . . It's what Clare has been telling me all along . . . This isn't getting us very far is it . . . I want Tom to start coming here and I don't want you staying for supper . . . I'm not forbidding you. If I did you would probably just sneak over anyway . . . " he shuffled his papers around, pressed down a key or two of the old typewriter, and without looking at me, added, "Just go if you want to go. Just go and let me work in peace . . . "

As I left I slammed the door behind me, and stomped down the road to Tom's house. I was still fuming when he opened the door.

"Boy you look pissed! What's up?"

"Never mind! I don't want to talk about it!"

He stood aside. "Okay, okay. Don't bite *my* head off."

"Well, we going to get stoned or not! Well? Are we?"

4. TOM'S STORY

It took me a long time to get use to Tom's silences; if I ever did. Prying details about anything out of him was nigh on impossible. Yet, I would not say he was secretive either. Reticent certainly. He expressed intimacy in the way most adolescent males do, more by sharing activities than by talking, while I always had been a verbal person. That same afternoon another side emerged. The light was fading from his room. I was playing a childish game with his face, stretching his cheeks and eyes to make a mask, pulling at his mouth and ears, squeezing his lips together, his nostrils shut, babbling on about this or that, He looked serene; his hand toyed with me. I would feel a surge of excited energy and suddenly press my lips roughly against his, or pinch his shoulder. If lying together naked can be a condition of soul, being in bed with Tom was a rite of passage. I asked dreamily:

How come Lansing slapped you in the face over in Kingston the other day and who were all them people with you? What was going on and how come you were there and why didn't you come home with us? I didn't want you getting involved. *Involved? Involved in what? That's stupid. It can't be the reason. Come on. What? What? Tell me. Tell me. Tell Danny all. Take it from the top* . . . From the top. Phew. How long you got? *Hours, days, weeks, months, years* . . . Okay, okay. And stop poking me will you. *From the top* . . . From the top. Right. How about just after I got here? *Fine.* Well, see it went this way . . . I had this big fight with Mom about staying out too late and she got so mad I walked out of the house and hitched a ride over to Kingston. *When was that exactly? Come on.* You mean minute and second? I don't know. I never know shit like that. Wait a minute. Hold on. Don't start again. No tickling. School had just started, so I guess it must have been around the first week of September. *Before the school Halloween party?* Oh yeah, way before that. It must have been a Sunday too because Ma was home the night I walked in about eleven thirty twelve or else

134

none of this would have happened. Anyway, she threw a shit fit about me being down the road at Lansing's and coming home after ten and I was really pissed at her too, like I'm sixteen and she still has to tuck me in bed every night, so I thought, I'm not going to put up with this bullshit. I'm getting out of here. I heard from Lansing or Donny there was this crash pad over in Kingston where kids could just walk in off the road and stay the night no questions asked so I decided I'd go there. *Kingston? Where? I never heard of such a place.* Yeah, well, you wouldn't would you. *What's that supposed to mean?* Hey man, take it easy. I wasn't trying to insult you or nothing. Just that it's not your world. I mean, drugs and running away from home. *So you went?* Yeah. Lansing introduced me to this runaway kid who was selling a few sticks of shit for him now and then and I had his phone number somewhere in case I run out. I knew he was staying at the pad so I phoned him and he told me he'd meet me and show me where it was 'cause it was pretty hard to find, sort of tucked back in the middle of nowhere somewhere. So I did. *You mean that puny dirty little kid I seen you around with.* Yeah; Bobby. *Richie heard he was an Indian.* Well Richie would wouldn't he. I don't really know myself. I mean he says he is, but a lot of people say a lot of things about themselves they ain't. *His eyes look Indian.* His eyes? I never much thought about it. *Like crow's or raven's or blackbird's.* Sure. If you say so. Anyway, one of the girls over at the pad told me he told her he was Iroquois nation. Which is cool. He's got the cops after him for robbing a gas station, but he says he was just riding with these guys who did it and not him but if his father finds out he'd get the shit beat out of him so he's not about to go home. He's got some relatives somewhere upstate in the mountains who can take care of him he says, but for the moment he's staying put at the pad. He was staying in some shelter on the lower East Side, but they ripped him off and wouldn't let him do drugs. He does speed and hash mostly. Man can he get high. I never saw anything like it. First he says he's going to run all the way to New York and the next he's popping a downer and lying around on the floor totally fucked. So anyway some guy staying at this shelter downtown tells him about this crash pad up here in Kingston which some guy or other runs and that's how he got here . . . So where was I? Oh yeah, meeting Bobby on the road and he takes me back there. And right away I found out he was selling dope around for Lansing and sometimes himself and not small change either. I mean hard stuff and all and there I am wondering who Lansing's source is like because I don't want to horn in on their territory so long as I can have some of the action cause I can see Lansing and even Bobby is scoring big I can tell you. I seen this wad of hundreds Lansing had hidden and it could choke a hippopotamus. Like he's found the mother lode all right. And that was only the start of the trouble . . . *Jesus! You mean you were running drugs that night?* Well, no. Not exactly. I'm getting to that . . . See. There's this other kid named Ford who gets involved about this time too. Everyone over there calls him Ford, but that's not his real name cause no one over there uses their real names, only shit like Tara, Jazz, Dawn, Tree. *Tree!* Yeah, well, what turns you on . . . Seems Ford told Tara he comes from some rich family and goes to some posh boarding school and sneaks away on weekends. His father's some sort of big-wig politician which is why he's got to use a different name so his father won't find out what he's up to and put him in military school. He's seen more and done more than most fifty-year-olds – from what he says at least. But you can see it in his eyes too. One thing I know for sure he can get all the shit he wants, I hear direct from the Big L. You name it and he can get it. Top stuff. Which is how it sort of all began because see when I was out on the Island I kind of had pretty good sources too. Nothing like what Ford or Lansing have going but not bad either and at lower prices. Except I'm kind of persona non gratis down there now so I ask Ford like can he make a run out there for me and it's sort of like setting up competition now isn't it? So Lansing and whoever their big boys really are, fuck are they pissed with me for horning in on their territory! So Big L starts making all these threats. Which is about where you and your father walked into the picture that night. *Fucking asshole Lansing.*

What was he threatening? That he'd get me for sure if I didn't toe the line, sell his shit, cut him in on my profits, maybe even divulge my sources. Shit like that. That Lansing's mean as snake shit. *Tell me about it. What were they going to do?* They didn't spell it out. They didn't have to now did they. *Jesus, Tom, you're going to get yourself beaten up for sure.* Yeah, well, maybe that ain't too far from the truth. *So what now?* Whadya mean? *I mean you gotta get yourself out of this somehow or you're gonna get yourself hurt. Jesus, I mean, you know, playing with these guys is like setting forest fires.* Hey, it's cool, man. Calm down. Don't worry. I'm working on it. I'm working on it. I got ways. *Man I got to go over and see this place! When we going?* Forget it. No way. No way I'm going to take you there. Like I said before I don't want you getting involved. *Not get involved, yeah sure, it's a little late for that ain't it?*

5. BREAKING IT OFF

The following week, as I was walking along the main road to school huddled over, protecting myself from the gusts of fine snow blowing horizontally across the pavement, I caught a glimpse of Reggie pulling out of the church driveway heading towards me at about two miles an hour. Even before he swerved the police car into my lane, I was sure that he had been waiting for me and was even more certain that it would again be about Tom. I searched through my mind trying to recall any occasion he might have glimpsed us together. Had I half observed him out of the corner of my eye lurking at the periphery of a moment, the mere ruffling of an instinct? Realizing I had not noticed him annoyed me as much as the thought of an impending lecture. As he rolled his window down, a cloud of cigarette smoke wafted into my face. His eyes were still puffed with half sleep.

"Still hanging out with that Corrigan kid I see."

Where *had* he seen us? I shrugged, waiting. His radio crackled. He turned it down.

"I seen the two of you hitching together the other day and yesterday it sure was you now wasn't it walking up his driveway big as life, so I asks myself, 'Now Reggie, I wonder if Tom there has told Danny the latest?' And you know what? I figured he hadn't."

He might have cruised by the end of North Road and seen me, that was possible, but where had he been the day we'd hitched home from Holland Corners? It was too cold standing there to play games, and I wanted to get to school before anyone would notice us talking.

I said, "Listen, I'd like to stand around talking Reggie – I really would – but I'm flag raiser this morning and got to go."

He threw the cigarette butt past me onto the road. I was half tempted to tell him not to litter, but held my tongue.

He said, "Like I tried to warn you, some heavy stuff is going down, way heavier than any of us first thought, and now I'm telling you there's no way Corrigan's not going to get himself into deep shit and drag you in after him you keep hanging out with him. I was sort of hoping after our little talk that you'd show some sense, maybe a little loyalty to the folks around here what supports you, but guess it just ain't going to be like that now, is it, and I sure as hell hate to have to put your good name in the same reports with them sleaze, but it looks like it may be coming to that don't it."

"There's no law against friendship, Reggie."

"Maybe that's what you call it, but I call it being used, and I sure know more about the world than you do."

I replied simply, "Friendship is friendship."

"Someone getting someone else in trouble . . . dragging their good name and reputation down into the mud . . . well, you can call it what you like but I sure as hell got my own name for it."

I glanced nervously down the road towards school. A few younger kids were already visible. The bell would ring soon. I had better hurry.

"I got to go, Reggie. Like I said, I got duties this morning."

His right hand was on the steering wheel, the motor idling, his left arm on the open window, his neck craned to stare up at me. "This whole thing's gonna blow up in your face. And you know what I think? I think – well, hell, I know – that friend of yours knows it's going to and doesn't give a tinker's damn about you or anybody else, maybe not even himself."

"I really don't know what you're talking about Reggie and I really gotta go."

"Yeah, well, you just get goin then, but when the Feds come knocking at your door asking questions don't come crying to me because I tell you it ain't going to be as friendly as when I come over."

I nearly laughed in his face. "Feds! In Madalin? Come on now."

He shrugged, "You believe what you like. I ain't about convincing anybody. But interstate trafficking is no joke I'm telling you, and any day now it'll be all over, so I guess you got some choices to make, don't you?"

Reggie must have caught a glimpse of something in his rear view mirror because he suddenly turned his head. Richie was walking towards us. I hadn't noticed him. He waved when I looked up.

I said. "You're going to get me in trouble with Sister if I don't go."

As if still showing his power, he held me there with some final words, "Corrigan's got some kind of hold over you, don't he? Sure as hell I can see that even if I don't know what it is. That's what I think. Anyway, I always liked you and you got my phone number. We can talk private any time, off the record, just you and me. I don't want to see you go down. Not you. You got too much of a future. But there's only so much I can do and then the ball's in your court. You come talk to me, it won't go no further. That's a promise."

"Thanks for the offer," I said.

"Well, I said what I got to say."

He rolled up his window and drove off.

The class had already started when I slid into my seat and spread out my pencils, note pad, and text book on the worn, wooden, knife-scarred desk top. It was nearing the start of Advent. Sister Francesca was asking for a volunteer to maintain the Advent candles and make the wreath. She wanted to know if anyone knew the origin of the word. A forest of hands waved in the air. I did not bother to raise mine. She called on me.

"Daniel. You didn't raise your hand. Am I to suppose that you either do not know the answer, or are not yet paying attention? Privilege does not mean irresponsibility, you know. Please pay attention, and while you're at it please stand up and answer the question."

Heads turned in my direction. On the first day of school we were seated alphabetically, but as the year waned we were shifted around according to achievement. Jacqueline and I vied for the highest grades. Today she sat behind me, the second seat of the first row, but after the next set of exams that could change.

I stood to attention. "Advent. From the Latin *venire* – to come, *adventus* – the coming."

Sister smiled her benevolent smile down on me, the one reserved for scholars and future priests. "Very good. I think you're already on your way to being a Latin expert."

This was, of course, her zillionth "veiled" reference to the possibility of my having a vocation. The nuns always thought that their best and brightest, not to mention best looking, all had to have vocations or else they would not have been so favored by God; wasting their genes on progeny rather than salvation, you might say.

She was in the habit of carrying a wooden yard stick, which she slapped against her palm or the folds of her habit. She paused in front of my desk, and brushed chalk off her long, black sleeve. Though it was a few years after Vatican II, the Sisters of St. Joseph had not yet decided to change their traditional habit for simpler, more modern dress. The idea of the habit had been to imitate the poor, but centuries later custom had divorced it from any such identification: the long black dress, black shoes and stockings, the veiled head, that strange starched white bib, the cincture and dangling, clacking rosary were about to be discarded, their meaning long ago obscured. She looked down at me, and asked quietly enough for no one else to hear, "Are you feeling well?"

The question startled me. Perhaps, as soon as she said it, if I was not already sick, I decided to feel sick. When had I become sick? My eyes burned, my forehead was warm, my mind went out of focus, a few beads of cold sweat ran down my side. I was biting my lower lip, which I had never done before.

She leaned a little closer. "You are looking a bit pale. Are you sure you didn't have a fever this morning?"

I looked up and smiled half-heartedly. "Thank you Sister. I'm all right."

At lunch time, just before our break, she came by my desk again and felt my forehead. By then I really was feverish. I had brought a sandwich with me to eat with the others, but I was feeling too nauseous to think of peanut butter and jelly.

"You're quite warm. I'm sure you have a fever. Come up to my desk and I'll give you your home work assignments. You had better get yourself right home. Richard! Come up here a moment. I want you to walk Daniel home. I'll phone your father and explain, but I want you to promise to get straight in bed."

I stood meekly by her large, nineteenth-century oak desk while she turned the pages of the illustrated history book trying to decide just how far she wanted me to read for the next day.

"If you're feeling up to it you should read to the end of the chapter, and we'll be doing questions one to ten for tomorrow's homework." She went through the other lessons. Closing the math exercise book she said, "Of course, the first thing is to take care of yourself, but as soon as you're better, I've been meaning to tell you, I want you to go and have a talk with Pastor. I've spoken about it with him already."

I did not feel much like protesting, which was perhaps her plan. I was certainly startled. Going to see Pastor usually meant some delinquency. She added by way of explanation, "There's things that I'm sure boys would rather talk about with a man. No arguments now. I want you to call him on your own and make an appointment. You know a priest is bound by God to keep things a secret. All you have to do is tell him that what you are saying is meant as confession. You remember the story we were told last week, don't you, about the priest who was shot to death because he wouldn't tell what had been told him in confession?"

She was not giving me a choice. I said I would.

I went home at noon. When I took my temperature I indeed had a fever of 102.4; headache, nausea and dizziness. I phoned Coach's office to say I would not be at practise, and now dutiful in illness, phoned Father to tell him I was home. Sister had already spoken with him. He said he would try to leave his office earlier than normal. His last class was at three. He had a student coming for some extra work, but he could cancel that. Was there anything I needed? Juice? Soup? He would stop and get me some ginger ale. If I thought of anything else, and I couldn't reach him, I could always leave a message with his secretary.

It was not much of a day to miss: cloudy, windy, and cold. The house was quiet. I welcomed being alone, the first of many such days in my life, as there must be in most people's, when solitude restores.

Everything had collected about me too rapidly, like a storm simultaneously arriving upon a spot from all directions at once. It is hard to think or see clearly in the middle of a maelstrom, as if I were being drawn into Tom's whirlwind without a will of my own. Maybe his troubles were normal for him and he could manage them. But they weren't for me, and I did not have to take responsibility for him.

I stretched out on the top of the bed with a quilt over me. Twelve thirty. The familiarity of my orderly room breathing with security. A green, carefully tended fern hung next to the window; grandmother's rocking chair with the needlepoint seat stood idle in the corner; rows of arrow heads lined two shelves. I had a knack, an instinct for finding them. An expert from the state historical museum in Albany, recognizing my talent, had asked me to go on hunts with his classes and I never failed to disappoint. They leapt out at me from the muddy stream beds as sure as if they were silver or gold, when no one else could see them; aligned now with little labels according to age. A photograph of mother in a silver art deco frame stood on my desk illumined by a chrome nineteenth-century lamp with blue glass shade. Not an ordinary boy's room. Too many books for that, not enough strewn toys, none of the airplanes hanging from the ceiling adorning Richie's room, or even the stale smells of solitary acts. Things put away. The clothing in the drawers neatly stacked. The pale green cotton drapes pulled partly shut, the blanket to my chin. I was shivering. The sky was pale gray out behind the bare black trees.

Tom knew his way around the drug world all right, I thought; enough to see a threat when it was coming. Or did he? He wasn't doing so well as far as everybody on the face of the earth was trying to tell me, and I only knew a fraction of the story. Why wasn't he telling me everything? That was what really bothered me. His not saying. I told him everything, but he held back, except for that once when he spilled a bit of it. Smoking a joint now and then with him was one thing, but when I was in his room the other day, and he pulled down that metal box from the closet shelf, there was a whole stash in it: plastic bags crammed full of what he bragged was the best stuff money could buy, different kinds of rolling papers, silver tweezers, lighter and tabs of things he had called bizarre names. He was sure into it in a big way. But I didn't have to be, and we could still be friends. Tom was Tom after all, and I was me. Why should I worry about him? He could probably take care of himself better than I could me. Not because he was older. That didn't have much to do with it. He had been around more, even if I had things to worry about that he didn't, like diving and the regionals in January. I couldn't afford getting stoned all the time while I was in training. It might affect my performance. Coach warned us not to smoke and he didn't even mean pot. If he ever found out there'd be holy hell to pay. Now and then was one thing, on special occasions or something. But every day! Maybe after I like won or something in Albany, because I sure as hell was going to try to win, maybe then and only then I could ease off a little, loosen up a little. We'd sure as hell have to be lots more careful though, use the woods again, and not the road unless we wanted busy-body Reggie breathing down our necks every time. Christ it seemed sometimes like everyone and their uncles was watching us every second. But that was Madalin. After all, I was just as nosy as the rest. Not to mention Richie! Now that the tables were turned I was getting a dose of my own medicine.

Well, whatever Tom and I were getting up to was nobody else's business, was it? No matter where he had learned all that shit, more even than my cousin a couple of summers ago when we were in Italy. And I thought he knew it all. Someone sure as hell had to teach you some of what Tom knew, unless he had a vivid imagination. But I sure as hell wasn't asking. It wasn't just that he was a few years older either. He didn't just know more, lots more, he knew secrets. Secrets with a big S. Maybe he had a revelation or something, like some angel come to him in a dream and showed him about nerves and making you jump right out of your skin, one minute thinking of everything under the sun and the next not thinking of anything if my life depended on it. Maybe it was the grass made you sort of lose your mind. I mean, okay, that was fine, but what was I going to do now, run over there every day? Blow my standing on the team? Yank the letter right off my jacket, figuratively, so to speak. No way buddy. His problem was his problem, not mine. He'd just have to get himself out of it alone – which was the way he got into it in the first place. How could I help him anyway? Especially with him not even telling me anything. He'd have to understand I got Responsibilities with a capital R. Once things cooled down and got back to normal, and the regionals were over, maybe, just maybe, we could know each other a little again but I doubted it. There was just too much on my plate right now to worry about him. I better get it all off my chest. Not on the telephone though with my nosy brother listening in all the time. Write him a letter! Not a bad idea. That way I wouldn't have to wait. Maybe we could establish a few conditions. Cool the drug thing, even if his stash was the best money could buy and his source wouldn't last forever. Quit hanging out with that Bobby kid, and start coming around more for dinner. Not every night, of course. He didn't have to be friends with Richie but he could at least say hello to take some of the pressure off me. We could never be seen in town together now, not with Reggie nosing around. Why couldn't people just leave you alone? There were a lot of things to straighten out. We'd have to draw up a contract or something. Get him to sign on the dotted line. And if he didn't? Well, his loss was his loss. Hasta la vista amigo. Yeah, a letter

144

would set things straight.

I went to my desk and after ten or fifteen drafts crumbled up and thrown carefully in the wood stove in the living room, managed the following:

> Dear Tom,
> Well, old buddy, guess we can't be friends anymore
> because there's ain't no ghost of a chance in hell of
> your cleaning up your act. Like, Stop using dope
> maybe? Or, Not hanging out with Lansing and the
> freak crowd at the crashpad? Yeah, right! There
> really is a man in the moon and he really does eat
> green cheese. I mean maybe if you did we could
> still be friends or something but I even got my
> doubts about that because everything's getting too
> weird. Spoiling my diving. The coach said so. You
> can ask him. See, nothing's fitting together for me
> anymore and I feel sort of out at the end of the
> high board with no water below. You're really
> something though. I know you are. You don't even
> know you are but I do. You're worth more than all
> of them and most everybody else put together even
> if you don't know so yourself and I can't think
> about anything else so I guess it's just better if I like
> wave off, say so long, adios amigo, see yah around,
> and like my grandma used to say, ciao bambino.
> Your ex-friendforever,
> Dan

I felt better after writing the letter. Despite my fever and the bad weather, I resolved to put on my warmest winter coat, scarf, gloves and cap, trudge over to Tom's and put the letter in his mailbox. I'd go by the road too, and if Reggie saw me again this time I'd give him the finger.

Of course, I did not. The rain was now particles of ice lashing my window. I was shivering with fever. But I would like to think that neither the weather nor my flu, but common sense and affection, held me back. I put the letter inside the book I was reading, and though I never threw it away, he never saw it either. There are letters in love you write, and letters you write and send. I had learned that early.

When later in the day he phoned I did not even think about whether or not I should get out of bed. I was glad to hear his voice. After dinner he came by to drop off a book and I was happy to see him.

It was a copy of *Dharma Bums*, his favorite book now after *Siddhartha*, or possibly before, because *Siddhartha* was about a loner but *Bums* was about friendship, so *Bums* was more 'radical'. He had marked a passage for me, and I thumbed through until I found it. *All over the West, and the mountains in the East, and the desert, I'll tramp with a rucksack and make it the pure way.* I don't know how much sense either the thought behind the words, or Tom's marking the passage, made to me that feverish day. Perhaps he was only reverting to his initial pattern of gift-giving, his gifts substitutes for words, bridges across that awkward, adolescent divide. My fever must have made me feel vulnerable. I muttered some kind of embarrassed thanks. 'The pure way.'

6. TROUBLE

My fever and flu lingered on to the end of the week, but by the Monday of Thanksgiving week I was well enough to return to school and training. Coach O'Malley was glad I was back. Williams wanted me to try something a little more complicated. As soon as I was changed I should come and see him. We had to set up a new schedule. I had already lost too much precious times, with only eight weeks left before Albany. Was I feeling okay? I assured him I was.

"Well then, get a hustle on, will you."

The smell of stale sweat and chlorine, the sounds of echoing cries and splashes from poolside, recentered me in the familiar. I felt as if I had been away a long time.

It was not until the end of the day, as I was returning from the showers to dress to go home that I noticed Tom's note, though I do not think it had been there earlier when I arrived. No one was around, but I still opened it furtively.

> Danny
> I need your help so can you come over after practise. Some deep shit's going down
> Tom

After practise, Mickey's father dropped me off in front of our house. I breathed a sigh of relief. No one was home. I stopped only long enough to put my books in my room and change, before heading out again. The snow bogged me down. Tom must have been waiting for me by the kitchen window. I did not even have to knock. He had the door open as I trudged up, banging my shoes against the side of the step to break loose the clods of wet snow. He looked distraught, his shirt was even buttoned wrong; he was biting the side of his hand, a nervous habit I had come to recognize as stress.

"God am I glad to see you. I guess you got my note. I couldn't wait around but nobody saw me put it there."

"Jesus, what's up? You look worse than I did when I had the flu."

"It's a fucking mess. Man, I don't know if I should even tell you."

He was heading down the hallway towards the stairwell, and I had to scurry after him after removing my shoes.

"What do you mean, not tell me? What's going on? You better tell me."

"Nothing except I'm going to get myself killed! That's all."

I leapt the steps two at a time; he had already made it to his room.

"What does that mean?"

He went straight to his closet and started throwing things backwards over his shoulder. The room was a bomb site, messier than I had ever seen it, if that was possible. Everything had been taken out of the dresser drawers and was scattered all over the room. Even the pictures had been taken off the walls; the bed-clothes stripped from the bed; the ceiling fixture loosened. My first thought was that the police had been there with a search warrant, but the rest of the house was orderly. Had someone broken in and been trying to steal something? I went over to the window, to get out of his way, and leaned back against the sill. The cold air seeped through the single pane, through my sweat shirt, chilling my back, but I did not move.

"Jesus, Tom. Your room looks like a war zone. What the fuck's going on?"

"I been searching everywhere. It's no use. I'm sure it ain't here. If it ever was. Oh man, if I don't find it . . . " He made a knife slash across his throat with his finger, and flung himself down on the stripped mattress. "Fuck. It's hopeless."

He told me the story in bits and pieces. There was this guy came around the crash pad now and again, real low-life named Luca, the kind usually has a scar on his face only this guy didn't, only looked mean, and him and O'Shea, the guy who owned the pad – sure I remembered who he was – they were definitely into some kind of shady goings-on, he didn't know exactly what, but Lansing thought O'Shea was laundering drug money for Luca through his rare coin business, but who could believe Lansing, even if it made sense, right? Anyway, O'Shea asked him, like months ago, when he first started hanging out there, could he stash this bag away for him somewhere safe and just give it back to him when he asked, which seemed simple enough at the time, so he said yes, don't ask him why, maybe he was trying to impress O'Shea or something, or maybe because O'Shea went on like how he was the only one around the pad he could rely on and trust to do something confidential, Bobby was so spaced out and Lansing, he wouldn't trust him with a rosary. Course there was always Tara, but she was like fifteen months pregnant and could hardly get up and down the stairs, and Ford, well he was the kind would rat on his mother if he thought there was something in it for him, not to mention all those others coming and going worse than Lansing some of them. So that sort of left him by a process of elimination. No, he didn't know what was in the bag, and no he hadn't been about to ask. Besides the bag had been locked with a padlock. The way he had ended up figuring it, you either did something for O'Shea or you didn't, but what you didn't do is ask too many questions, and it was kind of hard for him to say no when O'Shea had told him he could crash there any time and sort of gave him the key. But, if he was being honest with himself, he'd have to say he wanted to make O'Shea think he was cool, and belonged, you know, deserved a piece of the action, so he put the bag in a locker over at the bus station and everything was fine until Luca showed up a couple of days ago. He hadn't seen him for weeks and weeks and O'Shea comes to him yesterday and says, Hey, remember that bag I gave you to stash well I need it back like yesterday, and he figured it had to have something to do with Luca, O'Shea looked so panicky and shit, and right there he knows he's in something way deeper than he thought. He's got to deliver the bag direct to Luca like TONIGHT. Those are the instructions. Eight o'clock sharp. Trouble is . . . Trouble is he can't find the fucking locker key! Of course he'd looked everywhere, but it was *gone*.

"Christ, Danny, what am I going to do? I don't show up with the bag I'm going to get blown away. Those guys don't play around."

"Calm down will you. Did you look absofuckinglootly everywhere?"

"I even checked the toilet bowl . . . I'm not kidding. I must have gone over this room a zillion times. The worst is I think maybe someone over at the pad stole the key off me and like went and got the bag already, and if that's what happened then I really am dead meat and might as well head straight for the border."

"It's probably filled with counterfeit money."

"Don't say things like that. I'm scared enough as it is. I mean, if I don't produce it."

"It's one fucking mess."

I started pacing around the room. We could go through everything again but that could take hours, and he had made such chaos out of everything that we would probably never find it even if it was there somewhere. I shouldn't get involved. What was he talking about! Wasn't I involved already? I couldn't desert him like that right now at this moment.

I asked, "Where you going to meet O'Shea?"

"It ain't O'Shea. He said he was sending someone to meet me. In front of a bar in Kingston. Curly's. Along the tracks, down by the river."

I knew where he meant. "It's scary as hell down there! And going there at night . . . "

"Yeah, well, that's if we had the bag."

I was working on that. Did he at least remember which locker he put it in?

He didn't remember the exact number but it was in the middle on the end row and the door had a scratch or dent or paint on the lower half. He was sure he'd know it if he saw it again. What was I thinking?

I'd been to that bus station a thousand times. With the team. Going back and forth to matches. There were always the same security guards around. Especially weekdays. They been working there a hundred years or more and I talked to a couple of them a few times. People must always be losing their keys and they had to have a set of spares lying around. They couldn't be breaking open the lockers every time someone showed up with a problem.

"So?"

"So, if I go with you, one of them just might recognize me from the team, and I got my Jefferson ID pass with my picture on it I can show whoever is there and I even got a couple of clippings in my wallet which just might drop out."

The plan was for me to say that I had put my gym bag in a locker because I had to do some shopping at the mall. The stores didn't like kids bringing their bags in. They knew that was the honest truth. But then I went and lost the key and now I was real worried someone may have stole it or found it so I came right back to make sure my bag was still there because if I showed up tomorrow at gym without my gear Coach will throw a fit. Couldn't he please help me? I'd even be willing to pay the damage if they had to break the locker open. That wasn't the best part though. The best part was as we were walking over to the lockers I could slide into the conversation natural like this description of the bag so when he opened the locker he could see it was mine and all Tom had to do was tell me now what it looked like.

Tom had some objections. Couldn't he use the same story with the guard himself and keep me out of it? The whole point was getting him to recognize me, or at least believe I was with the team so he would trust me and open the locker without a big fuss. He still did not want me involved. But I was already, wasn't I? He reluctantly gave in.

I could see from Tom's window that the lights were on in our kitchen, which meant that Charlie was home. I telephoned and told him I was staying over at Richie's for supper so we could study together. I hadn't eaten at Richie's for awhile, but had done it often enough in the past not just to be believed now but for Father not to make much of it, or even be glad.

I also phoned Richie. "Hey, Richie. If anybody calls, I'm eating at your house. Right? I'll explain later."

The temptation of an explanation was enough to secure his cooperation.

Tom waited outside the bus station while I walked boldly up to the office window, pulled out my wallet, showed the guard my ID, and recited the story we had rehearsed. He swung around in his oak swivel chair and took a large key ring off a hook. As we walked through the deserted waiting room to the lockers, I slid the description of the bag into the conversation: mousy gray, smudged with grease marks, one of the leather straps pulled loose and looped around the other. He was concentrating on peeling off one key after the other around the large stainless steel hoop and wasn't listening to what I was saying. I switched to small talk about the team. We'd win the regionals by a good margin, Mickey the hundred-meter, the team the relay. The key worked on the first try. He grinned with satisfaction. The bag was lying there just as Tom had said. I pulled it out remembering that it would be heavy, and that I had to make it seem light.

"Gosh, thanks mister, you really saved my butt. Coach would've had my ass if I showed up without my gear. Maybe I can get you a couple of free tickets?"

"Forget it kid . . . "

Tom was shivering and stomping around in place, as I emerged triumphantly. His face lit up when he saw the bag.

"Any hitch?"

"No sweat. I don't know what's in it, but it's heavy enough for gold bars."

I handed it to him. We were running out of time and had better take a cab. He had enough money with him.

I had been to the warehouse district a couple of years before with my father and brother for an old train fair and still had a mental picture of smoking dumps, broken fences and street lights, a general dereliction that I now saw had not changed much. The cab driver was reluctant to take us down there on our own. It was foolhardy for two boys to be venturing into those abandoned streets at night in winter, and we should not be doing it. We had to show him our money first.

We passed not one living soul on all those abandoned blocks, the houses boarded up, turned into seedy brothels or singles bars. If anything went wrong and we got into trouble, I was thinking, we'd never find any help here. The potholes and rough road forced the cab driver to go at a snail's pace. Tom kept looking nervously at his watch. Behind the buildings I caught a glimpse of the dredged river jetty. There had been a loading dock there in the nineteenth century for whaling boats. A few empty coal barges were docked by the railway siding.

On our right were warehouses, on the left a despoiled building site smoldering in the icy rain, strewn with bottles, cans, derelict cars, doorless refrigerators. The cab stopped in front of the bar. The driver turned to look us over.

"You sure this is the place you want?"

Tom said it was. A red neon sign sputtered CUR-Y'S. It was nearly eight. No sign of anyone yet. We stepped under the overhang of the building but did not go inside, though the loud music and laughter seemed inviting enough. The wind banged a loose wire against the aluminum siding. I was cold to the marrow in a few seconds.

Some boats turned upside down lay off to the side, covered with tarpaulins and propped up on heavy wooden beams. Tom suggested that I hide behind one while he waited for the pickup alone, in plain sight. If Luca saw two people he might shy away and I would only be a few yards away if he needed help. I could see everything clearly from over there.

At precisely eight a new black Lincoln sedan came cruising down the hill. It glided silently to a stop about a hundred feet away, and blinked its lights twice. Tom started walking towards it, but stopped a few feet in front. The driver was gunning the motor, perhaps to keep it from stalling. He blinked the lights again. Tom did not move. The car window was rolled down. I could hear the man clearly.

"Bring the bag here kid."

"Where's Luca?" Tom said.

"Just bring it here, will you."

"You ain't Luca. He told me I should give it to him and no one else."

"He got detained so he sent me. Put it down on the ground right there and there won't be no trouble."

"You got some ID or a note from Luca or something you can show me? How do I know who you are?"

The car door opened and the driver stepped out. His collar was pulled up, his hat pulled down too far for me to make out any features.

"Like I said something important come up and Luca couldn't come himself. Don't do nothing foolish. Just put it down."

Tom had taken a few steps backwards. The man hesitated. Was he better off back in the car, or chasing him on foot? He started to get back in the car, changed his mind, came around the car door, but Tom had backed off even further.

"Drop it right there kid! I don't want to hurt you!"

He was fumbling in his raincoat, trying to get something out of the pocket. A blackjack? A gun?

As I was hiding behind the boat I had noticed some short lengths of metal piping and some long metal bolts lying nearby and I now grabbed as many as I could and scurried out, banging the pipe against the bottom of the boat and a nearby oil drum. I ran towards them shouting, and hurled one of the bolts as hard as I could. It whistled by the man's head. I threw another and it hit him in the shoulder. He slowed to a trot. Tom was up to me by then. I threw another bolt for good measure. It struck the man on the left cheek, stopping him in his tracks. He paused, pulled his handkerchief out, dabbed his cheek, shrugged his shoulders, went back to the car, slammed the door, and sped off, burning rubber. I was panting with excitement.

"You all right? The son of a bitch could have killed you. Didn't you see him reaching in his pocket? Why didn't you give him the bag?"

The red tail lights were already fading from view.

"Because he wasn't Luca. I didn't know who he was or who sent him but I wasn't about to give it to no stranger."

"What do you think's going on? Now what?"

"Come on. We got to get out of here before he comes back with reinforcements."

If we went inside the bar it might be the first place someone would check if he came looking for us. We could get trapped there. No one had heard the shouting, or if they had, had not come out to see what was going on. This sort of thing probably went on all the time around here.

Tom had noticed a small coffee shop about half a mile back up the road. He could phone O'Shea and find out if he knew what was going on, or had seen or talked to Luca. I agreed that we should get out of there right way. The music faded quickly as we ran back up the deserted road, a long, threatening few minutes to the café.

Not one car passed. It was cold and raining, but warm and bright inside. We slid onto stools at the counter. A large mirror in front of us allowed us to see the road. A young Hispanic boy about Tom's age came over to take our orders. There was a pay phone on the far wall. While Tom was calling the boy brought our order. What were we doing down here on a rainy school night? Maybe looking for action? I shook my head. I was nauseous from fear or excitement and pushed the plate away. Maybe we should have thought it through better before coming over here. Maybe it would have been better if Tom was not phoning O'Shea. What if he had sent this guy himself, to pull a fast one on Luca? I anxiously looked around, expecting the car to pull up to the door in a blaze of gun fire.

Tom came back to the booth and said that we had to sit

tight. O'Shea was on his way over to pick up the bag.

"He say what was going on?"

"No, he just said to wait. That I'd done right, and not to worry."

"We're sitting ducks here."

"I know. I don't like it either."

We had both ordered chocolate cake and coffee. Tom picked up his fork to eat his, but put it down immediately and suddenly said with great determination, "I'm going to see what's in this fucking bag."

"Jesus Tom, I don't know . . . "

He slid over a stool and put the bag between us, reaching in his pocket for his knife. Fear battled with curiosity.

I said, "I don't think you should be doing that. I mean, how you even going to get it open without them knowing? And what if it's a bomb?"

"They think I'm some patsy they can pull a fast one on they got another guess coming."

The worn brass padlock attached between the zipper and a metal loop gave little resistance. He spread the sides open, whistled.

"Oh shit, look at this."

The bag was stuffed with plastic sacks filled with a white powder under which I caught a glimpse of money. A gun lay on top, an old German war Luger, and a brown envelope, which he took out and opened but did not pass over to me. I could see there were strips of negatives in it.

"Jesus Christ," he said.

"What is it? let me see."

"No way."

His hand shook as he tried to finish his coffee. He had turned white. He put the envelope in his jacket pocket and said, "This is our insurance."

I lowered my voice. "There must be a million dollars worth in there. We should get out of here. Right now. Jesus Tom."

The boy was at the opposite end wiping glasses, but watching us.

I asked. "What are we going to do now?"

Tom kept his voice down. "I don't know. That fucking O'Shea! I bet he was setting me up!"

"For what?"

"I don't know."

"What are we going to do? I mean O'Shea is on his way over and what if he did set you up?"

Tom glanced at me. "I know. I was just thinking the same thing. Maybe the gun's loaded. If he tries anything funny I got protection. I mean, I'll hand it over to him if that's all he wants but he's got to come in to get it. I ain't going out to meet him. At least there's witnesses in here. I tell you one thing, I don't want you here when he comes."

"What do you mean?"

"Don't you got to call home or something. Go to the toilet. He doesn't know you're involved."

"What if he tries a fast one? I'm not going anywhere . . . "

"Look at it this way. I'm keeping you in reserve. Just in case. Go!"

It was already quarter to nine. Nine was the hour that Father expected me to be home when I was over at someone's house studying. He gave me half an hour leeway, but it was too far from where we were to be home by nine thirty. It seemed a million miles away. It was a good idea to phone, tell Father I'd be a little late, and call Richie to warn him to still cover for me. I went to the cash register to get some change and made the calls, but kept an eye on Tom from the far corner, for the second time that evening ordered to the sidelines.

Not ten minutes later Lansing walked in alone. I could not hear what they were saying, but Tom handed over the bag and Lansing left immediately.

"What happened?"

"Nothing much. O'Shea stayed in the car and Lansing came in to get it. That's about it."

The boy brought the check. Was there something wrong with the cake, I hadn't eaten it? Did we want a phone number maybe? This chick, she liked young guys. Especially if it was their first time. Didn't charge much.

We called another cab and I was home by nine thirty.

Father had not phoned Richie's house, as Richie told me the next day when I dropped over to give him the promised explanation, not of what had actually happened, but of some much more innocent fabrication.

Was it that same night or another that I overheard my father and brother discussing me? I attach it to that evening because it had the same sense of tension and aggression, the same dangers. Perhaps it happened days or even weeks later, but I doubt before.

My room was at the top of the stairwell. What drew me out that night? The mention of my name? Of Tom's? Long-established roles and habits? I had many times before perched on the third step from the top, out of sight, within hearing. Charlie was saying something about his friends making remarks about me and Tom doing drugs. Rumors were flying all over his school. The other night when I had come in, no doubt from Tom's, he was sure I reeked of pot. He had tried to talk to me about it, but I had told him to go to hell and kicked him out of my room. If O'Malley found out I was doing drugs I would be suspended from the team.

Father said he did not much like Tom and thought he was a bad influence. He had already tried to talk to me himself and I had been pretty defensive, which may or may not have meant that something was going on. He would have to try talking to me again. It was just that it was all so hard for him to take in. Hard for him to believe that with the first big match only a few weeks away, I would jeopardize not just it but being on the team itself with reckless behavior. Why, I ate, breathed and slept diving and the team. He didn't know what to believe. Maybe the kids at Charlie's school were just gossiping, he hated gossip. Sometimes he felt like moving us back to New York. Maybe he should have kept the job at Hunter, but he and Mother had wanted to raise us in the country.

Charlie said, "Sure. You never could believe he ever did anything wrong. I was always the one who you had to blame."

"Oh now, don't start. You know that isn't true. It's just that you're four years older. I don't know, maybe a father

157

expects more of the older son. But I always tried to be fair with you. With both of you."

"Fair. You know as well as I do that Danny never could do any wrong. It wasn't just you either. I mean, it's the nuns at school and the whole fucking village. Everybody thinks he's some kind of innocent boy wonder. You'd never be able to believe your little angel is sneaking off to get stoned, or worse. That's really it, isn't it?"

I heard a chair scrape, the faucet run. It must have been Father because the direction of his voice had changed when he spoke again.

"You're bitter. You're turning into something mean and bitter that I don't recognize. I mean, Danny is just Danny. Sometimes he gets into trouble and sometimes you do."

"Since when! When was the last time you admitted he was in the wrong? Ten years ago maybe when him and Richie broke Mason's window."

"Look. This isn't getting us anywhere. It's pretty late. Why don't we go get some sleep and talk about it in the morning when both of us are fresh?"

"Yeah. Like always when it comes to him. Walk away. Or go phone Clare and get her to make the decisions . . . You've never been able to talk about Danny. Ever since Mom died . . . Your precious angel. I know why too. It's because he reminds you of her. He looks like her and reminds you of her. Doesn't he? Doesn't he!"

But I could not listen to any more, and crept silently back to my room.

7. MEETINGS WITH RIGHTEOUS MEN

Two other incidents from the preceding or following weeks refuse to fall neatly into a symmetrical chronology. Disconnected, illogical; metaphorical fragments, particles of experience floating freely in memory, debris of the surrounding chaos.

I am walking over to Tom's house by the back way one late afternoon. But when? It is warm and there is no snow on the ground. The sun slants long shadows far across the brown dried ground; late afternoon. I have just emerged from the edge of the woods, passed the oak harboring our tree house on the other side of the stream, and have started along the west edge of the Episcopal church yard. To my right, half hidden behind a low, gray, fieldstone wall, is Trinity's graveyard. We made gravestone rubbings there for school projects. If I use the path through the dogwood bushes I can traverse the couple of hundred yards to the back of Tom's property unseen by Reverend Edgewater, further hidden from the prying back windows of the parish house by a square brick storage building and a seven-foot high stack of criss-crossed wooden railroad ties. I had often wondered why they were there, and what they were going to be used for. I never learned. As far as I know they are still there.

Was Edgewater waiting for me that day? I had been, and would be, in those woods hundreds if not thousands of times, but this is the only occasion he intercepted me. He was friendly towards me, but never too friendly, except that once when he heard me sing at a school pageant and said what a fine voice I had and wouldn't I like to be in his choir. If I had been born Episcopalian I might have ended up at some choir boarding school, all innocence and golden reed tones. He did not mention the choir again. It would not have been his place. He would have irritated the nuns.

The year before, he had stopped by our house to congratulate me about winning a diving medal. Why didn't I ever come to some of the films they showed on Saturdays in the church hall for *all* the village children? The Marx Brothers were on next week. But I never went. His was the only other church in the village. I had been taught to keep a respectable distance. Which perhaps makes this encounter all the more unusual, the more I think of it .

He was a vigorous, rotund, red-faced, balding man in his early forties, very old boy and proper about things. He had attended Andover, and Yale Divinity. He belonged to the right clubs. There was a cathedral in his future. One would have thought that a small parish in an out-of-the-way village was an unlikely place for an aspiring canon but that would have been a serious misjudgment. Many of the Hudson Valley aristocracy were Episcopalian, and ministering to old wealth, those with venerable connections and Wall Street firms, never did anyone's ambitions any harm. He had, I found out, coveted the post at Trinity, lobbied for it even, and for the moment was content to use it shrewdly as a base for building a solid future.

He had been working out of sight on the far side of the storage house and as I tried to scurry by he hailed me. He was wearing gray canvas work gloves and was stacking firewood. His cheeks had turned scarlet in the cold. He wore a ludicrously large racoon hat. He liked stentorian phrases and classical references. I cannot remember his exact words at that moment, but he would not have asked anything direct, such as, 'Out for a walk?' or 'Taking a hike?' or even, 'On your way to Tom's?' but in stained-glass tones, something more like, 'On your way to Pithias' house, young Damon?'

He removed his right glove to pat his brow with his spotless handkerchief. The sun focused a brilliant crystalline light upon us. All around there were black trees shorn of their leaves rustling like candy wrappings beneath my shuffling feet.

I see myself at that moment as standing precisely midpoint between my house and Tom's, but of course this is only metaphor tingeing memory. Midpoint might be a pause between past and present, a gathering. In some encounters our perceptions are heightened, awakened, on full alert, like a fawn ready to bolt. Sometimes, even if only for a split second before a dive, I had this vivid sense of being between, advancing to the edge of the board but not yet sprung. That same sense came to me as he greeted me and I stopped to talk.

It would have taken me some time to figure out what he was trying to say, so many twists and turns of phrase would there have been before he told me a certain story. He had had a special, older friend at boarding school when he was twelve and had felt very intensely about him. They use to meet after class in an abandoned greenhouse, sit together on boxes, share chocolate and tell each other their innermost thoughts. Then one day the other boy, whom he thought had 'manly virtue', had thrown his arms around him and kissed him on the lips. He had been 'utterly shocked by such crude attentions', and of course had nothing further to do with the 'venal person', whom, he later found out, was 'pressing his attentions at the very same time on another'. His own friendship, 'beyond the pale of a doubt' had been 'informed by the utmost purity and spiritual energization'. Alas this had 'proved to be one-sided'. Now that he was older if not old, he realized that sometimes youth can be 'carried away by fevers of emotions and passions of the moment'. He no longer judged his friend too harshly for 'being carried away by such uncontrollable fervor as is the necessary biological make-up of the procreative impulse'. He was 'grateful to that Higher Being that instils Higher Reason and spiritual motivations' that he 'had not succumbed' and had been able to learn such an essential lesson so early in life, 'the necessity of restraint for a life of continued virtue'. He might well have given in because 'boys indulge their whims, do they not?' They think 'no one witnesses.' Yes, he had seen many things. The base drives, two boys 'parading themselves like two Adams'. One of them always thinks, as he did with his precious friend, that he is the only special one, and can blind himself to the fact that the other 'may be motivated by lower impulses and driven to indulge with another what the pure and faithful thinks is only held for him.' He had thought about it for many years and – now would have come the moral of the tale – if he might indulge in an adage? 'Those who love the many, are doomed never to love the one.' One has to choose in life, after all, and he had learned the hard way that the way of devotion was to love one thing. Purity of heart. The Kierkegaardian imperative. What greater good was there for the human soul? Of course, when a boy is young, 'excitement moves him far more than virtue.' A worldly friend, for example, might be seen 'to have advantages over unworldly boys', but who was he to judge from his 'humble vantage point'? He pressed my shoulder earnestly and looked deeply into my eyes. 'Be watchful always, young Damon.'

I would have slipped away, back into the covering of woods.

This is juxtaposed in my mind with an encounter I had with Father Simone, even if the two events most certainly happened weeks apart. But events do not have to be sequenced linearly to be interconnected. The two conversations spiral past the same point of memory, so close to each other as to give the illusion that they are similar or the same. Indeed, I came to see everything about Tom as moving along a helix. Perhaps, however, because of my Catholicism, I could say that my talk with Simone had more weight?

I had been let out of school early for the appointment. Sister Francesca had suggested it, which meant it was unavoidable. On both days the air was still, cold, the sun blindingly bright, although this time I am walking straight west along the main road towards the rectory and the long shadow cast is of me. I squint, and press my wool mittens to my ears. I am walking in the street, very slowly, even though I may be late, kicking at sticks, stones. On my right a field, two new houses being built, the sound of carpenters hammering. On the left I pass the firehouse. The doors are open; someone is humming deep inside, hidden behind the red ladder truck. The rectory comes into view: the same tightening of breath I had felt on first glimpsing Edgewater. I start up the flag-stone walk to the front door. Yes, now I remember, the tall Norwegian pine in the church yard is already decorated with Christmas lights, and the lawn is powdered with snow.

The housekeeper opens the door; an elderly, stern Swiss woman named Mrs. Ritter whom people said had more piety than Simone. I was not more than five minutes late, but she glanced disapprovingly at her watch. She pronounces the F as if it were a V. "Vader is vaiting for you. In de sitting room."

I wipe my feet conscientiously on the doormat. She bangs the door shut, punctuating my tardiness. The smell of stewing green tomatoes, a sharper and more pungent smell than the red, beeswax, and cleaning liquid, a noxious mix.

Several religious reproductions adorn the hallway walls; a saccharin portrait of Jesus with long, light brown, flowing hair, Fra Lippi's Virgin, a Currier and Ives Christmas scene. She knocks and opens the door for me. A warm glow emanates from the sitting room. The Christmas tree lights are on. The room is warm. There is a tray on the coffee table with a tall glass of milk

162

and a plate of fresh chocolate chip cookies, a thermos jug containing coffee, paper napkins.

Simone is sitting in a large armchair beside the cold fireplace. A floor lamp casts a direct light on the breviary that he is reading. He holds up a hand. I wait. He puts a ribbon across the page, closes the book, kisses it, and sets it aside. He is wearing his brown Franciscan habit, not 'civvies' as I had expected. His legs are crossed. He smooths the folds from the cloth so that it falls evenly from his raised knee, meticulously picking off two pieces of white lint. His black shoes are polished to a high, military sheen. His bushy black eyebrows flare above his shrewd brown eyes; mid-fifties, intimidating, autocratic. He was the rector of the seminary in Brooklyn before a heart attack forced the quieter responsibilities of Saint Cecilia's.

He takes a purple and white stole off the table near his elbow. I am taken aback. Had he assumed that I was there for confession? I thought it was only for a talk. I look around for a prie-dieu on which to kneel but he gestures towards a straight-backed wooden chair so close to him that I have the uncomfortable feeling our knees will touch. I don't know what to do with my hands. I fold them in my lap. He kisses the stole, puts it around his neck, raises his hand.

"In nomine patris et filio . . . "

He still refuses to use the vernacular. The changes wrought by Vatican II will be slow in reaching his church.

I bless myself and mumble the formula quickly, "Bless me Father for I have sinned it has been one week since my last confession . . . "

The door to guilt and redemption, divine right and the individual life. I lied twelve times to my father, gossiped, lost my temper with my brother ten times, swore, played a mean trick on one of my team-mates, was lazy in school, gave in to impure thoughts and deeds, missed Mass on Sunday . . .

"But I was sick in bed with the flu so that doesn't count as a sin, does it Father?"

His hands had disappeared up the wide sleeves of his habit. He shook his head. It did not. Was there more?

I was tempted to steal candy from the general store and

money from my father but had not and I had played hooky and forged a note to Sister. That was months ago but I had forgotten to confess it before. I couldn't think of anything else. But for these and all the things I could not remember I was heartily sorry.

"And you promise God you'll try your best not to sin again?"

"Yes Father."

He uncrossed and recrossed his legs, nodded his approval, and said with a forced smile, "Help yourself to some milk and cookies, though I want you to remember that this is still confession. Mrs. Ritter made them this morning just for your visit, so don't forget to thank her when you leave. And pour me more coffee from the thermos while you're at it."

I unscrewed the cap and poured the steaming black brew into his extended cup.

"Sister asked me to have this talk with you because she was worried about you lately and thought you were at an age when it's easier to talk to a man. You remember my sermon on the Sacrament of Confession a few weeks ago?" I nodded. "In confession everything is a secret between you and God. The priest is only a mediator."

"I remember, Father."

He had told us a story about a priest being tortured to death by the communists because he wouldn't reveal what had been told him in confession. Of course, most of the time God didn't make such demands on us. We lived in a freer country.

"Do you know why Sister is worried?" A rhetorical question? Certainly a dangerous one. I did not answer. "She thinks you may have a vocation but are making bad friends. Do you think you have a vocation?"

"I don't know, Father. I mean I know she thinks I do. And I pray about it a lot."

"How old are you?"

"Thirteen. I'll be fourteen the 19th of January."

"High school is not the same as grammar, you know. There are far more temptations there. I was your age when I went to seminary. My generation thought differently about such things, and our family was very poor. My mother and father were immigrants. It was impossible for them to pay for a good education for me. The priesthood needs intelligent boys like you."

"My father thinks maybe it's better if I wait until I'm more sure it's what I want. Until after high school at least. I'm getting a scholarship to St. Francis. My brother is a senior there. He wants to be a lawyer. He's going to Fordham. If I don't become a priest I think I'd like to be an archeologist. I went to visit my aunt and uncle in Sicily two summers ago and they took me to see all these Roman ruins. I really liked that. I mean, digging around and finding old things. I'm good at finding arrowheads. This professor at the State University said I had a knack for it." I added ingratiatingly: "My mother is – was – Italian."

"What was her maiden name?"

"Acciardo."

He smiled benevolently. "A real southern name. There are fine archeologists in the Order, you know. We can use bright people like you. But waiting. I don't know if that's such a good idea. There are so many temptations. You have to cultivate a vocation. Water it, feed it like a delicate young plant, protect it from the strong winds. You'll need a lot of personal courage and fortitude to stand up to all the obstacles."

"It's just that right now I'm not sure. That's why my father thought it was better to wait . . . I pray about it at Mass every Sunday."

He nodded. "That's a good sign. The devil hates vocations and praying keeps him at arm's length. Please. Help yourself to more cookies. I can't eat any of them. My blood pressure and heart." I rose and took two more neatly on my white paper napkin. He waited until I was seated comfortably again.

"Now there's this other matter. About keeping bad company . . . "

Perhaps this was more difficult for me to discuss? But I had to remember – the priest was only a channel, as if he wasn't even there listening. I was at an impressionable age, an age at which friendship had a profound influence on my life, and even my future. Community was an essential part of salvation. And friendship was part of community. Now this friend of mine on the other hand – we both knew who he was talking about – he was an individualist, someone who went his own way through life making up his own rules. Of course, he did not want to judge, especially when so much of his information had come to him through rumor and was even contradictory. Take those reports about drugs, for example. Why, some people said that I wasn't involved, and some said I was, and what he wanted to know was, could we right there and then separate reality from rumor? Perhaps I had tried them once or twice? Out of curiosity? To please my friend? I reluctantly had to admit that I had.

He instantly exclaimed angrily, "That's very stupid and dangerous! Especially at your age! It's easy for boys to do rash things, without thinking about or even knowing the consequences. Didn't the Kitzel boy die in this very village a couple of years ago running his car into a tree playing some foolish game or other? And then they found out he was drunk! Have you forgotten the lesson of that already? What a terrible tragedy for his parents. Boys can do such wasteful things with their lives. Just to show off, or because of a dare. Is that what he did? Did he dare you?"

I did not answer.

He said more kindly, "You're too intelligent Daniel. You don't want to go around wasting your life now, do you?"

I replied meekly, "No, Father. I was just curious. I didn't know it was a sin though."

The stern tone returned, "We don't have the moral right to harm ourselves and that's precisely what you were doing! Life's too precious a gift to be thrown away on such nonsense. Does your father know about this?"

"No Father."

"He never asked you, or you never told him?"

"I never told him."

"In other words, you lied!"

I nodded, the Yes sticking in my throat.

"By their fruits you shall know them Daniel. By their fruits. You see what can come of bad friends?"

He leaned forward to take more coffee, his lips pursed, brow deeply furrowed from the strain of controlling his anger.

166

He continued, "Maybe you can tell me what you get from this friendship? I don't mean excitement or curiosity. I mean one spiritual thing you see in this person."

I thought, Tom was loyal. In his own way, truthful. He did not pretend he knew it all so maybe I could say he was humble. He cared about people. If I was a little jealous over Bobby, I could still see that Tom was looking after him. For his mother and me too in his own way. A long silence ensued in which I said none of this, aware of a radio being played low in the kitchen, the clock striking.

"Well?" he insisted.

I replied rather oddly, "He wants to be an artist. Like his grandfather."

"An artist?"

"Yes, Father."

He repeated it as a statement, "An artist."

I nodded.

He set his cup back on the tray. Through what process of logic I shall never know, he next asked, "Do you pray to the Blessed Virgin?"

I answered with relief, "Oh yes Father."

"If we turn our thoughts, our lives over to Our Lady she will always intercede for us. She is the most powerful Protectress we have. I want you to think about something for me – about joining the Sodality of Mary. Will you think about that for me?"

"Yes, Father."

"I want you to ask her help. She'll never refuse you if you open your soul to her. Pray to her for grace. For her intercession. You hear?"

"Yes, Father."

"Now then . . . " He looked at his watch; the deep frown had reappeared. "The church tells us that to receive absolution you must have the intention not to sin again. Do you have that intention?"

"Yes, Father."

"I want to give you some advice. You have other friends. I've seen you around the village with them. I know a small place like this can be limiting for a boy with so much life but you should spend more time with these other friends, and with your family too. You're good at sports. That's a gift from God, you know. Use it to resist temptation. Over time, with prayer and the help of our Blessed Mother grace will win out."

"Yes, Father."

"For your penance now I want you to make a novena to Our Lady of Fatima; every day for nine days ten Our Father's and ten Hail Mary's. Ask her for guidance. Have faith too that she'll always be there to comfort and help you."

This was a heavy penance, the heaviest I had ever received. But it was not the penance of mortal wrong, and I would not have protested.

"I want you to come see me again – but after the holidays are over. Do your best now and remember what I said about the Sodality. I'll ask your decision when we have our next talk."

"Yes, Father. I'll think about it seriously."

"The grace of Almighty God be always with you my son. Now make a good act of contrition."

"I confess to Almighty God . . . "

He raised his hand in blessing.

"Ego te absolvo . . . "

Part Four: Marrying

1. Thunderstorms

For days after the encounter in Kingston I had paranoid flashes.
As I was leaving St. Cecilia's one afternoon I noticed a strange,
dark-colored, four-door sedan idling outside the general store,
and I immediately ducked back into school thinking that it must
be the mob. A rather glamorous looking woman wearing sun-
glasses and a white silk scarf came out and drove off, most
probably a visitor to one of the Livingstone estates. A few evenings later a car stopped outside our house. I jumped up from
the floor where I was sprawled watching television and rushed
to the living room window – one of the village girls learning to
drive. Climbing the ladder onto the diving platform, I fanta-
sized some dark-suited thug hiding in the back row of the balcony,
jumping up and spraying the room with machine-gun fire. During class I would stare vacantly out the window and wonder
impassively what I would do if a car were to screech up to the
school walk as I was leaving. A big fat hairy arm would drag me
into the back seat. We would tear off in a cloud of dust and I
would never be seen again.

What I could not get out of my mind, and what gave my
fears their semblance of reality, was that, just as the mobster
spun his car around on the gravel, the headlights caught me full
in the face. No doubt he could recognize me again, and it would
be an easy matter for him to find me. There were not that many
schools in the area and all he had to do was wait outside each of
them in turn until he spotted me coming out one afternoon.

In tandem with the flashes came seizures of restlessness
and manic energy. I could not sit still in school, fidgeted in my
seat, broke pencils in half, accidentally knocked my books on

169

the floor, laughed at remarks that no one else found funny – loud, awkward snorts in the still classroom – frantically swam my exercise laps as if pursued by sharks down the watery lane. The most innocent of images could trigger an arousal: the angels in a reproduction of a Botticelli nativity scene that Sister pinned to the bulletin board for Advent; or, less innocent perhaps, the drawings in the first year Latin text book that Pastor Simone had lent me so that I could get a head start on high school, its pages filled with the near naked bodies of oiled youths, their long, banded hair reminding me of Tom. I was falling in love, though I could not articulate it at the time.

Despite, or because of this, my diving actually improved. The coaching with Williams in Albany the first Saturday of December went better than I, or O'Malley, had expected. On the drive up there Coach had been worried. He sat next to me in the bus. I looked a little peaked. Was I over the flu bug? My diving had been pretty uneven the past weeks. Was something bothering me? How did I feel about today? Did I want to talk about it? Anything?

I reassured him I felt fine.

Being out of the Valley and in a new environment was helping to pull me out of myself. The State University the previous year had opened a new sports facility and pool. The building, the locker and shower rooms, the blue tiles on the walls, even the water seemed sharper, harsher. The huge arc lamps buzzed overhead, infecting us with nervous energy. From the diving tower, the Olympic-sized pool shimmering below beckoned me to a higher professionalism. As I stretched out my arms, breathed my yoga breaths, emptied my mind, I could feel myself shifting smoothly into form like a tuned race car.

On the drive back O'Malley struck a different tone. Our performance was his affirmation. He clapped me on the shoulder. I had been on today. Williams had said he was impressed; wanted me training extra hours, every day now. There was hard work ahead. Was I up to it?"

I replied modestly, "I think so, Coach."

I also began keeping a diary that first week of December, and so from this point can begin accurately to date events, the trip to Albany, and what was to follow soon afterwards. Was it Williams's belief in me, the excitement of special coaching attention; or, was it the encounter in Kingston, the sexual awakening and desire, the pubescent longing, or even my growing isolation with Tom and having no one to turn to for advice, that acted as the catalyst for a verbalization of feeling. It was, however, a natural event that triggered it.

I was sitting up in the tree house one afternoon, trying to write a school paper. This in itself was a bit odd. It was a very cold day and I had never gone up to the tree house in this weather to do homework, or even to play for that matter. It was dangerous to climb the icy branches after a freeze, I had been warned about it often enough. But I did that day.

The temperature was hovering at the freeze point. I was huddled on the floor of the hut, my back against the north wall to shelter me from the wind. As I looked out over the edge of the half wall through the barren trees I could see a great black cloud-bank mounting on the horizon, its fringe hung with long, black, dread-lock twisters. I was counting the seconds between the bolts of lightning and the thunder, each count shorter as the storm rolled towards me. I turned to a blank page in the lined notebook. My hands were cold and I was shivering slightly, but I did not think about putting on gloves or leaving. As the storm gathered towards me, now filling three-quarters of the sky, I suddenly began to write a description of the storm, and then as if seized, as if it were writing me, I lost all sense of what I was doing. A burst of hailstones on the sheet of tin above my head startled me and sent me scurrying.

Cold and wet, I went back to my room, and hid the notebook at the back of my closet. It was not until later that evening that I took it out and read through the two or three water-blotted pages I had hurriedly scrawled in a broad hand helter-skelter across the page with little respect for the ruled lines, with many exclamation marks, and words printed bold – messages boiling up from the hidden mind? I have cleaned them up a bit, but this is more or less how I wrote them:

3:33 P.M., Saturday, December 7, 1968, Tree Fort, Woods, Madalin, Hudson Valley, New York State, USA, Earth

WEIRD storm coming right at me with these HUGE! black clouds far as the I/eye can see & the air real heavy. I got to work at it to breath.

Almost on top of me now.

There's these long drooly strands hanging down in front like black spit!!

Lightning. One & two & three & four. Thunder. And here comes the wind in waves like the trains I can hear from my room with the windows open in summer. There it is NOW! The whole fucking tree is going to get ripped right out of the ground! Hail stones big as hardballs. I told Richie this tin roof ain't worth shit. Not afraid. Even calm inside which is the pretty funny part cause I'm right in the middle of it & it's happening all around me, but not to me and I feel safe cept I wish Tom was here and us lying inside his sleeping-bag with him stretched warm on top of me talking stuff in my ear which makes me feel secure . . .

I was going to put it back under the floorboard in the closet – the sign of something not just private, hermetic but dangerous? – but hit upon a risky alternative instead. The first rule of secrecy is ' hide in the open'. The passage was scrawled in the middle pages of my math notebook, which now became my diary, while I started a new notebook for math. Not only did I not change the label announcing 'Math Homework', and simply put it on the desk amidst my school books, but I also took the added precaution of stuffing a few loose pages of returned homework into the front cover, knowing that the big red A+s would be sure to put Charlie off, magic talismans which perhaps did prove effective because he never did tamper with it.

Sunday Dec 8, 9:56 P.M..

Horny as hell. Went to Tom's about 1:00 because he told me his mom was leaving about then and this time I made sure no one saw me.

So? Nobody home. Hope all it was was he's out practicing driving with his mother & looking at the scenery. Yeah right! In winter!

Kind of pissed me off for no reason so I went over to Richie's to get distracted. Played Monopoly in the kitchen with a few of his zillion brothers and sisters. Came home about 6 for dinner cutting through the field but T's lights still not on. No answer just now when I sneaked a call from the kitchen. Real Worried!!!

11:03 P.M. Jerked off twice but can't sleep and still no lights on.

Monday, Dec. 9. 6:00 P.M.

Still no T. So you'd think everything'd be off for me today, right? Wrong. Diving like brilliant if I say so myself! Weird. Coach said I made it look easy. Didn't even ripple the water on entry.

Wanted to brag about it, but still no sight of you-know-who in the usual spot after training so I go over there and Guess who opens the door? Bobby! At least with clothes on this time. I says real cool Is T-Bird home and he says equal cool No he ain't but would I like to come in like it's his house & he's alone there! So I say No way, polite like & get this, he says Hey wait a minute I got a note for you & hands me this envelope all sealed proper & not steamed open or anything foolish so he wasn't snooping. Of course I can see right away it's from T & sure as hell won't read it there with him looking over my shoulder. Thank him. Like we got to be civilized don't we?

Note pissed me off. Quote, quote 'working things out from the other night' & 'see you tomorrow the usual place and time' which means 5:15 out back of Jefferson & of course it's what he fucking leaves out that burns me up! Like where the fuck is he and what the fuck is going on? And what was Tonto doing in his house with his eyes all red? As if I didn't know. Even the end – 'I miss you Love Tom' – sort of ticked me off like it was crumbs or something.

Just read this over. Man I got it bad. Go and do five hundred push-ups or something, Danny Boy. This just ain't working out. It just ain't.

Tuesday, Dec. 10. 6:30 PM

Doesn't show. Waited until I almost missed my ride with Mickey's father. Went to his house. Nobody home. I feel WRECKED! Don't want to write anymore

Later. 8:16 PM.

T just phoned! Says he's sorry about not showing up. Can I go over right away. No way I can get past the guards and what the fuck's been going on and where was he? Which is when I notice car noises in the background so figure he's at least in the village calling me from the laundromat and I don't want to ask too much in case Charlie is snooping on the other line but I can hear him in his room so I risk a couple of questions and say, Tell me something now will you. But pretty much all I get is that O'Shea claims he didn't know what Luca had in the bag cause Luca lied to him and how sorry he was to get T involved which should have never happened in the first place but all that sounds like a crock of shit to me but I know better by now and don't say it. We make a plan to meet after school tomorrow and before we get cut off he says again he misses me and starts going on about all these things we're going to do when we get alone which makes me paranoid in case someone is listening in but like he knows turns me on too

Later.
Been thinking and thinking. All this weird shit going down. What a fucking mess. Inside my head too like I'm getting farther & father out until I'll never be able to come back. That's one side of it. The other side is sometimes with him I feel like centered which is one of his favorite words these days & he asks the other day what I thought about him and I said the way I feel is we're inside something together with everyone & everything else outside and it would be great if we were a railroad and could build 1 station here & 1 there with tracks in between station to station connecting everything back & forth not just between him and me either but him & me and everything & he says he didn't expect that answer

Wednesday, Dec 11. 9:59 PM
Big fight! T real upset! Me too!
So we meet like we said. That part goes all right. He was waiting out back of school. But soon as he launches in again about O'Shea and Luca and shit it starts going wrong. O'Shea claims Luca lied to him about what was in the bag & that Luca & him had concocted this dumb plan to test Tom or something with a bag full of newspapers so later on they could trust him to do big shit like be a money courier!!!
But what really pissed me off was He was telling me like he believed it himself! So I started shouting at him right there as we're walking along the road – like I KNEW I shouldn't – You fucking believe that shit and you better get your head examined & You must be the biggest dumb motherfucking ass in the whole country! Bad. Real

bad.

Course he doesn't believe it, he starts hollering back. What do I think he is? What's my problem? How come I'm so ready to believe he's some kind of PATSY?

Which is when I should have shut up but I don't & I say It all sounds like such bullshit and what am I supposed to think! & how come he can't tell me like BEFORE he goes & disappears & I even have to get letters from some little shit ass Indian twirp instead of direct from him!

So, that's what's eating me, he says, I'm jealous. Which really really steams me. Like I'M jealous! No way I'm jealous. All I want is to know what the fuck is going on that's all and where was he anyway? I mean he was like missing two whole days and everything he told me about O'Shea he could've found out in one five minute phone call. So, that's when I finally find out he was up in Albany! Albany no less! What the fuck were you doing in Albany & seems he heard that some low life runs a boxing school there has the crap on Luca and he had to wait around until the guy showed and then didn't learn anything he didn't already know.

So I ask him How come you didn't ask me to go with you? Like we're supposed to be not just friends but FRIENDS? He gets all bent out of shape over that one and says sarcastic Yeah, so maybe I can get you expelled for cutting school? And thrown off the team too? Jesus Danny don't you know I don't want you getting your life screwed up and swears he's trying to get himself out of it all soon as he can and he already got me more involved than he should.

So by now we're about at his house and I'm thinking Do I go in or do I not go in? cause I'm still pretty ticked off when all of a sudden I think right out of the blue Why am I so upset? Which makes me all moody & quiet. Tom is just Tom I figure.

So we go inside & he tries to make it up to me and shit & when we're up in his room lying around in the dark listening to music like he goes and contradicts himself in a big way, propped up on his elbow leaning over me fiddling with my cock & me about to cream all over him again, which is when he says how there's this party Saturday over at O'Shea and how maybe this is the chance for me to go and see for myself what's going on? And how maybe that's better than my making up a story in my mind and then holding it against him? So I say natural like, Sure why not. When is it? Saturday night he says. Course there's no way Dad's going to give permission and course I'm going to have to promise my life for the next umpteen million years to Richie to cover for this one! Who knows how, I'm going man, I'm going.

2. The Christmas party

I recorded in my diary the elaborate ruse I used to trick Father into allowing me to be out that Saturday night, concocting one fabrication in order to cover another. I told Mickey that I was meeting this girl in Kingston who had the hots for me. I had hit on her in a diner. Only thing was, Father would never let me go if I told him the real reason. Of course Mickey'd back me. Anything to help a buddy score. If I wanted, he'd even be at my house when I did the asking, but I figured that was going too far. In turn, I told Father that one of the team was having a Christmas party Saturday. Everybody would be there. Even Coach was invited. Mickey and I were riding together. Father did not much like it that I was seeking permission at the last minute. Reluctantly, he agreed to let me go, but only on condition that I be home by ten, not one minute later, and leave a number where

I could be reached. Oddly enough it was the number of the crash pad that I left by the hallway phone. After Tom's 'disappearance' I had made an issue of his giving it to me. I must have rationalized my lies to Father by telling myself that he had the real phone number, so he really knew where I was if he wanted me. Therefore, I was 'sort of telling the truth'.

Perhaps still odder is the fact that we rode over to Kingston with my 'arch-enemy' Lansing. Tom was still too young to drive at night. His mother did not work the night shift on weekends, but he certainly would not have wanted her to know where he was going. I did not record, nor do I remember if Tom told me, what excuse he used with her, but I certainly remember protesting against our going with Lansing. He would probably be stoned out of his mind, or drunk, and would crash us into a tree. He liked to speed. For sure we'd get pulled over by the state troopers. They'd find hash, or worse, in the glove compartment and bust all of us. Tom reasoned simply that it made sense to ride with him because he was going door to door and maybe he'd let something slip about Luca and the contents of the gym bag. He had never heard Lansing say much of anything about me, one way or the other, at least not in his hearing. Convenience and curiosity prevailed.

We met him by the stone wall at the edge of the woods next to the church yard. The pine scrub there was thick enough to hide us from Reggie, or anyone else driving by. He pulled onto the shoulder right on time, at exactly six; leaning over to pull up the chrome button and push open the door for us. We lost no time getting in. I slid across the cold, plastic, front seat into the middle. The slushy roads were dangerously slippery, the tires threadbare. We skidded onto the shoulder, into the other lane, as we headed out towards the bridge. The car was too warm, the Hendrix music too loud. Toys and baubles dangled from the chrome molding along the edge of the windshield, from the stem of the rear view mirror, and the visors: a plastic rabbit's foot; a gaudy clown's head; a miniature skull, of a squirrel perhaps; a wooden rosary; a swastika badge; a gold Sicilian horn suspended from a tangled gold chain; the broken-off head of a papier mâché devil – talismans of a superstitious mind, a mind at the edge of possession. He frightened me. His thick hands pounded the wheel rhythmically. He was sweaty, smelled sickeningly sweet; his clothes dank and musty. The heat and odors, the clank and rattle of the trinkets made me nauseous. Thankfully, Tom cracked open a window.

Lansing leaned past me to ask him, "Anymore Acapulco Gold left? Or did you and Shitface here use it all up?"

"Yeah, well, whatever . . . scored something else almost as good . . . "

Tom reached into his shirt pocket and pulled out three joints, handing one to me and one to Lansing. I put mine in my pocket, but Lansing rolled his between his thick fingers, smelled the length of it as one would a Havana cigar, fished a stick match out of his jacket vest pocket, and struck it with one hand on his thumbnail, John Wayne style. I thought, my God he's going to drive while he's stoned. He took a long wheezing hit.

"Not bad. Not bad at all . . . You smoking or what Fuckface?"

I said, "Don't be so formal. Call me Danny. I'm saving mine for later."

"Yeah, well, whatever, Butthead."

I glanced over to see if I could read his sly grin. There was no way of believing that it was friendly. Everything about him always seemed to me aggressive and menacing. He was looking straight forward down the road, his face too thick and jowled, too bloated by drink and drugs, to be penetrable. Great, gray sacks weighed down his colorless eyes. The grass, or whatever else he was on, loosened his tongue. He rattled on. No need to save anything. Folks were bringing all kinds of shit. Acid, hash, quaaludes. Ford even copped some peyote buttons. Chicks galore. Who knows? Maybe he'd feel generous and fix me up with someone. Lose my cherry. Bring our little village angel down from the top of his Christmas tree. Or was I morally against a good lay? If he put it that way I probably was. On principle. He laughed, and leaned over to say to Tom:

"This friend of yours's too good to be true. Like right from kindergarten. Man, I could tell you shit."

Tom said, "Keep your eyes on the road, will yah. We want

to get there in one piece."

"Yeah sure." He deliberately swerved the car, to prove who was in charge.

Tom wanted to know how someone named Ellie was doing. Apparently, she had been mugged the week before by some Kingston creeps. Lansing said that he and the guys had gone over to this pool hall where they knew they hung out and had beaten the crap out of them. And got her money back for her too. They'd think twice before messing with anyone from 'the Pad' again.

I squeezed against Tom so that not even the outer edges of my clothing would be touching Lansing, and lapsed into a defensive fantasy – Tom and I fulfilling our dream of disappearing together into the distant mountains. He poked me out of my reverie and asked if Luca had been around lately? Lansing frowned. O'Shea was mostly going to see him now. Tom insisted. Did he think he'd be there tonight? How would he know. It was important; there was something they had to discuss.

Lansing said sharply, "Then don't ask me, ask Paddy."

The area of Kingston we were entering was a maze of cone-shaped hills and narrow gullies interconnected by twisting lanes criss-crossing each other and sometimes themselves, rising and dipping precipitously in ever more tangled strands. Even though situated within the city limits, the geography not only isolated it, but also gave it an eerie cohesion, like Dogtown above Glouces-ter.

I lost my sense of direction within a couple of minutes. There were too many sharp inclines, too many privet hedges, interminable series of S-shaped curves, innumerable intersections looking the same. The grades were so sharp I heard the metal scraping of our back bumper on the asphalt. I knew that if I walked in a straight line in any direction I would probably come out into one or another of the city districts. But how could any-one maneuver a straight line out there?

Occasionally the lights of a house, buried in tangles of un-dergrowth and woods, would flicker between the rows of cedars. It was still early, but we did not pass one car, nor see one soul. Children should have been out sledding. There was snow on the shaded slopes of one or two of the steep hillocks. In Madalin we would have been tobogganing. Someone surely should have been strolling his dog after dinner, shovelling his walk, or scattering rock salt?

We turned up a steep, potholed, slippery driveway. The back wheels spun. Lansing raced the motor and we slipped and slid up into a parking area next to a large Victorian house, freshly painted yellow and white and in good repair. A columned porch ran around the two sides facing us. French doors were open, so was an upstairs window. Two different rock songs, played simultaneously at top volume, battled each another from different upstairs windows. Hendrix and the Doors. A girl was shouting; a loud male voice was telling her to shut up.

Lansing mumbled something about the back door being permanently locked because some jackass months ago had lost the key, so we went in by the front. The hallway was rather grand. An Italian marble floor, wide, elegant stairway, an ebony banister curving up gracefully out of view. The red runner looked new. I could hear people shouting to each other or talking but not a soul was visible. The living room to my left was crammed with cardboard boxes, but devoid of any furnishings. This part of the house was unheated and smelled of wet, moldering paper. Tom saw me staring. O'Shea was a rare coin and money dealer and used the room for storage. If I asked him O'Shea would be all too glad to give me the grand tour. Some of the boxes were open. The one closest to hand was packed with some kind of oriental currency with high numbers on it.

"How much do you think's in there?" I whispered.

O'Shea had bought up all this Taiwanese money in great quantities in some interregnum period in the late forties, when he was still working for British intelligence, or so he said. It wasn't worth anything now, but it might be in the future. He was negotiating with the Bank of Taiwan to buy it all back so that none of it might accidentally find its way onto the black market. He could stand to make a fortune on the deal, except the government there wasn't even remotely interested. In the meantime they used it to play poker.

Lansing left us in the entrance and went lumbering up the

staircase. Tom and I made our way down a narrow, side hall towards the back of the house. A door opened into the kitchen. There was a blast of warmth from a wood stove, the smell of game bird roasting and fresh bread. Every light was on, but the room was empty. Someone must have liked yellow. The walls were mustard with white trim, the curtains canary yellow with white stripes. Two imitation Tiffany lamps hung over a pine banquet table piled with some of the evening's food: a cut-glass bowl filled with fruit, assorted salads, olives, celery and carrot sticks; white dishes with gold rims, crystal glasses, and silver candelabra. I had been in the main house of the commune down by the river in Madalin and everything there was extreme poverty and simplicity. That was the image I had formed in my mind of the crash pad, and none of this conformed. It made me feel confused and shy.

I heard footsteps on a back stairway. A pine farm door at the far end of the room banged open against the wall. The girl I had seen in the woods with Tom and Bobby so many weeks before entered. She was carrying a baby wrapped in a white blanket. She came over and kissed Tom.

"I heard the car. Glad you came. I wasn't sure you would. I mean, you ain't been around for ages. So, this is the famous Danny . . . " She extricated a warm hand from the blanket.

"Tara – Dan."

"Tom can't shut up about you." She folded the blanket back so I could see the baby's face. "His name is Tree." She had eaten some morning glory seeds and had him out in the yard under the big beech tree, and while she was in labor had thought that the tree was the most beautiful thing in the world; when he was born, she had decided that was what she had to call him.

She cooed down at him, and then said to Tom. "Ellie know you're here?"

"Don't think so. We just got here."

"I was just going to change him. I'll tell her you're here."

We took off our jackets and hung them on a coat stand in front of the now permanently locked back door. Others were drifting in. Who was Ellie? Just a friend, Tom said.

A stocky man, middle to late forties, who I knew must be

O'Shea, approached us. He was wearing a white shirt and a red tie decorated with white snowmen, but no jacket; his dark hair was closely cropped and graying; his thick horn-rimmed glasses magnified his blue eyes. On his left hand he wore a gold graduation ring with a fake ruby, on his right hand two gold bands. He was soft spoken. I needed to lean close to hear. His handshake was dry and firm.

"Well well, about time I meet the one and only Danny. I've been asking Tom for weeks to bring you by. He talks about you endlessly you know, but keeps you well hidden. Now that you've broken the ice you're sure to be a regular I hope. We're just one big happy family around here."

"Tom says you sell money?"

He laughed. "Sell money. Sounds rather peculiar when you put it that way. You had to come in by the front way so you would have noticed the boxes. I'll give you the grand tour for sure if you like."

His eyes had strayed to my neck. My shirt was open a couple of buttons. Wanting to look cool, I had decided to wear my gold chain and cross but no undershirt.

"Now that's a Maltese cross I see there around your neck. How did you come by that? You don't see many boys walking the streets of this fine country wearing such a thing now do you."

"It was a gift. From my aunt and uncle. They live in Sicily . . . This is a great house. Do you own it?"

"I bought it several years ago when the market was low, but it's a white elephant I can tell you. There's always something wrong with the bleeding place. Too hot in the summer. Too cold in the winter. The heating bills would give my dear mother a heart attack, even with these wood stoves. Too many rooms, too many holes in the roof, too little insulation, too many drafts. The windows don't fit properly, the doors creak. I must have been drunk or out of my mind when I signed the contract on this one. Still, it's a rather grand place and a bit loveable, don't you know."

I agreed that it was. "You're Irish, I guess?"

"Belfast. Born and raised there. But I spent the last few

years in London. Had the business there, before coming here. You never do lose the accent I suppose."

"I was in London once, a couple of years ago. But only for two or three days. My father knew some French professor and we stopped over so he could visit him. It was nice. I'd like to go back."

"It's your mother's side that's Italian."

I nodded. "Her maiden name was Acciardo. She died when I was little. I still have aunts and uncles and lots of cousins there. In Agrigento . . . That's in the south, in Sicily."

"I know it. The Valley of the Temples. Sun. Sea. Great food. A marvellous place. A paradise on earth really. Did you stay long?"

"Two months."

"Two months, bejesus! Then you really did get to know it."

"It was really hot. A few days it got over a hundred degrees. Way hotter than here. But we went swimming every day so it was all right. My uncle's house is right near the sea. You can walk right to it."

"That surely must have been a glorious place for you, liking swimming as you do. I can see how you might have even fallen in love with the place. You know we do that sometimes, fall in love with places. You could say you were in your natural element. And in the Mediterranean. For two whole months." He laughed. "You're a lucky one, all right. I'll tell you a little secret. I wouldn't mind having a wee house there some day myself to get out of the foul weather. That summer must have been an important time for you. Someday you'll have to go back to see just how much."

I was impressed. Few people had understood my attraction to Sicily, beyond the maternal blood and gene pull. He seemed to grasp it immediately, perhaps because he had been there.

"It was the first time I was on my own. I mean, my father brought me there but he could only stay a week or so because he had to go to a conference. In Paris. My aunt came back here with me at the end of the summer. I wanted to go back this year

184

but I think I'll be in training and probably won't get any further than Albany."

"Albany instead of Agrigento. Not a fair trade I'd say. I've heard how serious you are about your diving. We're planning to come and see you in January." I must have looked surprised because he added, "Didn't Tom tell you?" I shook my head. "I'll have to have a talk with that boy. Anyway, we are. You can count on it."

"Thank you," I replied politely.

"You know, this Acciardo. Well I made a few friends in that part of the world but I don't think I met any Acciardos. What does your uncle do?"

"He's an archeologist. That's what I want to be. But my aunt is the Acciardo. She's my mother's oldest sister. My uncle's name is Palermo."

"Well, I don't think I know anyone by that name either, at least not in Agrigento. Wyant is English, isn't it? Have yah any relatives there now?"

"Not any more. Dad's family has been here since like before the Mayflower. His mother, she died before I was born, was a DAR. My other aunt, my father's sister, lives in Utah. We don't see her much. She married a Mormon and looked up the family for us because they have this belief they can save the dead by praying for them? So she did all this genealogy stuff and found out that great-great-great-grandfather Wyant was a doctor and maybe invented forensic medicine. At least, my brother thinks he did. He wrote some books even. Father has all of them. They're real interesting. With illustrations of all these weird things. Creepy knives to cut people open, formulas for poison and sh – stuff-like that. Father says I shouldn't look at them because they'll give me nightmares, but I did and I didn't get any nightmares."

"Well, you wouldn't now, would you?"

"Why?"

"You're too sophisticated to be bothered by scientific illustrations now. Anyone can see that about you."

Being English and Italian, he thought, was a good combination because the cold rational north and the passionate emotional south counter-balanced each other. England, after all, represented Arcadia; Sicily, he supposed, Thalassa and the sea.

"Being partial now I'd have to say that Irish and Italian might have been a better mix, being as I was brought up Catholic, but we can't always have perfection now can we?"

I looked around for Tom. He had drifted off to the other side of the room and was talking to the girl I assumed was Ellie. She had her arm around his neck. I had seen her kiss him on the lips.

Several joints had been lit and were being passed. Someone I did not know had brought me one. O'Shea was telling me that somewhere in all those stacks of boxes and loose money he had some Fascist lire and perhaps I'd like a stack or two as a souvenir. Someday it would be collectible, no doubt even valuable. He had to circulate a bit now, but perhaps later, on our tour, we could look for them. They'd be somewhere, in one of those rooms.

I had not noticed the kitchen filling up. Fifteen or twenty people had already arrived, mostly teenagers. I noticed a boy slightly older than myself watching me. When he caught my eye he weaved his way over and introduced himself. This was Ford. Tom told me later that people thought he was beautiful, and like most beautiful people lived a special life, but that never occurred to me. His mouth sagged with too much self-indulgence; his mannerisms were too self-conscious. He was holding a joint and handed it to me before even speaking.

He finally asked, "We've seen each other around somewhere haven't we?"

I replied, "You were with Tom one night by the gas station. My father and I were giving him a ride."

"That was some evening."

I had the odd impression that he really knew where he had seen me, and that the question meant something else. I replied simply, "Yeah, it looked like it."

"I saw you talking to Paddy. He comes on a little strong sometimes."

"I don't know. He's all right."

He ignored what I had said. "The funny part is he thinks

he's being subtle and so lays it on all the more."

I said, "Maybe he's just being Irish or something."

"What do you mean?"

"You know, blarney and shit."

"Yeah sure, his heart's in the right place."

I was not sure whether he was being sarcastic or not. An excess of grass spiked with hash had started to make me feel dizzy. I had not eaten anything since morning. He must have seen me waver a bit because he took me by the arm and led me through the blurring bodies to the other side of the room where there was an old, tattered sofa set near the woodstove. The springs had long gone and I sank into it nearly to the floor. The declivity slid Ford against me. He handed me another joint. The windows were closed, the shades drawn, the doors closed to keep out draughts and hold in the heat, the room stuffy, pervaded with pot, body and food smells. Ford asked me if I wanted some wine, but I did not. Where was Tom now? Or Tara, or O'Shea, or anyone familiar for that matter? The noise level had risen to a din. I closed my eyes. The springs of the couch sank again. Ford returning. He handed me a plate of food.

"You look like you could use something to eat."

I glanced over. He had green eyes, I noticed. I didn't know anyone else with green eyes. He narcissistically tucked a lock of his brown hair behind his ear. I envied his flawless skin. Neither his aristocratic nose, nor his sharp forceful chin, showed the slightest disruption. Even his nails were perfect, manicured. His lower lip was too full, the kind that can easily contrive a pout. Perhaps it was one of the nuns who had said once that too full a mouth spelt trouble. There was something weak or bland about his looks. They lacked the oddity, the intensity, the imbalance I found attractive in Tom. He put me off.

He noticed that I was staring at Tom and Ellie, whose hand was now being generous with Tom's ass. Oddly though, Tom had gripped his chin in his right hand. His eyebrow was raised in concentration; he was staring at Ford and me. I waved. Without breaking his pose or expression, he turned away.

Ford said, "They were a number once, you know. Back in August. He kind of dumped her, or her him. I never got it straight."

Ellie wouldn't tell him what happened, but he knew Tom was just coming around mostly for the sex. Drugs too of course. But he was more interested in fucking his way through all the chicks here, so maybe Ellie didn't mean to him what he meant to her. Come to think of it he was fucking his way through some of the guys too. Like Bobby and him were also a number. He knew for a fact because Bobby's room was next to the one Paddy let him have when he stayed over.

I hurriedly changed the subject. How many people were living here? There was quite a crowd now. He wasn't sure, maybe eight or nine. It could change every day. After we were finished eating maybe I'd like to see the house? He could show me around.

He added, "I even got some great hash upstairs. We can share it . . . "

He took the empty plate from me. Would I have gone with him that evening? He had already taken my arm to help me to my feet. But through my growing haze I heard my name being called. I looked around. Bobby was maneuvering through the crowd towards us. Ford seemed annoyed that he was interferring.

"Oh Jesus, here comes that creep Indian."

Bobby flopped down next to me, breaking Ford's hold. "Hey man, how you doing? Didn't think horses could drag you here."

He grabbed my hand in one of those complicated multi-step handshakes everyone was doing then. "Hey Ford. What's up with you? When did they let you out? I thought you had to stay at that posh school of yours all weekend for some fancy doing or other."

"The Christmas play you mean? It's next weekend."

"Did Lansing find you? He was looking everywhere for you a few minutes ago."

Ford shook his head.

"He mustn't've seen you over here."

Ford seemed annoyed. "Where did he go?"

"Upstairs, I think. It sounded important."

Ford hesitated, perhaps unsure whether to believe Bobby

or not, or whether or not he had really lost some sort of advantage with me. Disgruntled, he dislodged himself the rest of the way from the sunken springs. "I'll only be gone a couple of minutes, then we can have that tour, okay?"

I nodded.

Bobby said instantly, "Bad news, that guy. You got to watch out for him."

"How come?"

"He sucks up to people and then sticks it to them soon as their backs are turned." I must have looked taken aback because he added, "Yeah. He thinks he owns everyone and can use them for whatever he wants. You know because his family's got all this money. Ford ain't his real name even."

"What is it then?"

He shrugged. "Ask Paddy. I hear his father's some kind of bigwig in Connecticut or New Jersey. You ought to be careful. He seen you and Tom around a few times and was going around asking all these questions."

"What kind of questions?"

"What your last name was. What house you lived in. Shit like that."

"So? We're in the phone book. And there ain't much to know. All he has to do is ask."

Ford liked power games. Playing sides against the middle. Tom had horned in on his sources and had to watch out. People like Ford only looked out for themselves. If you kept that in mind they were easy to figure out sometimes.

He added, "You know, come to think of it I wonder if it was such a good idea you coming over here tonight . . . "

I scanned the room again. So far as I could see it was just a bunch of stoned teenagers trying to balance white paper plates and look cool. It did not feel threatening. O'Shea had gone up to Tom; I saw him nodding about something.

I managed to extricate myself from the sofa. My mouth was dry and I went in search of something cold to drink.

I was beginning to focus on persons or objects to the exclusion of everything around, as if the thing itself was of the greatest importance. My vision was also slowing down. Paddy had his arm around Tom's shoulder, the way two males take each other into their confidence. They were moving with infinite slowness towards the side door, O'Shea's hand on the small of Tom's back, guiding him through the shoals. Lansing stood beside the closed door to the hallway through which we had earlier entered, arms folded, smoking a cigarette, raising his hand with great deliberation, tilting his head back at bit. He struck me as being shrewder than I had realized. Ford was walking slowly across the room towards Lansing. I noticed that he did not touch anyone as he moved across the room. Maintaining the isolation of his own body space; separating himself from the crowd? He jerked his head towards O'Shea and Tom, and Lansing nodded. I turned around 180 degrees to look back at the sofa. Bobby was weaving through the arboreal bodies towards me. His face or rather his intensely anxious expression rushed at me; alarmed me. Ford was talking now to Lansing. O'Shea and Tom went through a side door, O'Shea turned in the doorway to survey the room. Catching Lansing's eye, he nodded and Lansing nodded back. The door swayed eerily behind them. Ford turned. Seeing me, he grinned and started towards me but Bobby intervened.

"Come on. Hurry up! Don't ask any questions. Just follow me."

He handed me my jacket.

3. Out of body

Bobby held open a swinging door. We passed through into a pantry lined both sides floor to ceiling with enamel white shelving, every inch crammed with stacks of worthless foreign money held with brown paper bands. A second swinging door led into a back vestibule, perhaps originally intended for the gardener; just inside there was a sink, and just outside there was a small shed. Tom and O'Shea must have only been a few feet in front of us. I could not see them, but their voices travelled clearly in the cold air. Paddy was saying that he was glad Tom had brought me along, that he had liked meeting me, and hoped I would visit frequently. To my surprise Lansing answered, with a quip about my being more hip than he had thought. Perhaps he had exited through another door? And where then was Ford?

Their voices began to fade down the sloping yard. Bobby and I followed cautiously, scurrying into the shadow of a large oak tree. There was a powder of snow to soften our step. The cold was a shock. It brought me back somewhat to reality, and to fear. I pressed my back against the tree, reminded of my own woods, the tree fort and things familiar, a long way off. I could not hear them anymore, or see them when I darted a glance around the side of the trunk. My eyes had adjusted. There was a partial moon. High thin clouds diffused the light, the trees and bushes crystallized with ice. From the house, faint sounds of rock music and voices were still audible. We slid down a slight incline to a clump of pine shrubs. The music, the lights from the house receded; their voices became all the more distinct.

Lansing was saying, "Just wait until you see *his* stash . . . out of this world."

Tom: "Where're we heading anyway?"

O'Shea: "I had these brick shelters built, for extra storage, you know, a few years ago, just after I bought the place. They're a bit further down there beyond those pines. You can't see them yet."

Lansing: "You'd need a bazooka to break into them."

O'Shea laughed. "I might have overdone it. Putting on steel doors and all."

Tom: "How come you built them so far from the house?"

O'Shea: "There's an old service drive down there goes into the main road. It'd be easy to unload directly into them, I figured."

Lansing: "He installed this expensive security system."

O'Shea: "I spent a bloody fortune, come to think of it. For the money I could have bought myself a whole bank."

Tom: "I still don't see why we're out here."

O'Shea: "My fault. I should have explained, of course. I never keep *real* money in the house anymore. Your payment's here, and we can put the envelope here too and be sure it's safe and sound."

The yard sloped more steeply. The house must have been at the crest of a hill, though I had not noticed it in the dark as we arrived. Bobby and I were in a formal garden, hiding behind clumps of cedar and frozen rose beds. I thought I heard a car way down further below. If the road curved past there, it gave us a way of escape. I could see the lights of another house out far beyond the trees, high up on another hill.

Bobby motioned for me to crouch lower, pointing to a large garden statue that would continue to afford us cover. The storage houses were in plain view, each about an eight-foot cube. The red tile roofs, the wider than normal overhangs, the surrounding ice-laden conifers, made the structures look alpine. Bobby had taken us around to the far side. What was going on? What were they up to? Why all the caution? But we were too close to them to risk a question.

Lansing was saying how he was going to clear out and go to Mexico and live for a few years like a king, have himself a good vacation, some place warm, away from this fucking winter, this shithole Valley.

Keys rattled.

O'Shea asked Tom, "You did bring back everything in the envelope now like a good lad, didn't you? You didn't go and do anything foolish and hold any back, or make any copies, now. Not after you gave your word."

Tom said indignantly, "I keep my word. Everything's right here in my coat. This isn't a very good place to keep them. It's way too damp. I hope you don't expect me to guarantee anything once you've got them."

"You'd be right if I hadn't installed climate controls in each of them. What did I say? Spared no expense. Money is just paper after all and I wasn't about to lose my stock from moisture or rats . . . But I hope you're not telling me you want to back out now, at this late hour?"

"No. I was just wondering."

"Good lad. Fair enough. It took an awful lot to work this out for you, you know. You were in way over your head. In serious danger you realize. Let it be a lesson to you. You don't want to be playing around with these boys, Tom."

"Like I said, they keep their end of the deal and back off, and I keep mine. Like we agreed."

Lansing said sarcastically., "If it weren't for Paddy here they'd have iced you. You owe him."

"Now Teddy, no need to rub anything in."

"Sure, Paddy. Sure."

No one ever called Lansing by his first name. It sounded so strange.

A metal door grated. A bright light suddenly illuminated the area.

Lansing said, "Hand 'em over so I can check 'em."

"They're all there. Eight strips. Thirty-six frames each."

O'Shea's voice was muffled, coming from inside one of the vaults.

"Tom, come in here a minute and check the other stuff we were talking about while Teddy there checks the negatives."

Lansing said almost immediately, "Hurry up will you. I'm freezing my ass off. Everything's here."

Bobby and I had scurried down to the back of one of the vaults. Tom's voice was just on the other side of us.

"Jesus I never knew you had this much shit. There's enough here to get all of Jefferson stoned. There's a fucking arsenal too. Jesus. Machine guns. Rifles. Man, that looks like boxes of grenades. Where'd you get all this?"

From the direction and clarity of his voice it was clear that Paddy was now standing outside again.

"That's a long story. Let's just get this business here cleared up, and maybe I'll tell you about it later. First I got to make dead sure on your grandmother's grave that we're not going to learn a few months down the line that you made some copy negatives or that a few prints just happened to turn up in the bottom of some drawer and for a few hundred extra you'll turn those over too?"

"I told you I wouldn't and I didn't. I keep my word."

"Nothing personal mind you. You know I have to ask."

Lansing suddenly intruded. "It's his skin anyway, ain't it? If he's stupid enough to make copies and they find out, he's history."

Tom insisted, "Like I said, I gave you everything. You've got my word on it. I know who I'm dealing with. I'm not stupid."

"I know you're not, Tom. I know that sure as we're standing here."

Lansing said, "Come on, let's do what we got to do and get out of here."

O'Shea suddenly raised his voice and said loudly, "Do you hear that boys? The lad here is dealing straight with you! I told you he would."

A deep, accented strange male voice suddenly responded, "Yeah, well we got orders."

Bobby gripped my arm. I might have cried out, but he put his hand over my mouth. He held up two fingers, but I had already heard the footsteps of two people approaching.

The same man, closer now, said, "So, you're the smartass, eh? Too bad, a nice boy like you with such a future gotta make so much trouble. You shouldn't have messed around with things you don't know."

Still inside one of the vaults, Tom said defensively, "So, what the fuck's going on?"

O'Shea said with such sickening sweet false sincerity that a cold chill went through me, "I really am sorry about this, Tom. I liked you a lot you know. And I tried to warn you. You'll not be able to say I didn't try to warn you, but you were always playing with fire. You know that."

Lansing added derisively, "I said all along you was stupid. What did I tell you guys? Didn't I tell you Paddy here was true to his word? That he'd deliver the son of a bitch? Didn't I?"

The man said, "Sure. You done good kid. Luca always rewards people who do good for him. Now, you two scram. We got a little unfinished business here with this wise guy."

Tom: "What unfinished business? What are you guys talking about? I don't know what's going on."

O'Shea: "Now, Sal, really, haven't you forgotten one little thing first? A matter of a little wee envelope perhaps?"

"The boss he said we got to wrap up the details first neat and proper like before we hand over it over. That's what he tells us, right Guido?"

"Right, Sal, that's what he said."

O'Shea: "That was not the agreement between Luca and me. What I worked out with your boss was you hand over the money and I hand over the lad here. Very neat and simple it all was too. And a man of his word, your boss. So, I'd say, hand it over first."

"Yeah, well maybe he changed his mind, and maybe the boss needs his own guarantee he's getting all the goods, cause he give us different orders."

"Five thousand up front. The rest later. That's the agreement and that's the way it's got to be."

"Like you got a choice."

"I think I do, you know. We could lock Tom here in this vault for a bit and all go up to the house while I telephone Luca myself and then we'll see if he's breaking his word or not."

Lansing: "Jesus, Paddy, just hand the motherfucker over to them will you. He ain't worth it."

"Well you see, Teddy, I happen to know that Luca is a man of honor and what I think now is that these two here are playing their little personal game with me and it isn't working out the way they thought, and when Luca finds out, well, I don't think he's going to like it that you boys took matters into your own hands, now will he? So, you want to hand over the money now or do I have to go back to the house and make a phone call."

"You're a wise guy too, huh? All of you, wise guys. Guido, give him the envelope."

"But Sal. When the boss finds out he's gonna take it out on us."

I suddenly recognized the second voice. Guido was the driver of the car that night down by the docks.

Sal: "Shut up will you. Just hand it over. We got the kid as guarantee."

Guido: "Can you beat that. Just look at this. The fucking guy has got to count it."

O'Shea: "It's all here."

Sal: "Okay kid. You and us, we're going to take a little

ride. Have us a little conversation. Luca ain't been too pleased about some of the shit you been pulling. Like maybe you need being taught a lesson. We got a few things to discuss. Easy now. Don't make no trouble."

Were they going to beat up Tom, torture him, dump his body in the river? What could we do? I was terrified, in a cold sweat. I glanced around for Bobby. Without my noticing, he had silently disappeared. I felt completely deserted, frightened, and powerless.

Tom was obviously frightened. "Where you guys taking me? What's Luca want? I gave everything to Paddy. I told you. I gave him everything." He added plaintively, "O'Shea? What's going on?"

"I'm afraid it's out of my hands Tom. I really do regret this, but I'm afraid you just went too far."

Tom said, "You tell them. I'm not going anywhere. Paddy . . . "

O'Shea said half-heartedly, "The boy wouldn't try to cheat you and you'd know where to find him. Why don't we all just leave here on friendly terms?"

Sal: "We got our own ways of making sure."

Tom: "I'm not coming out of here. And I'm not going anywhere with you guys."

Guido shouted, "Watch out Sal! He's going for one of those guns!"

"Jesus bloody Christ, don't shoot!" O'Shea cried. "Those guns aren't loaded. Put it down Tom. Put it down!"

From the sounds of the commotion that ensued, the sounds of a scuffle and Tom's shouts, I surmised that Lansing had grabbed him and dragged him out of the shed.

"You can fucking have the worthless little bastard. He ain't worth arguing over. I tell you Paddy. Leave well enough alone. He ain't worth all the effort."

By then, I was just about hysterical. I looked around in vain for a stick, or discarded rake, or anything, to repeat my performance of that other night, but there was nothing.

O'Shea said, "Everybody calm down now. Let's not do anything rash here. Why don't we just all go back to the house

196

and have us a little wee drink together and if things need solving a few shots of whiskey will do the trick better than any means of yours for sure. I'm a believer in a good fire and a good brew on a cold night, aren't you now lads?"

But Lansing must have already delivered Tom into their hands because Tom said, "Christ. Stop them Paddy. Can't you see they're not listening!"

I heard a sudden blow. "You fucking shut your mouth kid. He fucking tried to bite me!"

O'Shea said sternly, "Lay off the boy now. I tell you, there's no need for this . . . "

I heard scuffling, everyone talking at once. Above the confusion I also heard Bobby shouting my name: "Danny! Everybody! Now! Now! Danny! Danny! Everybody! Help! Help! Leave him alone! Leave Tom alone! Come on! Everybody. Danny! Help! Help! Come on!"

I rushed out from around the side of the shed.

Bobby screamed again at the top of my lungs. "Tom! Tom! Get out of there!"

Guido cried out, "Jesus Christ. He stabbed me! The little fuck stabbed me in the arm! Who the fuck is this? Where's the fucking gun? Sal! I dropped it! Fucking shit. I'm bleeding."

In a flash I took in everything. Lansing was holding Tom by his hair and shaking him. Tom was shouting and trying to free his hands. Guido was holding his arm, blood pouring from between his fingers, but he was backing off. Bobby had jumped on Sal's back and was trying to get a stranglehold on him. I lunged with all my force against Lansing's back, kicking him wildly, and managed to wind him and knock him off balance by the force or shock of surprise.

I shouted, "Run Tom! Run!"

Tom turned around and around in a circle, completely confused, but he must have seen Guido's gun lying on the ground, because he dove for it. Sal, shaking off Bobby with some ease, kicked at Tom's head but missed and slipped on the ice. They rolled around on the ground trying to get the gun. Where was O'Shea? Where was Lansing? I swirled, but too late. Lansing grabbed me by the collar and hit me on the side of the face with his open palm. He was breathing heavily. I could smell his foul sweat. He hit me harder. My head reeled, but he did not let go. He shook me by the collar as a dog would a rabbit. He was breathing heavily in my face, his breath reeking of stale beer. His face was contorted with rage and hatred. He hit me again with his open palm on the right and then the left ear. My head spun. I had begun to bleed profusely from several cuts he had opened above my right eye, my lip, my nose. My hands were free. I tried to protect myself, but he was a huge person in a white rage, like a wounded bear. I tried to wipe my eyes, but he wouldn't let me. He was not saying a word, but he was wheezing, his enormous hulk heaving and smelling like rancid meat. I think I must have been going into shock because I was very calm, not at all afraid. In fact, I was even worried whether Tom or Sal was going to get the gun. Lansing was cursing me under his breath, "Motherfucker know-it-all, had this coming a long time." A gun went off twice. I had to get free to help Tom. Where was Bobby? I said something stupid to Lansing, something like I didn't believe in violence, that it never solved anything, something that must have made him angrier because he began to hit me even harder. Everything was blurring. I remember slipping on an ice patch; I remember Lansing holding me by the coat so I could not fall down or get free; I remember Bobby flying through the air to tackle Lansing and being kicked to the ground, I remember thinking that he was going to kill me for sure, that I was going to die, and that I would not be able to set any records in Albany. Perhaps the blows had begun to affect my sight. The last thing I remember seeing as if in some horrible dream was Ford step out from behind a tree and walk off with O'Shea back towards the house . . .

I am out of my body, ten feet above myself, watching myself struggle to free myself from Lansing. I am seeing everything that is happening with complete clarity. I feel very peaceful, not a shred of fear. As soon as I focus on something, I am there, with no discernible motion or passage of time. I do not go from here to there, nor from one second to the next. When I am aware, I am present, whatever I am aware of is in the process of happening.

I calmly give myself instructions from ten feet above me. "Walk slowly towards that tree. Don't run. Keep walking. You'll be all right. Stay calm and you'll be all right." Lansing loses his grip on my jacket for a split second and I fall down. I say to me, "Get up again. Just keep walking. Towards that tree. You'll be all right . . . "

I am above Tom. He has been able to grab the gun, and hits Sal on the side of the face with it, not hard enough to knock him out, but hard enough to stun him. He fires another shot into the air. Guido is clutching his arm, he runs towards the road. The same black four-door sedan is parked at the beginning of a dirt driveway. I hover one inch from the car window and peer in. Guido is trying to take his arm out of his coat sleeve so that he can tie a handkerchief around his bleeding forearm. Sal is running down the dirt path towards the car. He looks in a rage.

Bobby kicks Lansing in the back of the knee and his leg buckles. As he totters, Bobby kicks him in the groin. He doubles over. My face is covered in blood. With the same great calmness, the I above me watches myself sinking to the ground. I say to me again, "You'll be all right." Lansing is struggling to his feet. Bobby kicks him again. Tom is looking around wildly and calling my name, clutches his head and runs over to me. He grabs me as I begin to fall, repeating my name over and over.

I am hovering level with Tom's eyes and am aware of moving very slowly towards him, towards his face, to within an foot, an inch, a millimeter, and still closer, to the very edge of his skin. It offers no resistance and I keep going, inside him. But the pace dramatically changes. It is black all around me. I am moving at a tremendous speed, a kind of ultra-speed far beyond the speed of light because there is no matter to move, a velocity expanded beyond the confines of velocity, that cannot be measured as we measure it. I am travelling inside an incomprehensibly vast space towards a goal, a particular point, or meeting. I am not at all afraid or uncomfortable about travelling through such a vastness in such a manner. It seems normal, natural. I know that the sense of infinite vastness and trans-speed is necessary to the awareness.

As I approach this place, or state, a point of light grows brighter and brighter taking on form, that of a person, that of Tom. He is moving towards me at the same trans-velocity and from some vast distance just as I have been moving towards him. No sooner is his whole translucent body, or being, completely formed before me than I am aware that we are both moving slower and slower, still towards each other. The light that is around each of us seems to merge into one light. I feel a great joy around me, as if it were part of the spirit of place. We are still moving towards each other at an infinitesimal rate now. Tom is as joyous looking as I know I am. We move closer and closer towards each other, closer still, up to the edges of each other, as if we were one with the motion itself. A motion which does not have beginning or end and cannot keep us from joining into each other . . .

I open my eyes. I am lying huddled on the back seat of a moving car.

4. Only connect

Tom is driving, his jacket wrapped around me, a nest of familiar smells. Whose car is it? Where are we going? I try to raise myself to look out the window, but my head and arm hurt too much to manage even so simple an act as wiping the frosted glass. The car is warm. I lie back on the seat, dizzy and disoriented, jarred by the thump of tires over the pavement cracks. Bobby is sitting next to him, their voices an anxious counterpoint to the steady drone of the motor.

Bobby: "Where we going, man?"

Tom: "I don't know. I need time to think."

"We can't just keep driving around. What if those guys are after us already? They weren't fooling around you know."

"I know that."

"It looks pretty bleak out there. Where the fuck are we?"

"9W going north; almost at Cementon."

"Jesus Christ, Cementon. Like they're probably making

shoes for us already."

"Don't say things like that!"

"Lighten up will you. And fucking slow down. All we need's for us to get stopped for speeding. You only got a junior license don't you?"

"Okay, okay."

"What the fuck got into you? Jesus, stealing their car with their own gun. Luca ain't never going to forgive you until you're six feet under."

"I panicked, I guess. All I could think of was what if they came back for us. We'd be like sitting ducks out there."

"And me going along for the ride. I ought to have my head examined."

"You want out, I'll stop the car any time."

"Yeah sure, right here in the middle of nowhere. What time is it?"

"Ten to nine."

"More like nine going on midnight. I can't even see any lights on. And I thought Quebec was bad. Man, what a mess. What a fucking mess."

"Who asked you to get involved in the first place! Not to mention getting Danny involved."

Bobby had overheard bits and pieces of phone conversation between O'Shea and Luca but, as they had taken place on different occasions over several days, he had not put it all together in his mind until tonight. Luca had to make sure his men were on time or the plan wouldn't work . . . Lansing was bringing Tom . . . He had thought of a way to get Tom down to the sheds . . . Ford's dad would pay . . . They could do whatever they liked with Tom but not on O'Shea's land. When he saw O'Shea and Lansing easing Tom out the door, it had all clicked.

Tom said, "The dirty sons of bitches. If we ever get out of this I'm going to get even with the whole fucking bunch of them."

"Don't even think *if*! We got to get out of it even if we need the whole shitass army to do it. I mean did you see what was in them sheds? A fuckin' arsenal! I knew some heavy shit was going around there. But this."

"That fucking bastard traitor O'Shea."

"*And* Teddy. *And* Ford. Don't forget Ford. I seen him down there the whole time you know."

"Ford! You sure?"

"Course I'm sure. He was right down there the whole time hiding behind a bush just watching it all like he was getting off on it or something. He's a real pervert."

"Man. If Ford was down there . . . "

"That Teddy's a crazy son of a bitch. What's he got against Danny? I thought for sure he was going to kill him. He's a real psycho."

"Yeah, a sick motherfucker . . . "

Tom glanced back at me. With some effort I raised my left arm to look at my watch. I had held it in front of my face to protect myself from Lansing's blows. It was bruised and swollen, but I could move and put pressure on it, so I did not think it was broken, but the watch crystal was, its dial frozen at 7:57.

Bobby asked, "How much gas we got?"

"Half a tank."

"That's not going to get us to Canada."

Tom slows down for a junction. Bobby has found a map in the glove compartment. Route 23a would head us west into the Catskills: Palenville, Haines Falls, and Tannersville. If we continue north along this road a couple more miles we'll hit the Thruway entrance – Albany and the Northway into the Adirondacks and Canada, south to New York. Route 23 intersects there; east back across the Hudson, to the Berkshires, or downriver home to Madalin.

There is a hamburger joint at the crossroads. Bobby says we should risk the stop, get something to eat and drink, come up with a plan. That lawyer friend of his, the one who helped him when he was down and out in the city, he had a cabin back up the Kauterskill Creek. It was only another thirty or forty miles. He'd only been there once but he thought he could find it. He'd have to phone Ed first, to find out where the key was, and get the codes for the security system so we wouldn't have the cops down on us. It was set way back. You couldn't see any lights from the road. There was even a barn where we could hide the car. Nobody, but nobody, would find us until spring.

Tom found a dark place at the far end of the parking lot. Bobby would go in alone so he could keep the car running. If they had it, herbal tea with lots of honey for me, coffee for himself. He turned the ceiling light off so it would not go on when Bobby opened the door.

A teenage couple came out as Bobby went in, talking and laughing loudly. Their arms were so tightly wound each other around each other that they stumbled as they hurried through the rain. They crossed to an old wreck, drove off in a cloud of exhaust and noise. There were several trailer trucks, parked at the opposite end parallel to the road, but no police cars. Near us, two large metal trash containers which in warm weather would have smelled too badly for anyone to park there. No one had bothered to put any lights here. The racoons could raid the bins unseen.

I slid over the seat into the front.

"You okay?"

I shrugged. "I feel weird. How did I get in the car? You carry me?"

Tom shook his head. "You walked there. Don't you remember?"

"No."

"You said you were okay."

"I don't remember saying anything either."

"You remember any of it?"

"I remember Lansing . . . and falling down . . . " My voice choked up.

"You don't have to talk about it."

I touched my swollen lip, winced, "Everything hurts. My arm's all swollen. I can move it though."

He helped me off with my jacket, and turned on the overhead light for a second. The forearm from wrist to elbow was black and blue and swollen.

"Jesus, look at it. It looks really sore."

"What if I can't swim again, Tom?"

It *was* just bruised, it would be okay in a few days. "Just look at you," Tom added. "You're covered in blood! I blame myself Danny. Christ, I'm so sorry!"

There was a mirror on the reverse side of the passenger's visor. I was deathly pale, there was a cut above my eyebrow, the right corner of my lower lip twice its normal size; a raw wound on my cheek; the front of my shirt and jacket were covered in dried blood. My face had a haunted expression, as when drops distend the retina. He helped me back into my jacket.

Was I sure I was okay? Maybe we could find a doctor somewhere nearby. He didn't know Lansing was going to go crazy like that. He'd looked around everywhere for me but Lansing had been blocking his view. When he had seen what was happening he'd rushed over and knocked Lansing out of the way; Bobby had kicked him in the groin. He shouldn't have agreed to let me come tonight. He blamed himself. It was all his fault.

I found myself in the ironic, if difficult position of reassuring him. If Tom lost control, all would be lost. It helped calm me down.

"Everything'll be all right, Tom. You'll see. It'll all work out. I don't blame you . . . I wouldn't have missed it for the world."

I glanced out the window, wondering if Bobby was on his way back to the car, and changed the subject. Where were we going? What were we going to do now? I was not sure about going to this Ed's cabin. Someone had told me once that the Catskills were Mafia country. They kidnapped young girls.

Tom said that Bobby had also mentioned some boy scout camp up in the Adirondacks, but I had not overheard that. What did I think about going there? Some of his people were occupying it as part of a lawsuit to get the land back. Ed was their lawyer, which is how Bobby met him. It was four or five hours drive but if we were careful we could make it. Or we could ditch the car in Albany and take the first bus or train out. Go west. Maybe Berkeley or Big Sur. Rough it in the Pacific Northwest. Find us a cabin. Or build one. He had some money on him and he could ask his grandfather or father to wire him funds in San Francisco. We could make it work. We really could. The important thing was to stick together. We could even dump the car right here. One of those truckers was bound to be going upstate and would give us a ride. Make Buffalo tonight, stay in the Y, in a few days be wading in the Pacific. If I wasn't up to it, we'd find a motel somewhere. Get some rest until I felt better. He'd take care of me. It would all be okay.

The door of the restaurant was brightly lit by a large overhead lamp. Bobby came out, and paused to pull up his collar. He was carrying our food and drinks in a shallow cardboard box. I only had a few seconds, I thought.

It is hard for me to judge my state of mind from this safe distance, but I must surely have been in shock from the beating and loss of blood, the grass, hash and wine. I had played with my life, without thinking, without appreciating it.

The if's lined themselves up to infinity – if Tom had not panicked; if it had been a normal party; if I was with Richie, or home watching television, or in bed with Jacqueline or that made-up chick I had used as an excuse with Mickey; if I had not had that second joint, or that glass of wine; if I had never met Tom.

I glanced over, and saw Bobby huddle and begin his fifty-yard dash to the car. The impossibilities prevented me from seeing the possibilities. The final if, saving me from the endless others. If I told Tom what I wanted to do before Bobby reached the car then everything would be all right and it would be the right thing to do. It was another of my magic games, perhaps it was the last. I really believed it.

I turned to him and said, "I can't face things right now, Tom. I mean, I feel weird and I just can't deal with any of it. Let's go to your house. Please, let's just go to your house."

"Jesus, Danny, that'd be the first place they'd look for us. And what about the car? I mean they'd see it parked in my drive big as life."

"We can ditch the car in Lansing's back yard. They'd never think of looking there Tom. Not with all them other cars. We don't have to put any lights on . . . We'd be okay."

Bobby was almost at the door. If Tom did not say yes before he opened the door all was lost. I was on the verge of hysteria.

"Please Tom! Please. Let's just go to your house. I can't deal with any of this. I can't."

He said simply, "Okay Danny. We can go to my house.

We can go home."

Bobby looked in the front window and when he saw me sitting there he automatically got in back. He was all excited. Ed had said that we could stay in the cabin. It was a great place. We'd love it.

When Tom told him what we had decided he looked disgusted. He was certainly not going to go down into Madalin with us. Ed was driving up next weekend, and he would go north to the camp with him. If it worked out he might stay there for the winter, or go back to the city with Ed. Tom said he could come with us, but Bobby said he'd be all right. He walked back across the lot to the restaurant and we waited until we saw him come out with one of the drivers. As he was stepping up into the rig he turned and waved. We would not see each other again for thirty years.

I am standing at Tom's bedroom window looking out through the trees at our house. It is about four a.m. and I have not returned home yet. Tom is sleeping peacefully. He closes his door and his mother doesn't look in on him, so she doesn't know I'm there. I'm wrapped in a blanket, kicked off by one of us onto the floor. My mind is racing, hyperactive, restless, disturbed, words at the tip of my tongue, thoughts too disturbing to allow, perhaps a delayed reaction, perhaps the aftermath of shock, a flock of chaotic feelings beating against the wall of mind.

It had started as we were driving over the bridge to our side of the river, on the final leg to Madalin. I had been watching the lights of Olana, Frederick Church's Moorish mansion, loom towards us from a hilltop opposite, visited several times with various school classes, signalling a return to my territory, to familiar ground again. Tom had his arm around me but we were not saying much. As we reached the center of the bridge I glanced downriver. The lights of a freighter, parked or plying its way, were visible, but not the lights of Madalin, still a few miles off.

I said, "We're going full circle."

Indeed, from the moment we had left, to the time that we would be back again, we'd have gone full circle. But we had not yet completed it.

He nodded.

I added, "I have to phone home."

"You can call from my house. It isn't even ten yet."

I shook my head and said, "There's a phone booth at the crossroads in Manorton. I can call from there."

He looked puzzled but did not ask me why and made the turn into Manorton. The phone booth was at the corner of North Road, the end of Tom's road. Why did I want to call from there?

Father answered on the third or fourth ring.

I tried to sound buoyant, "Hi. We're having car trouble. I'm not going to get home on time."

"Where are you? I'll come pick you up."

"I think I should help out here. Besides we'll probably get it going again before you could even get here."

"How far are you? I don't mind going out."

"Oh I don't know. Miles. It's better if I stick around and help."

"Well, if that's what you want. How late do you think you'll be?"

"I don't know. I'll phone again if it's going to be much later."

"You okay? Your voice sounds strange."

"It must be the connection . . . I got to go. I don't have any more change."

"Call me in half an hour if you're still stuck and then I *will* come and get you. Where did you say you were?"

But I hung up without answering.

Lansing's house was five hundred yards or so north of Tom's. We parked the car without incident, if not without fear, a hundred feet or so past the house behind a large shed among several car wrecks and body parts, fenders, doors, bumpers. Large stacks of used tires further concealed it. We scurried across the street and ducked through the woods to Tom's back door.

My feet are cold. I turn from the window. Had it been the thought or threat of completing the circle that set my mind racing? His mother turns the heat down before she goes to bed. I put on Tom's socks.

He helped me undress and ran a bath for me, careful when he slipped my undershirt over my bruised arm; motherly when he helped me step into the steaming water. Would I be all right alone for a few minutes? There were some things he wanted to do. My shirt and jacket were covered with blood. He'd wash and dry them for me; they'd be done before his mother returned from work. He'd make me some more herbal tea, the real thing this time. Was the water too hot? Was I really okay? His solicitude was apologetic but affectionate.

I settled into the water. There was a clothes line above my head with a few wooden pins clinging to it, but no negatives. He had built a wide shelf over the toilet on which he stored his developing chemicals in plastic bottles. A piece of plywood, hidden behind the door, could be placed over the sink as a work bench. I had helped him two or three times. I knew where everything was. It all oriented me, like points on a compass. He had not pulled the black-out shade, nor turned on any lights. I heard the washing machine start, heard him rummaging around the kitchen, heard him talking to someone on the phone. I slid my head beneath the water.

He tucked me in bed from my bath; I handed him the white Turkish towel from beneath the covers, suddenly shy. He closed his bedroom door carefully, pushing on it firmly until he heard it click shut. He had not turned on any lights. Did I want the shade up? I did, I said. There was enough light to watch every move of his nightly ritual. He lined up the gold wrist watch, the gold chain, the assortment of wrist bands side by side on the dresser top. Was he afraid his native messiness would prevent him from finding them in the morning? He wore no rings.

He sat on a straight back chair two feet opposite me to remove his socks, but stood to remove his shirt; seized it at the bottom and peeled it off with one easy lift. He reached behind his head to unfasten the band. He tilted his head back and shook his hair loose, like some wild animal shaking off water. The gesture aroused me.

He faced me, but did not look at me. Was I already an extension of him? His old faded jeans had buttons. He undid them with great concentration, balanced on each leg to remove them, heaved them onto the same chair. His body was not what it seemed when he was clothed, but more refined, lithe. I liked knowing that about it. It made it more mine. His legs and thighs had a sheen of reddish gold hair. He wore white boxer shorts, distended with a large erection. He removed them quickly. His cock leapt up like some exuberant acrobat proud from a stunt, a long curved, dancing verticality, eager.

He pulled the cover open to slide in next to me. Earlier he had bandaged my right arm, laying it tenderly on a pillow like an infant in a manger. My head rested in the crook of his arm. He whispered in my ear. How sorry he was. How it would never happen again. How things would be different now. He knew they would. He promised. He was so sorry. His warm breath seeped into me. He smelled faintly of freshly ground coffee.

Should I dress and go home? Should I crawl back into the sleeping-bag, drape myself in his arm and leg? We had never spent a whole night together. Thinking about him had aroused me. We could spend the night together. We could spend the next night together; and the next. I return to the window, restless, wide awake.

Is it my nervous energy that awakens him? My thoughts? The missing place beside him growing cool? He sits up.

"Danny? You there?" he whispers.

"I'm over here, by the window."

"You okay?"

"I couldn't sleep. My mind's going a mile a minute."

"You still upset?"

"Sort of . . . "

"Why don't you come back to bed? The room's kind of cold. We can talk about it?"

"I don't know . . . "

"You don't have to. Not until you're ready. It's okay . . . "

He struggles out of bed now. He is naked. He comes over and puts his arms around me. Am I hungry? Do I want something to drink? He could get us something without waking his mother up. How long have I been standing there? Why didn't I wake him up? Am I worried about going home? I take his hand to hold him there. I still feel shaky. Do I have to go home? I don't know if I can face it yet.

"You been through a lot . . . Maybe I shouldn't talk about it."

I had thought that I was going to die. I had thought it was the end but I had not been afraid. I had felt peaceful and calm, floating out there alone, above everything, but I had not been afraid. Was that so wrong? Everybody said you had to be afraid. But I was even glad. Was this the thing I'd been holding back? I felt glad she died when she did, she was in so much pain. I wanted her to die and I was glad. Was that so wrong?

I begin to cry. I turn around and put my arms around him.

"I love you Tom. I love you."

I am crying uncontrollably now.

"It's okay, Danny. It's okay. I love you too. I'll always love you. I always will."

5. MEETING WITH FORD

In those few remaining days of December two more events could be said to complete the cycle begun with my first glimpse of Tom, one a closing, the other an opening, of sorts.

Tom walked me home that night, some time before dawn. Father was asleep on the sofa; the television on, the pattern sputtering white noise. I went up to bed without awakening him. He looked in on me sometime in the early morning, but I pretended to be asleep. When, at noon, I wandered downstairs for breakfast, careful to wear a long-sleeve shirt over my bandaged arm, I was moody and defensive. He tried to question me about the night before. Why did I have a cut above my eye? What time did I get home? Where was I anyway? But I refused to break a sullen, defiant silence. When he pressed me, I stormed out of the room. He told Clare on the telephone that if I thought I could get away with staying out until all hours of the night making him half sick with worry when I wasn't even fourteen yet, I had another guess coming. If I was angry he was feeling angrier; hurt, and betrayed. If he had idealized me, or my innocence, held me on the proverbial pedestal, I had brought myself crashing down.

I woke up anxious about Tom. I had to see him, or at least be reassured by his voice. What if they had ambushed him on the way home after he had left me? What if nothing had been real – those things that had happened, those things we said? What if he didn't feel the same way today – and never had? I did not so much doubt Tom, or want his reassurance, as the reassurance of Reality. Everything could change in a flash, time alter anything on a whim.

I waited until Father was safely ensconced in his study before phoning. He picked up the receiver on the first ring.

"I was just about to call you. You okay?"

"Yes."

"Your arm and shit?"

"It feels better. The swelling's gone down a bit."

"You free to talk?"

"Not really."

"Your brother?"

"Not home."

"Father?"

"Study."

"Did he say anything about last night?"

"What do you think. Don't ask."

"That bad?"

"Worse. Can you come over? We could study together in the kitchen."

He paused. "Is that such a good idea?"

"I don't care if it is or not!" My voice deflated. "So, is that a no?"

"No. It wasn't a no. I'm just not sure the timing is right."

"I don't care! I want to see you. I meant what I said last night."

"I did too. It's just . . . "

"Just what?"

"There's some things I should take care of today. You know . . . "

I didn't want him to talk about it, didn't want to hear. He promised to be at my house by four.

"Bring your homework. Stay for dinner. I'll ask Dad."

Before he could voice another, impending hesitation, I shouted as loud as I could, "Dad! Tom's coming over to do his homework! Can he stay for dinner?"

A pause . . . A simple, "Yes!"

I settled unwittingly that day on the strategy of trusting Tom to sort out the mess for us, while staying out of it completely myself. But a flotsam and jetsam of information floated by me, like the debris I watched from the rocks, caught in the Hudson's tidal flow. I noted most of it in my diary, belying my diffidence.

Before coming over that afternoon, Tom sneaked back through the woods to see if Luca's car was still in Lansing's yard; it was not. Some days later, still before Christmas, Richie told me that Lansing had 'taken off for Florida'. Although it falls out of the chronology of this story, months later in September I pasted in my journal a newspaper article reporting Lansing's arrest in Miami on armed robbery charges, and another article, February the following year, reporting his conviction and jail sentence. I also noted Tom's remark – meant as a reassurance? – that he had 'the low-down on O'Shea, witnesses and all', about some under-age girl. Perhaps it was Tara. Bobby had phoned him from the cabin. He'd 'seen and heard enough around there over the months to fry the whole lot of them.' From an entry dated December 20th, and from the meeting with Ford soon afterwards, I think I can deduce that Ford's father paid off Luca. What Tom said exactly was 'he's getting his pay-off like he wanted so he won't give a shit about small fry like us.' So, I wonder if everything might have been resolved sooner, had the holiday not intervened. Tom was at his grandfather's for Christmas, and it was not until Saturday, the 28th, that the lunch with Ford took place, at a colonial inn in a town near Madalin. This I did record in my diary in some detail. Tom did not just want me to be there, he said I 'had to be there'.

We arrived on time precisely at one and gave our names at the reception desk. The inn had been opened in 1770 as a coach stop on the land route between New York and Albany, between the port and the fur trade of the Mohawk Valley. The building had undergone various renovations and additions, but it still retained a great deal of the simple elegance of the best of colonial structures. It had always been an inn, the oldest continuous inn in the state.

Ford was waiting for us by the reception desk, elegantly dressed in a white turtleneck cashmere sweater and crushed gray corduroys. Tom's jeans were torn at the knee, mine were the old paint-stained ones. The restaurant was on the ground floor; the guest rooms were above. We went together to the back where there were booths. A man was already seated as we approached, a large menu hiding his face. Tom and I slid into the same side, Ford and the man opposite. He lowered the menu, but did not acknowledge us even with a nod. He was heavy-set, wore a dark gray suit and blue tie, had a carefully trimmed beard and large horn-rimmed glasses. Ford said simply that this was his father's lawyer, without giving us his name. He nodded, but not at us, and frowned. The waitress came. The man said Tom and I could order whatever we wanted, he would pay the bill. They each ordered a drink.

The lawyer immediately asked Tom to hand over the envelope but Tom said he wanted to see the letter of guarantee first. No letter, no envelope, the same envelope that had been wrestled and fought over that terrible night. The man pulled up a black briefcase from off the seat next to him, took a parcel wrapped in brown grocery paper from it, and passed it to Tom.

A piece of brown cord held it. Tom had trouble undoing the knots. Ford was tense; the lawyer impatient. Tom opened it, and did a visible double-take. He slid it across the table to me. It was stuffed with used hundred dollar bills.

Staring at us over the top of his glasses, the lawyer said that 'the Senator' was unwilling to give Tom a letter. He just wouldn't do that. He certainly wanted the whole thing to end right here and now, cleanly, with no loose ends, but he just wasn't willing to put anything in writing. The Senator also wanted his word that everything was here. He glanced at me, and said this went for me as well.

If he was assuming that I knew all the circumstances, he

was wrong. I did not even know Ford's real name, and this was certainly the first time I had heard that his father was a senator. I kept silent.

The lawyer continued that Ford's father was offering the money as a show of good faith, and because, "you've been put to a lot of trouble by . . . him." He wanted him to have it for his college fund. It was the senator's way "of reassuring you that the whole matter will stop here, and that the other parties have been – well – called off you might say. If you're willing to cooperate."

Tom remained cool, he had not even counted the money. "What guarantee do I or Danny have that it'll stop once I hand over the negatives? The Senator's friends might have different ideas."

"If he had wanted to do it another way, you, well, wouldn't be here now, would you? That's about all the guarantee you need. Is it a deal or not?"

Tom flicked through the bills. "How much is here?"

The lawyer looked angry. "Does it matter?"

"It might."

Tom told me later that he had asked because he was curious how much Ford's father thought Ford was worth, or at least Ford's reputation. If it had been a paltry amount he might not have believed the lawyer.

The man bit his lip, visibly struggling with his anger. He finally shrugged and said, Five thousand."

I tried to keep my adolescent cool, hide my utter astonishment. To a thirteen-year-old boy, in the late sixties, that was an extraordinary fortune.

Tom reached into his coat, which he had put on the seat between us, pulled the envelope out of the inside pocket but did not hand it over. He put his hand on top of it.

"The money's fine but I want one more thing first. From you, Ford . . . Everybody in the whole state, except Danny here, thinks I robbed the liquor store blind that night but you know what really happened, don't you? So I want Danny to hear it from your own mouth. No story, no negatives."

Ford looked panic-stricken. He glanced sideways at the

lawyer, who shrugged. "I'm not going to do that," he whined.

The lawyer turned angrily towards him. "Jesus Christ, just tell him what he wants to know. You don't think I'm going to go back to your father and tell him you blew the whole thing because of your stinking vanity!"

Ford nearly choked on his words, but he did tell us. Lansing had put him up to it. Tom was 'horning in on his territory', selling dope to some of Lansing's customers. He wouldn't turn over his sources to him either, so Lansing figured if he took Tom out of circulation he'd be 'protecting his business interests', so he set it up to make the robbery look like Tom did it and helped spread the rumor himself. Lansing even went out and bought a wool jacket like Tom's. Made Ford wear it the night of the break-in. Ford had told Lansing the police would know easy it wasn't Tom's jacket as soon as they did tests but Lansing said it didn't matter cause you were the outsider and everybody'd blame you anyway. He could also go to Tom afterwards and tell him he'd better take over things for him awhile, until the heat was off his. Which he did, and he guessed it worked, because 'Lansing didn't say no more about it' after that. He added, "Lansing did it to get even. Sort of show you who was boss. So you'd cooperate."

Tom wondered why Ford went along with it? What had he gotten out of it?

"The school concession. Lansing said I could do it for him. He said he would cancel you if he had to . . . " He glanced fearfully at the lawyer, and added, defensively, his voice rising, "He said he was going to tell you himself who did it, so's you know it was a warning not to fool with them ."

"He did too."

"What? . . . Then why? . . . "

The lawyer put his hand on Ford's arm and said to Tom, "Okay, so you got your story. The envelope."

Tom slid it over to him. He rifled through the contact sheets quickly, whistled.

"Jesus Christ, Ford! Wait 'til your father sees these. He's going to send your ass to military school for sure after he sees these." He put a white silk scarf around his neck. "Come on.

Let's get out of here. You two can stay and finish. I'll take care of the bill out at the desk."

We had ordered meals, but they hadn't yet arrived. As they were sliding out of the booth Ford turned a look of pure pouting malice on Tom and me and I wondered how anyone could have thought that he was even vaguely handsome, and whether we might not hear more from him in the future.

After they had gone I slid into the seat opposite. Lowering my voice, I immediately asked him why he'd made Ford tell about the robbery. "Man, you had him sweating."

"Yeah. He deserved it too. Setting me up like that."

"I can't believe you even asked. How come?"

"I figured I owed it to you, Danny."

"How – owed it to me?"

"After all I put you through. How can you even ask? It was the least I could do. So you wouldn't have any doubts."

"I always knew you didn't do it. I didn't have any doubts. I told you that a million times. You didn't have to prove it."

"The way I figure it is, it was one of the few times you could get certainty about something. So why not? I mean the little son of a bitch deserved it. Man did you see his face? That was worth more than the money!" He lowered his voice, "Jesus. Can you believe it? Five thousand dollars. Sitting right here on the fucking table. What are we going to do with it?"

"What do you mean we?" I laughed.

"Half of it's yours."

I started to object, but he interrupted. He had a brilliant idea. We would go on a trip together that summer. The trip of a lifetime. Unless we were grounded for life and his mother and my father never let us do anything again. With that much we could go anywhere we wanted. I thought he would say, to the West Coast, to the mountains, but he said, "We can spend the whole summer in Europe with this much."

"We could, couldn't we . . . " We could go to Italy and stay with my aunt and uncle. Spend the whole summer there. Swim the whole day. Lay around. Eat stuff right off the trees. My father would let me do that. I'm sure he would . . . "We could have this absofuckinglootly incredible adventure like you never

216

seen before!" I desperately wanted to do it, but a doubt crept in and I added, "How we possibly going to get them to let us do it together, let alone explain where we got the money?"

"Hey, cross those bridges when we come to them . . ."

If we wanted to do it, we'd find a way. Maybe he could get his father to send him another thousand. No wait. He had a better idea. His grandfather would cover for him. He'd been going on for a couple of years about his seeing Paris.

I said, "Maybe we can earn enough to tell people we made it all ourselves, then the rest would be gravy."

If I saved the Christmas money I had just received, and if we both got part-time jobs, even if I had no idea when I could fit it into my training schedule, especially with the match coming up in January, we could probably get the basic expenses together by June. No one would have to know how much we really had. We didn't have to tell anyone either. I already had three hundred from Christmas and that was not even counting what I was going to get for my birthday in January. We could go to Paris first. My father would love that. I could tell him I wanted to get a head start on my French before high school. He'd let me do it. I just knew he would. Five thousand would buy us this incredible trip. We'd have to keep it quiet for awhile though. If we asked them now, no way they would give us permission, but a few months down the line, who knew?

And I asked him, "Would you really do it?"

He nodded, and blushed. "A proper honeymoon, hey Danny . . . "

"You mean not just a one-night stand shacked up in some cheap motel. We nearly did you know."

He laughed. "I know."

As we were getting up to leave the restaurant I asked him if he thought the whole mess was over. With Luca and everybody? We were in a public space, but he put his arm around me.

"Yeah Danny, it's over. And what's over is over."

6. DINNER WITH TOM

I also recorded in my diary that Father invited Tom for a 'Christmas dinner' a couple of evenings later, on Monday the 30th. Father suggested this particular evening himself. I also noted that the three of us were alone. Tom's mother was on the night shift until the first of the year, but by then she was also seeing a doctor from the hospital. Charlie had a steady girlfriend and was spending all his free time at her house. He did not like Tom very much, and was to create a lot of trouble in our relationship several months later. Even if he was not at Jennifer's I think he would have made some excuse not to be home. As it was Father's idea and choice of evenings, and Clare was not there either, I can only assume that Father wanted it this way.

Tom arrived at the front door sporting a new sheepskin coat. I was standing at the opposite end of the hall when Father opened the front door. The porch light shone down full on him, accenting his smooth, broad forehead and oriental cheekbones, his aquiline nose, his skin reddened from the cold. He wore the same deerskin vest, the same white shirt with ruffled sleeves, that he had on the night of the school party, when, emerging up the circular staircase of the school library to where I was telling fortunes in the loft, he appeared to be, then and now, someone stepping out of time to find me. The long, tied-back, glistening hair, the eighteenth-century style clothes I had come to learn were not so much affectations as projections of an internal image, generated perhaps from some colonial, or classical, origin – Pathfinder or Deerslayer – or even from some psychic alluvial layer still lower, *erastes* to my *eromenos* reborn. We looked shabby by comparison. Father's old sweater was spotted with pinhole burns from burning bits of pipe tobacco raining from the bowl; my jeans were the ragged ones blotched with the white paint used to redecorate the bathroom the previous summer. The knee showed through.

Father had three Chagall lithographs and two superb Picasso etchings on the living-room walls, which he had bought in

Paris in the 1950s for even then substantial sums. They would prove to be worth a tidy fortune by the time Charlie and I inherited them, along with the book collection. Tom impressed Father by knowing what they were. His grandfather, he explained, had a Picasso print portfolio. But Chagall?

We ate somewhat formally in the dining room. I was afraid that Father had only asked him over as an excuse to discuss all that had happened, but that turned out not to be true. The conversation panned between them.

Father: "You were living with your grandfather before moving here?"

Tom: "Only for the last six months. Before that we had an apartment in town. He had a heart operation and my mother took a leave of absence from her job to take care of him. He's okay now though."

Father: "To tell you the truth I didn't know his work all that well until recently, but I looked up a couple of monographs about him and I like it a lot. There's even a couple of paintings of you, at least I think they're of you."

"He did six or seven of me when I was ten or so. Not counting drawings and watercolors. During the summer mostly. On the beach and stuff."

I interjected, "There's one in his living room."

"I'd like to see it."

"Sure. Come over any time you like."

"Danny says you made some fine drawings yourself."

Tom shrugged. "They're okay."

"What do you mean okay! They're great. You should see them. Four-feet square hands and feet. And eyes. He's even got them pinned up on the ceiling of his bedroom."

"Do you want to be a painter or photographer? I heard you were serious about photography."

"A photographer I think."

"He's got this great idea for a book."

"It's okay. I mean. I haven't worked it out or anything."

He had told me about his book project several weeks before. *True Teen* . "Not the phoney, sentimental crap you see around but kids shooting up and shit like that." I had seen some of the images; a teenage boy hustler lingering on a Times Square street corner, tough-guy cigarette dangling from the corner of his mouth; a frightening shot of an emaciated, strung-out girl inserting a needle into her strapped forearm. He wanted to make 'an anti-high school yearbook'. Everything that was left out of people's lives. Yearbooks were such 'sentimental crap. Rose-colored glasses.' The real stuff was out there under everyone's noses but people just didn't want to see it.

He added, "I showed some of the shots to Grandfather but he didn't like it that much. He says my stuff's too violent for him. He's a romantic." He glanced at me before adding that he had come up with another idea just for his grandfather, while he was there for the holiday. A book about Paris. An American in Real Paris. Not lovers on bridges and kids playing in the Tuileries. More the new spirit which was barricades and student riots. Except he had to go there first.

Father observed that both books were really the same idea; Paris was just something else that Americans romanticized. Perhaps he did so himself. Tom's instincts might be right. Paris was certainly not the romantic city of Hemingway and Fitzgerald anymore. If it had ever been. It had changed radically since he had lived there in the late forties. French life had been more accessible, more visible. There had been more street life, which was why it had been so popular with the documentary photographers in the fifties. People seemed to have moved inside. Whole areas of the city were being torn down, but not to make it a better place for people; it was getting less, not more liveable.

"It's a kind of decadence I suppose," Father added.

Tom hesitated. "I don't just mean Paris . . . " His brow furrowed. He was making it up as he went along. "It's Berkeley, Columbia, Paris. Like all of history is . . . not exactly different . . . but *erupting*. All of a sudden there's this anger coming out. It's like . . . a world eruption. I don't know how you photograph that though."

Father said, "You have to find out why first."

"People are afraid. That's what I think."

"Why?"

"They might not survive. Like it's all about . . . Big S . . .

Survival . . . Anyway I'm trying to save up money so I can go there this summer and see for myself."

"Your grandfather lived in Paris immediately after the war, didn't he? I remember reading it somewhere. So did I, but a little later. That's how I met Danny's mother. We were both exchange students. We were seeing each other, and one night on the Pont Neuf we fell in love. It sounds a little silly to say it that way, but that's really the way it happened. It was something you were supposed to do in Paris in those days. Buy warm chestnuts. Walk in the rain. Fall in love on the Pont Neuf. I've been back there a lot over the years, because of my research and yes, well, it has changed a lot over twenty years. It seems more corrupt. Indochina, then the Algerian war corrupted the French. In and out of government. Like Vietnam is doing here I suppose. The French have this stubborn, authoritarian, puritanical, violent streak which nobody is supposed to speak about. God knows what it will be like in another ten years. You should definitely see it before any more of it is lost. While there's still some of the old atmosphere and glamour left. The Paris spirit Americans loved seems to be dying. Everywhere. I guess, in your terms, not surviving."

Tom shook his head. It was not just atmosphere he was talking about. "Nobody knows anymore whether *anyone* will survive." He suddenly shrugged, less from indifference, than from an inability to take the thought further. He added, "Grandfather said he might give me some of the fare . . . " He laughed, "If I shape up."

I added, for good measure, "Shaping up to see Paris. Life could be worse. I'd be jealous."

Father thought that if Tom did get to Paris he should think about going to Italy too. Take the Grand Tour like in the old days. Every young gentleman had to do it to be properly educated in the world. He added, "Danny's mother's side of the family lives in Sicily you know, but probably he told you all about it. We can give you their address if you think you'll get that far south." He added suddenly, "Danny's mother liked to draw. She used to sit in the Luxembourg Gardens for hours with a sketch book on her lap, even though she was there to study language. I tried to encourage her, but she thought of herself as an amateur. It was common for young women in the nineteenth century to do amateur drawings, especially if you were English and upper class, but not the Italian-American daughter of an immigrant in the 1940s. She was rather good too, but her poetry was better."

Tom said to me, "You didn't tell me your mother drew and wrote poetry."

I hadn't, but I insisted I had.

Father pushed his chair back, and reached over to take up the dirty plates. "Drawings, photographs, book projects. It sounds like there's a lot to see and talk about when I come over to your house. How about tomorrow at ten?"

Tom was taken aback. "Well . . . Yeah . . . I guess."

Father laughed, "Don't worry. I don't bite."

"Oh I didn't mean that. It's just that there won't be time to make any prints and you'll have to look at contact sheets."

"That'd be okay."

I objected that I would be at Jefferson for training at ten, and why couldn't they wait until late afternoon. For good measure, I said to Tom, "He's ruthless you know. You should hear what he says about my English papers. Cuts them to pieces."

Father laughed. "Forewarned is forearmed I suppose. I *am* a harsh critic. Especially when it comes to art and literature. You don't have to go around telling everyone though, Danny."

"You can't be worse than my grandfather."

Father stood up. "It's settled then? Tomorrow at ten."

Tom said he would have things out for him when he arrived.

"Good. Now, if you guys will clear the table we can have some dessert."

We carried the plates into the kitchen.

I walked Tom home that evening, but did not linger at his house, though he would have been alone and Father might have allowed it. I hurried back home, curious to find out myself what Father had to say about the evening. He was standing at the sink doing the dishes when I entered. I hung up my jacket, and took up a towel to dry.

"Tom's pretty excited about your going there tomorrow. He showed me some of the photographs he wants to put in his book. They're really good."

Father nodded. "The anti-yearbook. I'm looking forward to seeing them."

The house was quiet. I had left the back light on. From the window over the sink I could see the bird feeder Father had planted in the lawn atop a two-by-four, looking pallid and desolate. We tried to feed the birds all year round, chickadees and nuthatch, and in spring extraordinary masses of yellow finch, and bluebirds. The switch was next to the back door. I turned it off. Father was drying his hands.

"An awful lot has happened to you recently." It was not a question. I shrugged. "You haven't said much about it." I did not answer. "No more bad dreams?"

"No."

"I'd like to know what happened. From you. Hear it first from you instead of someone else. When you're ready to tell me."

"Okay."

"You've been so quiet lately, a bit pale. Clare says I should leave you alone, that you'll talk about it in your own good time. I hope you feel you can?"

I shrugged, not really able to say anything.

"You know, when you didn't come home that night, all I could think of was losing you." He stopped himself, tried to sound brighter. "Clare's been sticking up for you. I told her she should say some of the things to you herself."

"I know." I suddenly realized what I had given away, and added, quickly, "I mean I overheard you . . . once."

He interrupted, "It's all right. Don't be so defensive. I know you were listening. Like always."

"You knew?"

"Of course, I've always known. You've been sitting on that third step for years. The Listening Post I call it. We'll have to put a memorial plague on it. Danny the Snoop eavesdropped here."

"You mean the whole time you knew and you never said?"

He nodded. "I don't know about the whole time, but at least since you were four."

"But I heard everything."

"I suppose you did."

"How come you never said anything?"

He shrugged. "I liked it."

"That's weird. Why did you like it?"

"It's not really so weird. It was your way of being in the family. After all, so long as you were sneaking down to that step you were a part of things, weren't you? You were even doing it a few days ago – listening to Clare and me talk about you! I guess it was, well – comforting. I thought maybe things wouldn't turn out too badly around here."

Things had happened to me. They were the way they were. I was not sure they could be called good or bad. I said, "I still think it's weird. Like officially I'm not supposed to know something but unofficially it's okay?"

Father laughed. "It's part of being a child. Finding out all those things children aren't supposed to know but find out anyway. When you were listening the last time – I almost hate to say this – I didn't feel comfortable about it anymore. I wanted to go into the hall and tell you to come down. But then I thought maybe it still wasn't the right moment. I was still too angry. When you were five, or even twelve, it was – well – a game, you on the stair. But maybe we have to go further now . . . I don't know . . . I want there to be something between us in the future."

To tell the truth, I was feeling defensive. I said angrily, "You think I need a shrink. I'm not crazy. I don't need no shrink."

I threw down the dish towel, but before I could say anything else, or walk away, he put his hands on my shoulders.

"This conversation is not about blame." He bent his head to try to see in my eyes but I kept twisting this way and that to avoid his gaze.

"Look at me, will you. You're all closed up about things. I don't know what happened that night. I'm not even sure I want, or have, to know. I do know though that you're not about to stop your friendship with Tom. Well, are you?" I tried to break away, but he held his grip and said, " No. Don't walk away. Not this time. We've got to start somewhere. This Tom, he's like a wild animal. He hasn't got any discipline at all. I don't even know if I can trust him. But we both know he's not about to vanish into thin air. Well is he? It doesn't mean that you have to shut down, or that we have to grow apart. I don't want that to happen."

"I know you never liked him. No one did. No one *does.*"

"That's not true. It was never a question of liking or disliking. It's just that he's, well, a law unto himself. God only knows what will come of him. And you, if you keep hanging out with him. Why won't you look at me? What are you afraid of?"

"I'm not afraid. But you hate him. Why won't you just admit it? You hate his guts. Just like Charlie does. You're no different. You're just like all the rest."

Father looked shocked. "I don't hate him. I'm angry with him . . . and you . . . but that's a far cry from hating him. I'm angry with him because he *is* talented and wasting it on drugs and bloody stupid adolescent rebellion. His mother must feel the same way, and God alone knows what his grandfather thinks. But no, I don't hate him."

I shook his hands off my shoulders, and turned away, but did not walk away, filled with rage, conflict, and remorse.

"No one ever gave him a chance. Not even you. Right from the start. Just because he wasn't born in this fucking hole in the ground! Like accusing him of robbing that fucking old zombie's liquor store when I know for a fact he didn't do it. I even know who did it. Not even Richie trusted him."

"Is that why you dumped Richie? And all your friends for that matter?"

"That's not fair. I didn't dump no one. I'm not like that! See, you don't know me at all. I see Richie every day at school. I eat every fucking lunch with him! And I drive to practise with Mickey don't I? That's just like you. You're always turning things around. It's just what I've been saying. Just look what you're doing. Blaming Tom for things that aren't even happening!"

"Richie was coming here every day. I haven't seen him for weeks."

"It's just because he's got such a fucking big mouth and I couldn't trust him not to go around blabbing everything."

"About what? Why are you hiding everything? You mean about Tom, don't you? Why not say it?"

"What do you have against him? What!"

"He doesn't have any boundaries and he doesn't want you to have any boundaries. I'm afraid of what he's doing to you. You're the kind of person who needs boundaries. Just look at you for Christ's sake. I've never seen anyone with your discipline. You're only – I should say almost – fourteen and you live by a schedule! I don't even have to wake you up and get you out of bed to make sure you leave the house on time for school or your training. You have all this motivation and discipline. God alone knows your brother doesn't. And he'll have to have some, at least, if he ever wants to be a lawyer. Jesus Danny. It's just the three of us and you and Charlie are already on the outs!"

Father rarely used profanity. I said, "I suppose you're going to blame that on Tom too. He hates Tom. He hates everything I do. He's jealous all the time."

"I'm just trying to hold this family together and if that means having Tom around then your brother will have to learn to live with it."

"I don't believe you. That's what Clare told you to think and feel, but that's not what you think!"

He became quite angry, "Yes, that *is* what I think!"

He turned away from me. Neither of us spoke for awhile, and then for the second time in just a few minutes he pulled himself together, and summoned up the energy. He came over to me again, and again put his hands on my shoulders. I give him credit for not giving up. He shook me a bit, and bent his head again to catch my eyes.

"Please look at me Dan . . . I'm not going to say this again. You can bring Tom here every day for dinner if you like. Do you understand?"

I mumbled, "He doesn't want to come every day."

"You're still not listening to what I'm saying."

I was even more confused, and mumbled, "What then? I know Tom's a problem . . . I know . . . " but I could not get out much more than that. Cold sweat trickled down my sides. I wanted to slap him in the face. I wanted to reassure him. I wanted to shout and run away.

He said, "I know I can't protect you. I know. But don't clam up on me. Of course, I want everything to be all right. God alone knows I want everything to be all right." He suddenly shook me roughly. "It'll be all right. I tell you it will."

"No it won't. It never will be."

"It will if you let it. Tom's not about to go away, is he? I mean, that's not what you want is it? You've formed this bond with him and he's not just going to vanish like smoke in thin air. I can see that. But you don't have to do stupid things."

"Nobody understands him. He's not what anyone thinks . . . "

"What then?"

I looked him defiantly in the eye. I had gone cold with fright but I managed to look him in the eye, even if my voice was too loud and shrill.

"What do you want from me? What do you want me to say?" Once again, I knocked his hands off my shoulders and turned away.

He said angrily, "It's not what I want you to say . . . " He paused to collect himself, then said wearily, as if defeated, "Nothing . . . Just nothing."

It felt as if I were losing everything. I was terribly afraid and upset. I said in a near whisper which he nonetheless heard clearly, "I don't know what you want from me. Tom's my friend . . . I love him . . . I love him. Don't you understand. Can't you understand?"

"I don't know why you always have to pick such difficult things. I don't know where you get that from . . . I wish you could go an easier way. I really do. But I don't suppose you ever will. Maybe it's just your way. I don't know. But I don't think you ever will."

"I don't know either, I don't . . . "

But I was too upset to continue. He came over and put his

arms around me. I tried to say something else, but could not manage it.

He said quietly, "It's okay. It's okay. I think I can understand. I'll try, Danny. I will . . . I'm glad you said it. I'm glad it's out."